THE FIRST EAGLE

BOOKS BY TONY HILLERMAN

FICTION
The Shape Shifter
Skeleton Man • *The Sinister Pig*
The Wailing Wind • *Hunting Badger*
The First Eagle • *The Fallen Man*
Finding Moon • *Sacred Clowns*
Coyote Waits • *Talking God*
A Thief of Time • *Skinwalkers*
The Ghostway • *The Dark Wind*
People of Darkness • *Listening Woman*
Dance Hall of the Dead • *The Fly on the Wall*
The Blessing Way • *The Mysterious West*
The Boy Who Made Dragonfly (for children)
Buster Mesquite's Cowboy Band (for children)

NONFICTION
Seldom Disappointed
Hillerman Country
The Great Taos Bank Robbery
Rio Grande
New Mexico
The Spell of New Mexico
Indian Country
Talking Mysteries (with Ernie Bulow)
Kilroy Was There
A New Omnibus of Crime

THE FIRST EAGLE

TONY HILLERMAN

HARPER

NEW YORK • LONDON • TORONTO • SYDNEY

HARPER

A hardcover edition of this book was published in 1998 by Harper-Collins Publishers.

THE FIRST EAGLE. Copyright © 1998 by Tony Hillerman. All rights reserved. Printed in the United States of America. No part of this book may be used or reproduced in any manner whatsoever without written permission except in the case of brief quotations embodied in critical articles and reviews. For information, address HarperCollins Publishers, 195 Broadway, New York, NY 10007.

HarperCollins books may be purchased for educational, business, or sales promotional use. For information, please email the Special Markets Department at SPsales@harpercollins.com.

FIRST HARPER PAPERBACKS EDITION PUBLISHED 2021.

Library of Congress Cataloging-in-Publication Data has been applied for.

ISBN 978-0-06-304953-6 (pbk.)

21 22 23 24 25   LSC   10 9 8 7 6 5 4 3 2 1

ACKNOWLEDGMENTS

All characters in this work are fictional. Especially let it be known that Pamela J. Reynolds and Ted L. Brown, vector control specialists of the New Mexico Department of Public Health, did not model for the two vector control characters in *The First Eagle*—being too amiable and generous for those roles. They did try to educate me on how they track the viruses and bacteria that plague our mountains and deserts and even modeled PAPRS for me. Thanks, too, to Patrick and Susie McDermott, Ph.D. and M.D. respectively in microbiology and neurology, who tried to keep my speculation about drug-resistant microbes close to reality. Dr. John C. Brown of the University of Kansas Department of Microbiology provided a reading list and good advice. Robert Ambrose, a falconer and trainer of raptors, informed me about eagles. My friend Neal Shadoff, M.D., helped make the medical

ACKNOWLEDGMENTS

professionals involved sound professional, and Justice Robert Henry of the U.S. Tenth Circuit Court of Appeals advised me relative to the federal death penalty law. I thank them all.

THE FIRST EAGLE

ONE

THE BODY OF Anderson Nez lay under a sheet on the gurney, waiting.

From the viewpoint of Shirley Ahkeah, sitting at her desk in the Intensive Care Unit nursing station of the Northern Arizona Medical Center in Flagstaff, the white shape formed by the corpse of Mr. Nez reminded her of Sleeping Ute Mountain as seen from her aunt's hogan near Teec Nos Pos. Nez's feet, only a couple of yards from her eyes, pushed the sheet up to form the mountain's peak. Perspective caused the rest of the sheet to slope away in humps and ridges, as the mountain seemed to do under its winter snow when she was a child. Shirley had given up on finishing her night shift paperwork. Her mind kept drifting away to what had happened to Mr. Nez and trying to calculate whether he fit into the Bitter Water clan Nez family with the grazing lease adjoining her grandmother's place at Short Mountain. And then there was the question of whether his family would allow an autopsy. She remembered them as sheep camp traditionals, but Dr. Woody, the one who'd brought Nez in, insisted he had the family's permission.

At that moment Dr. Woody was looking at his watch, a black plastic digital job that obviously hadn't been bought to impress the sort of people who are impressed by expensive watches.

"Now," Woody said, "I need to know the time the man died."

"It was early this morning," Dr. Delano said, looking surprised. It surprised Shirley, too, because Woody already knew the answer.

"No. No. No," Woody said. "I mean exactly when."

"Probably about two A.M.," Dr. Delano said, with his expression saying that he wasn't used to being addressed in that impatient tone. He shrugged. "Something like that."

Woody shook his head, grimaced. "Who would know? I mean, who would know within a few minutes?" He looked up and down the hospital corridor, then pointed at Shirley. "Surely somebody would be on duty. The man was terminal. I know the time he was infected, and the time he began registering a fever. Now I need to know how fast it killed him. I need every bit of information I can get on processes in that terminal period. What was happening with various vital functions? I need all that data I ordered kept when I checked him in. Everything."

Odd, Shirley thought. If Woody knew all that, why hadn't Nez been brought to the hospital while there was still some hope of saving him? When Nez was brought in yesterday he was burning with fever and dying fast.

"I'm sure it's all there," Delano said, nodding toward the clipboard Woody was holding. "You'll find it there in his chart."

Now Shirley grimaced. All that information wasn't in Nez's chart. Not yet. It should have been, and would have been even on this unusually hectic shift if Woody hadn't rushed in demanding an autopsy, and not just an autopsy but a lot of special stuff. And that had caused Delano to be summoned, looking sleepy and out of sorts, in his role as assistant medical superintendent, and Delano to call in Dr. Howe, who had handled the Nez case in ICU. Howe, she noticed, wasn't letting Woody bother him. He was too old a hand for that. Howe took every case as his personal *mano-a-mano* battle against death. But when death won, as it often did in ICU units, he racked up a loss and forgot it. A few hours ago he had worried about Nez, hovered over him.

Now he was simply another of the battles he'd been fated to lose.

So why was Dr. Woody causing all this excitement? Why did Woody insist on the autopsy? And insist on sitting in on it with the pathologist? The cause of death was clearly the plague. Nez had been sent to the Intensive Care Unit on admission. Even then the infected lymph glands were swollen, and subcutaneous hemorrhages were forming their splotches on his abdomen and legs, the discolorations that had given the disease its "Black Death" name when it swept through Europe in the Middle Ages, killing tens of millions.

Like most medical personnel in the Four Corners country, Shirley Ahkeah had seen Black Death before. There'd been no cases on the Big Reservation for three or four years, but there were three already this year. One of the others had been on the New Mexico side of the Rez and hadn't come here. But it, too, had been fatal, and the word was that this was a vintage year for the old-fashioned bacteria—that it had flared up in an unusually virulent form.

It certainly had been virulent with Nez. The disease had gone quickly from the common glandular form into plague pneumonia. The Nez sputum, as well as his blood, swarmed with the bacteria, and no one went into his room without donning a filtration mask.

Delano, Howe, and Woody had drifted down the hall beyond Shirley's eavesdropping range, but the tone of the conversation suggested an agreement of some sort had been reached. More work for her, probably. She stared at the sheet covering Nez, remembering the man under it racked by sickness and wishing they'd move the body away. She'd been born in Farmington, daughter of an elementary schoolteacher who had converted to Catholicism. Thus she saw the Navajo "corpse avoidance" teaching as akin to the Jewish dietary prohibitions—a smart way to prevent the spread of illnesses. But even without believing in the evil *chindi* that traditional Navajos knew would attend the corpse of Nez for four days, the body under the sheet provoked unhappy thoughts of human mortality and the sorrow death causes.

Howe reappeared, looking old and tired and reminding her as he always did of a plumper version of her maternal grandfather.

"Shirley, darlin', did I by any chance give you a long list of special stuff we were supposed to do on the Nez case? One thing I remember was he wanted a bunch of extra blood work. Wanted measurement of the interleukin-six in his blood every hour, for one thing. And can't you just imagine the screaming fit the Indian Health Service auditors would have if we billed for that?"

"I can," Shirley said. "But nope. I didn't see any such list. I would have remembered that interleukin-six." She laughed. "I would have had to look it up. Something to do with how the immune system is working, isn't it?"

"It's not my field either," Howe said. "But I think you're right. I know it shows up in AIDS cases, and diabetes, and the sort of situations that affect immunity. Anyway, we shall let the record show that the list didn't reach your desk. I think I must have just wadded it up and tossed it."

"Who is this Dr. Woody anyway?" Shirley asked. "What's his specialty? And why did it take so long to get Nez in here? He must have been running a fever for days."

"He's not a doctor at all," Howe said. "I mean he's not a practicing physician. I think he has the M.D. degree, but mostly he's the Ph.D. kind of doc. Microbiology. Pharmacology. Organic chemistry. Writes lots of papers in the journals about the immune system, evolution of pathogens, immunity of microbes to antibiotics, that sort of stuff. He did a piece for *Science* magazine a few months ago for the layman to read, warning the world that our miracle medicines aren't working anymore. If the viruses don't get us, the bacteria will."

"Oh, yeah," Shirley said. "I remember reading that article. That was his piece? If he knows so much, how come he didn't see that fever?"

Howe shook his head. "I asked him. He said Nez just started showing the symptoms. Said he had him on preventive doxycycline already because of the work they do, but he gave him a booster shot of streptomycin and rushed him right in."

"You don't believe that, do you?"

Howe grimaced. "I'd hate to," he said. "Good old plague used to be reliable. It'd poke along and give us time to treat it. And, yeah, that was Woody's article. Sort of don't worry about global warming. The tiny little beasties will get us first."

"Well, as I remember it, I agreed with a lot of it," Shirley said. "It's downright stupid the way some of you doctors prescribe a bunch of antibiotics every time a mama brings her kid in with an earache. No wonder—"

Howe held up a hand.

"Save it, Shirley. Save it. You're preaching to the choir here." He nodded toward the sheet on the gurney. "Doesn't Mr. Nez there just prove we're breeding a whole new set of drug-resistant bugs? The old *Pasteurella pestis,* as we used to call it in those glorious primitive days when drugs worked, was duck soup for a half dozen antibiotics. Now, whatever they call it these days, *Yersinia pestis* I think it is, just ignored everything we tried on Mr. Nez. We had us a case here where one of your Navajo curing ceremonials could have done Nez more good than we did."

"They just brought him in too late," Shirley said. "You can't give the plague a two-week head start and hope to—"

Howe shook his head. "It wasn't two weeks, Shirley. If Woody knows what the hell he's talking about, it was more like just about one day."

"No way," Shirley said, shaking her head. "And how would he know, anyway?"

"Said he picked the flea off of him. Woody's doing a big study of rodent host colonies. National Institutes of Health money, and some of the pharmaceutical companies. He's interested in these mammal disease reservoirs. You know. Prairie dog colonies that get the plague infection but somehow stay alive while all the other colonies are wiped out. That and the kangaroo rats and deer mice, which aren't killed by the hantavirus. Anyway, Woody said he and Nez always took a broad-spectrum antibiotic when there was any risk of flea bites. If it happened, they'd save the flea so he could check it and do a follow-up treatment if needed. According to Woody, Nez found the flea on the inside of his thigh, and almost right away he was feeling sick and running a fever."

"Wow," Shirley said.

"Yeah," Howe agreed. "Wow indeed."

"I'll bet another flea got him a couple of weeks ago," she said. "Did you agree on the autopsy?"

"Yeah again," Howe said. "You said you know the family. Or know some Nezes, anyway. You think they'll object?"

"I'm what they call an urban Indian. Three-fourths Navajo by blood, but I'm no expert on the culture." She shrugged. "Tradition is against chopping up bodies, but on the other hand it solves the problem of the burial."

Howe sighed, rested his plump buttocks against the desk, pushed back his glasses and rubbed his hand across his eyes. "Always liked that about you guys," he said. "Four days of grief and mourning for the spirit, and then get on with life. How did we white folks get into this corpse worship business? It's just dead meat, and dangerous to boot."

Shirley merely nodded.

"Anything hopeful for that kid in Room Four?" Howe asked. He picked up the chart, looked at it, clicked his tongue and shook his head. He pushed himself up from the desk and stood, shoulders slumped, staring at the sheet covering the body of Anderson Nez.

"You know," he said, "back in the Middle Ages the doctors had another cure for this stuff. They thought it had something to do with the sense of smell, and they recommended people stave it off by using a lot of perfume and wearing flowers. It didn't stop everybody from dying, but it proved humans have a sense of humor."

Shirley had known Howe long enough to understand that she was now supposed to provide a straight line for his wit. She wasn't in the mood, but she said: "What do you mean?"

"They made an ironic song out of it—and it lived on as a nursery rhyme." Howe sang it in his creaky voice:

"Ring around with roses,
pockets full of posies.
Ashes. Ashes.
We all fall down."

He looked at her quizzically. "You remember singing that in kindergarten?"

Shirley didn't. She shook her head.

And Dr. Howe walked down the hall toward where another of his patients was dying.

TWO

ACTING LIEUTENANT JIM Chee of the Navajo Tribal Police, a "traditional" at heart, had parked his trailer with its door facing east. At dawn on July 8, he looked out at the rising sun, scattered a pinch of pollen from his medicine pouch to bless the day and considered what it would bring him.

He reviewed the bad part first. On his desk his monthly report for June—his first month as administrator in charge of a Navajo Police sub-agency unit—awaited him, half-finished and already overdue. But finishing the hated paperwork would be fun compared to the other priority job—telling Officer Benny Kinsman to get his testosterone under control.

The good part of the day involved, at least obliquely, his own testosterone. Janet Pete was leaving Washington and coming back to Indian country. Her letter was friendly but cool, with no hint of romantic passion. Still, Janet was coming back, and after he finished with Kinsman he planned to call her. It would be a tentative exploratory call. Were they still engaged? Did she want to resume their prickly relationship? Bridge the gap? Actually get married? For that matter, did he? However he answered that question, she was coming back and that explained why Chee was grinning while he washed the breakfast dishes.

The grin went away when he got to his office at the Tuba City station. Officer Kinsman, who was supposed to be awaiting him in his office, wasn't there. Claire Dineyahze explained it.

"He said he had to run out to Yells Back Butte first and catch that Hopi who's been poaching eagles," Mrs. Dineyahze said.

Chee inhaled, opened his mouth, then clamped it shut. Mrs. Dineyahze would have been offended by the obscenity Kinsman's action deserved.

She made a wry face and shook her head, sharing Chee's disapproval.

"I guess it's the same Hopi he arrested out there last winter," she said. "The one they turned loose because Benny forgot to read him his rights. But he wouldn't tell me. Just gave me that look." She put on a haughty expression. "Said his informant was confidential." Clearly Mrs. Dineyahze was offended by this exclusion. "One of his girlfriends, probably."

"I'll find out," Chee said. It was time to change the subject. "I've got to get that June report finished. Anything else going on?"

"Well," Mrs. Dineyahze said, and then stopped.

Chee waited.

Mrs. Dineyahze shrugged. "I know you don't like gossip," she said. "But you'll probably hear about this anyway."

"What?"

"Suzy Gorman called this morning. You know? The secretary in the Arizona Highway Patrol at Winslow. She said one of their troopers had to break up a fight at a place in Flagstaff. It was Benny Kinsman and some guy from Northern Arizona University."

Chee sighed. "They charge him?"

"She said no. Professional courtesy."

"Thank God," Chee said. "That's a relief."

"May not be over, though," she said. "Suzy said the fight started because Kinsman was making a big move on a woman and wouldn't stop, and the woman said she was going to file a complaint. Said he'd been bothering her before. On her job."

"Well, hell," Chee said. "What next? Where's she work?"

"Works out of that little office the Arizona

Health Department set up here after those two bubonic plague cases. They call 'em vector control people." Mrs. Dineyahze smiled. "They catch fleas."

"I've got to get that report out by noon," Chee said. He'd had all the Kinsman he wanted this morning.

Mrs. Dineyahze wasn't finished with Kinsman. "Did Bernie talk to you about Kinsman?"

"No," Chee said. She hadn't, but he'd heard a rumble on the gossip circuit.

"I told her she should tell you, but she didn't want to bother you."

"Tell me what?" Bernie was Officer Bernadette Manuelito, who was young and green and, judging from gossip Chee had overheard, had a crush on him.

Mrs. Dineyahze looked sour. "Sexual harassment," she said.

"Like what?"

"Like making a move on her."

Chee didn't want to hear about it. Not now. "Tell her to report it to me," he said, and went into his office to confront his paperwork. With a couple of hours of peace and quiet he could finish it by lunchtime. He got in about thirty minutes before the dispatcher buzzed him.

"Kinsman wants a backup," she said.

"For what?" Chee asked. "Where is he?"

"Out there past Goldtooth," the dispatcher said. "Over near the west side of Black Mesa. The signal was breaking up."

"It always does out there," Chee said. In fact, these chronic radio communication problems were one thing he was complaining about in his report. "We have anyone close?"

"Afraid not."

"I'll take it myself," Chee said.

A few minutes after noon, Chee was bumping down the gravel trailing a cloud of dust looking for Kinsman. "Come in, Benny," Chee said into his mike. "I'm eight miles south of Goldtooth. Where are you?"

"Under the south cliff of Yells Back Butte," Kinsman said. "Take the old Tijinney hogan road. Park where the arroyo cuts it. Half mile up the arroyo. Be very quiet."

"Well, hell," Chee said. He said it to himself, not into the mike. Kinsman had gotten himself excited stalking his Hopi poacher, or whatever he was after, and had been transmitting in a half-intelligible whisper. Even more irritating, he was switching off his receiver lest a too-loud response alert his prey. While this was proper procedure in some emergency situations, Chee doubted this was anything serious enough to warrant that sort of foolishness.

"Come on, Kinsman," he said. "Grow up."

If he was going to be backup man on whatever Benny was doing, it would help to understand the problem. It would also help to know how to find the road to the Tijinney hogan. Chee knew just about every track on the east side of the Big Rez, the Checkerboard Rez even better, and the territory around Navajo Mountain fairly well. But he'd worked out of Tuba City very briefly as a rookie and had been reassigned there only six weeks ago. This rugged landscape beside the Hopi Reservation was relatively strange to him.

He remembered Yells Back Butte was an outcrop of Black Mesa. Therefore it shouldn't be too difficult to find the Tijinney road, and the arroyo, and Kinsman. When he did, Chee intended to give him some very explicit instructions about how to use his radio and to behave himself when dealing with women. And, come to think of it, to curb his anti-Hopi attitude.

This was the product of having his family's home site added to the Hopi Reservation when Congress split the Joint Use lands. Kinsman's grandmother, who spoke only Navajo, had been relocated to Flagstaff, where almost nobody speaks Navajo. Whenever Kinsman visited her, he came back full of anger.

One of those scattered little showers that serve as forerunners to the desert country rainy season had swept across the Moenkopi Plateau a few minutes before and was still producing rumbles of thunder far to the east. Now he was driving through the track the shower had left and the gusty breeze was no longer engulfing the patrol car in dust. The air pouring through the window was rich with the perfume of wet sage and dampened earth.

Don't let this Kinsman problem spoil the whole day, Chee told himself. Be happy. And he was. Janet Pete was coming. Which meant what? That she thought she could be content outside the culture of Washington's high society? Apparently. Or would she try again to pull him into it? If so, would she succeed? That made him uneasy.

Before yesterday's letter, he had hardly thought about Janet for days. A little before drifting off to sleep, a little at dawn while he fried his breakfast Spam. But he had resisted the temptation to dig out her previous letter and reread it. He knew the facts by heart. One of her mother's many well-placed friends reported that her job application was "favorably considered" in the Justice Department. Being half-Navajo made her prospects for an assignment in Indian country look good. Then came the last paragraph.

"Maybe I'll be assigned to Oklahoma—lots of legal work there with that internal fight the

Cherokees are having. And then there's the rumble inside the Bureau of Indian Affairs over law enforcement that might keep me in Washington."

Nothing in that one that suggested the old pre-quarrel affection. It had caused Chee to waste a dozen sheets of paper with abortive attempts to frame the proper answer. In some of them he'd urged her to use the experience she'd gained working for the Navajo tribe's legal aid program to land an assignment on the Big Rez. He'd said hurry home, that he'd been wrong in distrusting her. He had misunderstood the situation. He had acted out of unreasonable jealousy. In others he'd said, Stay away. You'll never be content here. It can never be the same for us. Don't come unless you can be happy without your Kennedy Center culture, your Ivy League friends, art shows, and high-fashion and cocktail parties with the celebrity set, without the snobbish intellectual elite. Don't come unless you can be happy living with a fellow whose goals include neither luxury nor climbing the ladder of social caste, with a man who has found the good life in a rusty trailer house.

Found the good life? Or thought he had. Either way, he knew he was finally having some luck forgetting her. And the note he'd eventually sent had been carefully unrevealing. Then came yesterday's letter, with the last line saying she was "coming home!!"

Home. Home with two exclamation points. He was thinking of that when Kinsman's silly whispering had jarred him back to reality. And now Kinsman was whispering again. Unintelligible muttering at first, then: "Lieutenant! Hurry!"

Chee hurried. He'd planned to pause at Goldtooth to ask directions, but nothing remained there except two roofless stone buildings, their doorways and windows open to the world, and an old-fashioned round hogan that looked equally deserted. Tracks branched off here, disappearing, through the dunes to the right and left. He hadn't seen a vehicle since he'd left the pavement, but the center track bore tire marks. He stayed with it. Speeding. He was out of the shower's path now and leaving a rooster tail of dust. Forty miles to the right the San Franciscos dominated the horizon, with a thunderstorm building over Humphrey's Peak. To the left rose the ragged shape of the Hopi mesas, partly obscured at the moment by the rain another cloud was dragging. All around him was the empty wind-shaped plateau, its dunes held by great growths of Mormon tea, snake weed, yucca, and durable sage. Abruptly Chee again smelled the perfume that showers leave behind them. No more dust now. The track was damp. It veered eastward, toward mesa cliffs and, jutting from them, the massive shape of a butte. The tracks leading toward it were hidden behind a growth of Mormon tea and Chee almost missed them. He backed up, tried his radio again, got nothing but static, and turned onto the ruts toward the butte. Short of the cliffs he came to the washout Kinsman had mentioned.

Kinsman's patrol car was parked by a cluster of junipers, and Kinsman's tracks led up the arroyo. He followed them along the sandy bottom and then away from it, climbing the slope toward the towering sandstone wall of the butte. Kinsman's voice was still in Chee's mind. To hell with being quiet. Chee ran.

Officer Kinsman was behind an outcrop of sandstone. Chee saw a leg of his uniform trousers, partly obscured by a growth of wheatgrass. He began a shout to him, and cut it off. He could see a boot now. Toe down. That was wrong. He slid his pistol from its holster and edged closer.

From behind the sandstone, Chee heard the sound boots make on loose gravel, a grunting noise, labored breathing, an exclamation. He thumbed off the safety on his pistol and stepped into the open.

Benjamin Kinsman was facedown, the back of his uniform shirt matted with grass and sand glued to the cloth by fresh red blood. Beside

Kinsman a young man squatted, looking up at Chee. His shirt, too, was smeared with blood.

"Put your hands on top of your head," Chee said.

"Hey," the man said. "This guy . . ."

"Hands on head," Chee said, hearing his own voice harsh and shaky in his ears. "And get face-down on the ground."

The man stared at Chee, at the pistol aimed at his face. He wore his hair in two braids. A Hopi, Chee thought. Of course. Probably the eagle poacher he'd guessed Kinsman had been trying to catch. Well, Kinsman had caught him.

"Down," Chee ordered. "Face to the ground."

The young man leaned forward, lowered himself slowly. Very agile, Chee thought. His torn shirt sleeve revealed a long gash on the right forearm, the congealed blood forming a curved red stripe across sunburned skin.

Chee pulled the man's right hand behind his back, clicked the handcuff on the wrist, cuffed the left wrist to it. Then he extracted a worn brown leather wallet from the man's hip pocket and flipped it open. From his Arizona driver's license photo the young man smiled at him. Robert Jano. Mishongnove, Second Mesa.

Robert Jano was turning onto his side, pulling his legs up, preparing to rise.

"Stay down," Chee said. "Robert Jano, you

have the right to remain silent. You have the right to . . ."

"What are you arresting me for?" Jano said. A raindrop hit the rock beside Chee. Then another.

"For murder. You have the right to retain legal counsel. You have the right—"

"I don't think he's dead," Jano said. "He was alive when I got here."

"Yeah," Chee said. "I'm sure he was."

"And when I checked his pulse. Just thirty seconds ago."

Chee was already kneeling beside Kinsman, his hand on Kinsman's neck, first noticing the sticky blood and now the faint pulse under his fingertip and the warmth of the flesh under his palm.

He stared at Jano. "You sonofabitch!" Chee shouted. "Why did you brain him like that?"

"I didn't," Jano said. "I didn't hit him. I just walked up and he was here." He nodded toward Kinsman. "Just lying there like that."

"Like hell," Chee said. "How'd you get that blood all over you then, and your arm cut up like—"

A rasping shriek and a clatter behind him cut off the question. Chee spun, pistol pointing. A squawking sound came from behind the outcrop where Kinsman lay. Behind it a metal birdcage lay on its side. It was a large cage, but barely large enough to hold the eagle struggling inside it. Chee lifted it by the ring at its top, rested it on the sandstone slab and stared at Jano. "A federal offense," he said. "Poaching an endangered species. Not as bad as felony assault on a law officer, but—"

"Watch out!" Jano shouted.

Too late. Chee felt the eagle's talons tearing at the side of his hand.

"That's what happened to me," Jano said. "That's how I got so bloody."

Icy raindrops hit Chee's ear, his cheek, his shoulder, his bleeding hand. The shower engulfed them, and with it a mixture of hailstones. He covered Kinsman with his jacket and moved the eagle's cage under the shelter of the outcrop. He had to get help for Kinsman fast, and he had to keep the eagle under shelter. If Jano was telling the truth, which seemed extremely unlikely, there would be blood on the bird. He didn't want Jano's defense attorney to be able to claim that Chee had let the evidence wash away.

THREE

THE LIMO THAT had parked in front of Joe Leaphorn's house was a glossy blue-black job with the morning sun glittering on its polished chrome. Leaphorn had stood behind his screen door watching it—hoping his neighbors on this fringe of Window Rock wouldn't notice it. Which was like hoping the kids who played in the schoolyard down his gravel street wouldn't notice a herd of giraffes trotting by. The limo's arrival so early meant the man sitting patiently behind the wheel must have left Santa Fe about 3:00 A.M. That made Leaphorn ponder what life would be like as a hireling of the very rich—which Millicent Vanders certainly must be.

Well, in just a few minutes he'd have a chance to find out. The limo now was turning off a narrow asphalt road in Santa Fe's northeast foothills onto a brick driveway. It stopped at an elaborate iron gate.

"Is this it?" Leaphorn asked.

"Yep," the driver said, which was about the average length of the answers Leaphorn had been getting before he'd stopped asking questions. He'd started with the standard break-the-ice: gasoline mileage on the limo, how it handled, that sort of thing. Went from that into how long the driver had worked for Millicent Vanders, which proved to be twenty-one years. Beyond that point, Leaphorn's digging ran into granite.

"Who is Mrs. Vanders?" Leaphorn had asked.

"My boss."

Leaphorn had laughed. "That's not what I meant."

"I didn't think it was."

"You know anything about this job she's going to offer me?"

"No."

"What she wants?"

"It's none of my business."

So Leaphorn dropped it. He watched the scenery, learned that even the rich could find only country-western music on their radios here, tuned in KNDN to listen in on the Navajo open-mike program. Someone had lost his billfold at the Farmington bus station and was asking the finder to return his driver's license and credit card. A woman was inviting members of the Bitter Water and Standing Rock clans, and all other kinfolk and friends, to show up for a *yeibichai* sing to be held for Emerson Roanhorse at his place north of Kayenta. Then came an old-sounding voice declaring that Billy Etcitty's roan mare was missing from his place north of Burnt Water and asking folks to let him know if they spotted it. "Like maybe at a livestock auction," the voice added, which suggested that Etcitty presumed his mare hadn't wandered off without assistance. Soon Leaphorn had surrendered to the soft luxury of the limo seat and dozed. When he awoke, they were, rolling down I-25 past Santa Fe's outskirts.

Leaphorn then had fished Millicent Vanders's letter from his jacket pocket and reread it.

It wasn't, of course, directly from Millicent Vanders. The letterhead read Peabody, Snell and Glick, followed by those initials law firms use. The address was Boston. Delivery was FedEx's Priority Overnight.

Dear Mr. Leaphorn:

This is to confirm and formalize our telephone conversation of this date. I write you in the interest of Mrs. Millicent Vanders, who is represented by this firm in some of her affairs. Mrs. Vanders has charged me with finding an investigator familiar with the Navajo Reservation whose reputation for integrity and circumspection is impeccable.

You have been recommended to us as satisfying these requirements. This inquiry is to determine if you would be willing to meet with Mrs. Vanders at her summer home in Santa Fe and explore her needs with her. If so, please call me so arrangements can be made for her car to pick you up and for your financial reimbursement. I must add that Mrs. Vanders expressed a sense of urgency in this affair.

Leaphorn's first inclination had been to write Christopher Peabody a polite "thanks but no thanks" and recommend he find his client a licensed private investigator instead of a former cop.

But . . .

There was the fact that Peabody, surely the senior partner, had signed the letter himself, and the business of having his circumspection rated impeccable, and—most important of all—the "sense of urgency" note, which made the woman's problem sound interesting. Leaphorn needed something interesting. He'd soon be finishing his first year of retirement from the Navajo Tribal Police. He'd long since run out of things to do. He was bored.

And so he'd called Mr. Peabody back and here

he was, driver pushing the proper button, gate sliding silently open, rolling past lush landscaping toward a sprawling two-story house—its tan plaster and brick copings declaring it to be what Santa Feans call "Territorial Style" and its size declaring it a mansion.

The driver opened the door for Leaphorn. A young man wearing a faded blue shirt and jeans, his blond hair tied in a pigtail, stood smiling just inside the towering double doors.

"Mr. Leaphorn," he said. "Mrs. Vanders is expecting you."

Millicent Vanders was waiting in a room that Leaphorn's experience with movies and television suggested was either a study or a sitting room. She was a frail little woman standing beside a frail little desk, supporting herself with the tips of her fingers on its polished surface. Her hair was almost white and the smile with which she greeted him was pale.

"Mr. Leaphorn," she said. "How good of you to come. How good of you to help me."

Leaphorn, with no idea yet whether he would help her or not, simply returned the smile and sat in the chair to which she motioned.

"Would you care for tea? Or coffee? Or some other refreshment? And should I call you Mr. Leaphorn, or do you prefer 'Lieutenant'?"

"Coffee, thank you, if it's no trouble," Leaphorn

said. "And it's mister. I've retired from the Navajo Tribal Police."

Millicent Vanders looked past him toward the door: "Coffee then, and tea," she said. She sat herself behind the desk with a slow, careful motion that told Leaphorn his hostess had one or other of the hundred forms of arthritis. But she smiled again, a signal meant to be reassuring. Leaphorn detected pain in it. He'd become very good at that sort of detection while he was watching his wife die. Emma, holding his hand, telling him not to worry, pretending she wasn't in pain, promising that someday soon she'd be well again.

Mrs. Vanders was sorting through papers on her desk, arranging them in a folder, untroubled by the lack of conversation. Leaphorn had found this unusual among whites and admired it when he saw it. She extracted two eight-by-ten photographs from an envelope, examined one, added it to the folder, then examined the other. A thump broke the silence—a careless piñon jay colliding with a windowpane. It fled in wobbling flight. Mrs. Vanders continued her contemplation of the photo, lost in some remembered sorrow, undisturbed by the bird or by Leaphorn watching her. An interesting person, Leaphorn thought.

A plump young woman appeared at his elbow bearing a tray. She placed a napkin, saucer, cup, and spoon on the table beside him, filled the cup from a white china pot, then repeated the process at the desk, pouring the tea from a silver container. Mrs. Vanders interrupted her contemplation of the photo, slid it into the folder, handed it to the woman.

"Ella," she said. "Would you give this, please, to Mr. Leaphorn?"

Ella handed it to Leaphorn and left as silently as she had come. He put the folder on his lap, sipped his coffee. The cup was translucent china, thin as paper. The coffee was hot, fresh, and excellent.

Mrs. Vanders was studying him. "Mr. Leaphorn," she said, "I asked you to come here because I hope you will agree to do something for me."

"I might agree," Leaphorn said. "What would it be?"

"Everything has to be completely confidential," Mrs. Vanders said. "You would communicate only to me. Not to my lawyers. Not to anyone else."

Leaphorn considered this, sampled the coffee again, put down the cup. "Then I might not be able to help you."

Mrs. Vanders looked surprised.

"Why not?"

"I've spent most of my life being a policeman," Leaphorn said. "If what you have in mind causes me to discover anything illegal, then—"

"If that happened, I would report it to the authorities," she said rather stiffly.

Leaphorn allowed the typical Navajo moments of silence to make certain that Mrs. Vanders had said all she wanted to say. She had, but his lack of response touched a nerve.

"Of course I would," she added. "Certainly."

"But if you didn't for some reason, you understand that I would have to do it. Would you agree to that?"

She stared at Leaphorn. Then she nodded. "I think we are creating a problem where none exists."

"Probably," Leaphorn said.

"I would like you to locate a young woman. Or, failing that, discover what happened to her."

She gestured toward the folder. Leaphorn opened it.

The top picture was a studio portrait of a dark-haired, dark-eyed woman wearing a mortarboard. The face was narrow and intelligent, the expression somber. Not a girl who would have been called "cute," Leaphorn thought. Nor pretty either, for that matter. Handsome, perhaps. Full of character. Certainly it would be an easy face to remember.

The next picture was of the same woman,

wearing jeans and a jean jacket now, leaning on the door of a pickup truck and looking back at the camera. She had the look of an athlete, Leaphorn thought, and was older in this one. Perhaps in her early thirties. On the back of each photograph the same name was written: Catherine Anne.

Leaphorn glanced at Mrs. Vanders.

"My niece," she said. "The only child of my late sister."

Leaphorn returned the photos to the folder and took out a sheaf of papers, clipped together. The top one had biographical details.

Catherine Anne Pollard was the full name. The birthdate made her thirty-three, the birthplace was Arlington, Virginia, the current address Flag-staff, Arizona.

"Catherine studied biology," Mrs. Vanders said. "She specialized in mammals and insects. She was working for the Indian Health Service, but actually I think it's more for the Arizona Health Department. The environment division. They call her a 'vector control specialist.' I imagine you would know about that?"

Leaphorn nodded.

Mrs. Vanders made a wry face. "She says they actually call her a 'fleacatcher.'

"I think she could have had a good career as a tennis player. On the tour, you know. She always loved sports. Soccer, striker on the college volley-ball team. When she was in junior high school she worried about being bigger than the other girls. I think excelling in sports was her compensation for that."

Leaphorn nodded again.

"The first time she came to see me after she got this job, I asked for her job title, and she said 'fleacatcher.' " Mrs. Vanders's expression was sad. "Called herself that, so I guess she doesn't mind."

"It's an important job," Leaphorn said.

"She wanted a career in biology. But 'flea-catcher'?" Mrs. Vanders shook her head. "I understand that she and some others were working on the source of those bubonic plague cases this spring. They have a little laboratory in Tuba City and check places where the victims might have picked up the disease. Trapping rodents." Mrs. Vanders hesitated, her face reflecting distaste. "That's the flea catching. They collect the fleas from them. And take samples of their blood. That sort of thing." She dismissed this with a wave of the hand.

"Then last week, early in the morning, she went to work and never came back."

She let that hang there, her eyes on Leaphorn.

"She left for work alone?"

"Alone. That's what they say. I'm not so sure."

Leaphorn would come back to that later. Now he needed basic facts. Speculation could wait.

"Went to work where?"

"The man I called said she just stopped by the office to pick up some of the equipment she uses in her work and then drove away. To someplace out in the country where she was trapping rodents."

"Was she meeting anyone where she was going to be working?"

"Apparently not. Not officially anyway. The man I talked to didn't think anyone went with her."

"And you think something has happened to her. Have you discussed this with the police?"

"Mr. Peabody discussed it with people he knows in the FBI. He said they would not be involved in something like this. They would have jurisdiction only if it involved a kidnapping for ransom, or"—she hesitated, glanced down at her hands—"or some other sort of felony. They told Mr. Peabody there would have to be evidence that a federal law had been violated."

"What evidence was there?" He was pretty sure he knew the answer. It would be none. Nothing at all.

Mrs. Vanders shook her head.

"Actually, I guess you would say the only evidence is that a woman is missing. Just the circumstances."

"The vehicle. Where was it found?"

"It hasn't been found. Not as far as I have been able to discover." Mrs. Vanders's eyes were intent on Leaphorn, watching for his reaction.

Had they not been, Leaphorn would have allowed himself a smile—thinking of the hopeless task Mr. Peabody must have faced in trying to interest the federals. Thinking of the paperwork this missing vehicle would cause in the Arizona Health Department, of how this would be interpreted by the Arizona Highway Patrol if a missing person report had been filed, of the other complexities. But Mrs. Vanders would read a smile as an expression of cynicism.

"Do you have a theory?"

"Yes," she said, and cleared her throat. "I think she must be dead."

Mrs. Vanders, who had seemed frail and unhealthy, now looked downright sick.

"Are you all right? Do you want to continue this?"

She produced a weak smile, extracted a small white container from the pocket of her jacket and held it up.

"I have a heart condition," she said. "This is nitroglycerin. The prescription used to come in little tablets, but these days the patient just sprays it on the tongue. Please excuse me. I'll feel fine again in a moment."

She turned away from him, held the tube to her lips for a moment, then returned it to her pocket.

Leaphorn waited, reviewing what little he knew about nitro as a heart medication. It served to expand the arteries and thus increase the blood flow. Neither of the people he'd known who used it had lived very long. Perhaps that explained the urgency Peabody mentioned in his letter.

Mrs. Vanders sighed. "Where were we?"

"You'd said you thought your niece must be dead."

"Murdered, I think."

"Did someone have a motive? Or did she have something that would attract a thief?"

"She was being stalked," Mrs. Vanders said. "A man named Victor Hammar. A graduate student she'd met at the University of New Mexico. A fairly typical case, I'd guess, for this sort of thing. He was from East Germany, what used to be East Germany that is, with no family or friends over here. A very lonely man, I would imagine. And that's the way Catherine described him to me. They had common interests at the university. Both biologists. He was studying small mammals. That caused them to do a lot of work in the laboratory together. I suppose Catherine took pity on him."

Mrs. Vanders shook her head. "Losers always had a special appeal to her. When her mother was going to buy her a dog, she wanted one from the pound. Something she could feel sorry for. But with that man . . ." She grimaced. "Well, anyway, she couldn't get rid of him. I suspected she dropped out of graduate school to get away from him. Then, after she took the job in Arizona, he would turn up at Phoenix when she was there. It was the same thing when she started working at Flagstaff."

"Had he threatened her?"

"I asked her that and she just laughed. She thought he was perfectly harmless. She told me to think of him as being like a little lost kitten. Just a nuisance."

"But you think he was a threat?"

"I think he was a very dangerous man. Under the right circumstances anyway. When he came here with her once, he seemed polite enough. But there was a sort of—" She paused, looking for the way to express it. "I think a lot of anger was right under that nicey-nicey surface ready to explode."

Leaphorn waited for more explanation. Mrs. Vanders merely looked worried.

"I told Catherine that even with kittens, if you hurt one it will scratch you," she said.

"That's true," Leaphorn said. "If I decide I can be of any help on this, I'll need his name and address." He thought about it. "And I think finding that vehicle she was driving is important. I think you should offer a reward. Something substantial enough to attract attention. To get people talking about it."

"Of course," Mrs. Vanders said. "Offer whatever you like."

"I'll need all the pertinent biographical information about her. People who might know her or something about her habits. Names, addresses, that sort of thing."

"All I have is in the folder you have there," she said. "There's a report about what a lawyer from Mr. Peabody's office found out, and a report from a lawyer he hired in Flagstaff to collect what information he could. It wasn't much. I'm afraid it won't be very helpful."

"When was the last time she saw this Hammar?"

"That's one reason I suspect him," Mrs. Vanders said. "It was just before she disappeared. He'd come out to Tuba City where she was working. She'd called to tell me she was coming to see me that weekend. That Hammar man was there at Tuba City when she called."

"Did she say anything that made you think she was afraid of him?"

"No." Mrs. Vanders laughed. "I don't think Catherine's ever been afraid of anything. She inherited her mother's genes."

Leaphorn frowned. "She said she was coming to see you but she disappeared instead," he said. "Did she say why she was coming? Just social, or did she have something on her mind?"

"She was thinking of quitting. She couldn't stand her boss. A man named Krause." Mrs. Vanders pointed at the folder. "Very arrogant. And she disapproved of the way he ran the operation."

"Something illegal?"

"I don't know. She said she didn't want to talk about it on the telephone. But it must have been pretty serious to make her think about leaving."

"Something personal, you think? Did she ever suggest sexual harassment? Anything like that?"

"She didn't exactly suggest that," Mrs. Vanders said. "But he was a bachelor. Whatever he was doing it was bad enough to be driving her away from a job she loved."

Leaphorn questioned that by raising his eyebrows.

"She was excited by that job. She's been working for months to find the rodents that caused that last outbreak of bubonic plague on your reservation. Catherine has always been obsessive, even as a child. And since she took this health department job her obsession has been the plague. She spent one entire visit telling me about it. About how it killed half the people in Europe in the Middle Ages. How it spreads. How they're beginning to think the bacteria are evolving. All that sort of thing. She's on a personal crusade about it. Almost religious, I'd say. And she thought she might have found some of the rodents it spreads from. She'd told this Hammar fellow about it and I guess he used that as an excuse to come out."

Mrs. Vanders made a deprecating gesture. "Being a student of mice and rats and other rodents, that gives him an excuse, I guess. She said he might go out there with her to help her with the rodents. Apparently he wasn't with her when she left Tuba City, but I thought he might have followed her. I guess they trap them or poison them or something. And she said it was a hard-to-get-to place, so maybe she would want him to help her carry in whatever they use. It's out on the edge of the Hopi Reservation. A place called Yells Back Butte."

"Yells Back Butte," Leaphorn said.

"It seems a strange name," Mrs. Vanders said. "I suspect there's some story behind it."

"Probably," Leaphorn said. "I think it's a local

name for a little finger sticking out from Black Mesa. On the edge of the Hopi Reservation. And when was she going out there?"

"The day after she called me," Mrs. Vanders said. "That would be a week ago next Friday."

Leaphorn nodded, sorting out some memories. That would be July 8, just about the day—No. It was exactly the day when Officer Benjamin Kinsman had his skull cracked with a rock somewhere very near Yells Back Butte. Same time. Same place. Leaphorn had never learned to believe in coincidences.

"All right, Mrs. Vanders," Leaphorn said, "I'll see what I can find out."

FOUR

CHEE WAS NOT standing at the waiting room window just to watch the Northern Arizona Medical Center parking lot and the cloud shadows dappling the mountains across the valley. He was postponing the painful moment when he would walk into Officer Benjamin Kinsman's room and give Benny the foredoomed official "last opportunity" to tell them who had murdered him.

Actually, it wasn't murder yet. The neurologist in charge had called Shiprock yesterday to report that Kinsman had become brain-dead and procedures could now begin to end his ordeal. But this was going to be a legally complicated and socially sensitive process. The U.S. Attorney's office was nervous. Converting the charge against Jano from attempted homicide to murder had to be done exactly right. Therefore, J. D. Mickey, the acting assistant U.S. attorney charged with handling the prosecution, had decided that the arresting officer must be present when the plug was pulled. He wanted Chee to testify that he was available to receive any possible last words. That meant that the defense attorney should be there, too.

Chee had no idea why. Everybody involved had the same boss. As an indigent, Jano would be represented by another Justice Department lawyer. Said lawyer being—Chee glanced at his watch—eleven minutes late. But maybe that was his vehicle pulling into the lot. No. It was a pickup truck. Even in Arizona, Justice Department lawyers didn't arrive in trucks.

In fact, it was a familiar truck. Dodge Ram king cab pickups of the early nineties looked a lot alike, but this one had a winch attached to the front bumper and fender damage covered with paint that didn't quite match. It was Joe Leaphorn's truck.

Chee sighed. Fate seemed to be tying him to his former boss again, endlessly renewing the sense of inferiority Chee felt in the presence of the Legendary Lieutenant.

But he felt a little better after he thought about it. There was no way the murder of Officer Kinsman could involve Leaphorn. The Legendary Lieutenant had been retired since last year. As a rookie, Kinsman had never worked for him. There were no clan relationships that Chee knew about. Leaphorn must be coming to visit some sick friend. This would be one of those coincidences that Leaphorn had told him, about a hundred times, not to believe in. Chee relaxed. He watched a white Chevy sedan, driving too fast, skid through the parking lot gate. A federal motor-pool Chevy. The defense lawyer finally. Now the plugs could be pulled, stopping the machines that had kept Kinsman's lungs pumping and his heart beating for all these days, since the wind of life that had blown through Benny had left, taking Benny's consciousness on its last great adventure.

Now the lawyers would agree, in view of the seriousness of the case, to ignore the objections the Kinsman family might have and conduct a useless autopsy. That would prove that the blow to the head had caused Benny's death and therefore the People of the United States could apply the death penalty and kill Robert Jano to even the score. The fact that neither the Navajos nor the Hopis believed in this eye-for-an-eye philosophy of the white men would be ignored.

Two floors below him the white Chevy had parked. The driver's-side door opened, a pair of black trouser legs emerged, then a hand holding a briefcase.

"Lieutenant Chee," said a familiar voice just behind him. "Could I talk to you for a minute?"

Joe Leaphorn was standing in the doorway, holding his battered gray Stetson in his hands and looking apologetic.

So much for coincidences.

FIVE

"**SOMEPLACE QUIETER, MAYBE,**" Leaphorn had said, meaning a place where no one would overhear him. So Chee led him down the hall to the empty orthopedic waiting room. He pulled back a chair by the table and motioned toward another one.

"I know you just have a minute," Leaphorn said, and sat down. "The defense attorney just drove up."

"Yeah," Chee said, thinking that Leaphorn not only had managed to find him in this unlikely place but knew why he was here and what was going on. Probably knew more than Chee did. That irritated Chee, but it didn't surprise him.

"I wanted to ask if the name Catherine Anne Pollard meant anything to you. If a missing persons report was filed on her. Or a stolen vehicle report? Anything like that?"

"Pollard?" Chee said. "I don't think so. It doesn't ring a bell." Thank God Leaphorn wasn't involving himself in the Kinsman business. It was already complicated enough.

"Woman, early thirties, working with the Indian Health Service," Leaphorn said. "In vector control. Looking for the source of that bubonic plague outbreak. Checking rodents. You know how they work."

"Oh, yeah," Chee said. "I heard about it. When I get back to Tuba I'll check our reports. I think somebody in environmental health or the Indian Health Service called Window Rock about her not coming back from a job and they passed it along to us." He shrugged. "I got the impression they were more worried about losing the department's Jeep."

Leaphorn grinned at him. "Not exactly the crime of the century."

"No," Chee said. "If she was about thirteen you'd be checking the motels. At her age, if she wants to run off somewhere, that's her business. As long as she brings back the Jeep."

"She didn't, then? It's still missing?"

"I don't know," Chee said. "If she returned it, APH forgot to tell us."

"That wouldn't be unusual," Leaphorn said.

Chee nodded, and looked at Leaphorn. Wanting an explanation for his interest in something that seemed both obvious and trivial.

"Somebody in her family thinks she's dead. Thinks somebody killed her." Leaphorn let that hang a moment, made an apologetic face. "I know that's what kinfolks usually think. But this time there's a suspicion that a would-be boyfriend was stalking her."

"That's not unusual either," Chee said. He felt vaguely disappointed. Leaphorn had done some private detecting right after he'd retired, but that had been to tie up a loose end from his career, close out an old case. This sounded purely commercial. Was the Legendary Lieutenant Leaphorn reduced to doing routine private detective stuff?

Leaphorn took a notebook out of his shirt pocket, looked at it, tapped it against the tabletop. It occurred to Chee that this was embarrassing Leaphorn, and that embarrassed Chee. The Legendary Lieutenant, totally unflappable when he'd been in charge, didn't know how to handle being a civilian. Asking favors. Chee didn't know how to handle it either. He noticed that Leaphorn's burr-cut hair, long black-salted-with-gray, had become gray-salted-with-black.

"Anything I can do?" Chee asked.

Leaphorn put the notebook back in his pocket.

"You know how I am about coincidences," he said.

"Yep," Chee said.

"Well, this one is so strained I hate to even mention it." He shook his head.

Chee waited.

"From what I know now, the last time anyone heard of this woman, she was heading out of Tuba City checking on prairie dog colonies, looking for dead rodents. One of the places on her list was that area around Yells Back Butte."

Chee thought about that a moment, took a deep breath, thinking he'd been too optimistic. But "that area around Yells Back Butte" didn't make it much of a coincidence with his Kinsman case. That "around" could include a huge bunch of territory. He waited to see if Leaphorn was finished. He wasn't.

"That was the morning of July eighth," Leaphorn said.

"July eighth," Chee said, frowning. "I was out there that morning."

"I was thinking that you were," Leaphorn said. "Look, I'm headed to Window Rock now and all I know now is from some preliminary checking a lawyer did for Pollard's aunt. I couldn't reach Pollard's boss on the telephone and soon as I do, I'll go to Tuba and talk to him. If I learn anything useful, I'll let you know."

"I'd appreciate that," Chee said. "I'd like to know some more about this."

"Probably absolutely no connection with the Kinsman case," Leaphorn said. "I don't see how there could be. Unless you know some reason to feel otherwise. I just thought—"

A loud voice from the doorway interrupted him.

"Chee!" The speaker was a beefy young man with reddish-blond hair and a complexion that suffered from too many hours of dry air and high-altitude sun. The coat of his dark blue suit was unbuttoned, his necktie was slightly loose, his white shirt was rumpled and his expression was irritated. "Mickey wants to get this damned thing over with," he said. "He wants you in there."

He was pointing at Chee, a violation of the Dine rules of courtesy. Now he beckoned to Chee with his finger—rude in a multitude of other cultures.

Chee rose, his face darkened a shade.

"Mr. Leaphorn," Chee said, motioning toward the man, "this gentleman is Agent Edgar Evans of the Federal Bureau of Investigation. He was assigned out here just a couple of months ago."

Leaphorn acknowledged that with a nod toward Evans.

"Chee," Agent Evans said, "Mickey is in a hell of a—"

"Tell Mr. Mickey I'll be there in a minute or

so," Chee said. And to Leaphorn: "I'll call you from the office when I know what we have."

Leaphorn smiled at Evans and turned back to Chee.

"I am particularly interested in that Jeep," Leaphorn said. "People don't just walk away from good trucks. It's odd. Someone sees it, mentions it to someone else, the word gets around."

Chee chuckled. (More, Leaphorn suspected, for Evans's benefit than his own.) "It does," Chee said. "And pretty soon people begin deciding no one wants it anymore, and parts of it begin showing up on other people's trucks."

"I'd like to spread the word that there's a reward for locating that Jeep," Leaphorn said.

Evans cleared his throat loudly.

"How much?" Chee asked.

"How does a thousand dollars sound?"

"About right," Chee said, turning toward the door. He motioned to Agent Evans. "Come on," he said. "Let's go."

Officer Benjamin Kinsman's room was lit by the sun pouring through its two windows and a battery of ceiling fluorescent lights. Entering involved slipping past a burly male nurse and two young women in the sort of pale blue smocks doctors wear. Acting Assistant U.S. Attorney J. D. Mickey stood by the windows. The shape of Officer Kinsman lay at rigid attention in the center of the bed, covered with a sheet. One of the vital signs monitors on the wall above the bed registered a horizontal white line. The other screen was blank.

Mickey looked at his watch, then at Chee, glanced at the doors and nodded.

"You're the arresting officer?"

"That's correct," Chee said.

"What I want you to do is ask the victim here if he can tell you anything about who killed him. What happened. All that. We just want to get it on the record in case the defense tries something fancy."

Chee licked his lips, cleared his throat, looked at the body.

"Ben," he said. "Can you tell me who killed you? Can you hear me? Can you tell me anything?"

"Pull the sheet down," Mickey said. "Off of his face."

Chee shook his head. "Ben," he said. "I'm sorry I didn't get there quicker. Be happy on your journey."

Agent Evans was pulling at the sheet, drawing it down to reveal Benjamin Kinsman's waxen face.

Chee gripped his wrist. Hard. "No," he said. "Don't do that." He pulled the sheet back in place.

"Let it go," Mickey said, looking at his watch

again. "I guess we're done here." He turned toward the door.

Standing there, looking in at Chee, at all of them, was Janet Pete.

"Better late than never," Mickey said. "I hope you got here early enough to know all your client's legal rights were satisfied."

Janet Pete, looking very pale, nodded. She stood aside to let them pass.

Behind Chee the medical crew was working fast, disconnecting wires and tubes—starting the bed rolling toward the side exit. There, Chee guessed, Officer Benjamin Kinsman's kidneys would be salvaged, perhaps his heart, perhaps whatever else some other person could use. But Ben was far, far away now. Only his *chindi* would remain here. Or would it follow the corpse into other rooms? Into other bodies? Navajo theology did not cover such contingencies. Corpses were dangerous, excepting only those of infants who die before their first laugh, and people who die naturally of old age. The good of Benjamin Kinsman would go with his spirit. The part of the personality that was out of harmony would linger as a *chindi*, causing sickness. Chee turned away from the body.

Janet was still standing at the door.

He stopped.

"Hello, Jim."

"Hello, Janet." He took a deep breath. "It's good to see you."

"Even like this?" She made a weak gesture at the room and tried to smile.

He didn't answer that. He felt dizzy, sick, and depleted.

"I tried to call you, but you're never home. I'm Robert Jano's counsel," she said. "I guess you knew that?"

"I didn't know it," Chee said. "Not until I heard what Mr. Mickey said."

"You're the arresting officer, as I heard? Is that right? So I need to talk to you."

"Fine," Chee said. "But I can't do it now. And not here. Somewhere away from here." He swallowed down the bile. "How about dinner?"

"I can't tonight. Mr. Mickey has us all conferring about the case. And, Jim, you look exhausted. I think you must be working too hard."

"I'm not," he said. "And you look great. Will you be here tomorrow?"

"I have to drive down to Phoenix."

"How about breakfast then? At the hotel."

"Good," she said, and they set the time.

Mickey was standing down the hallway. "Ms. Pete," he called.

"Got to go," she said, and turned, then turned back again. "Jim," she said, "tired or not, you look fine."

"You, too," Chee said. She did. The classic, perfect beauty you see on the cover of *Vogue*, or on any of the fashion magazines.

Chee leaned against the wall and watched her walk down the hall, around the corner and out of sight, wishing he had thought of something more romantic to say than "You, too." Wishing he knew what to do about her. About them. Wishing he knew whether he could trust her. Wishing life wasn't so damned complicated.

SIX

IT SEEMED OBVIOUS to Leaphorn that the person most likely to tell him something useful about Catherine Anne Pollard was Richard Krause, her boss and the biologist in charge of rooting out the cause of the reservation's most recent plague outbreak. A lifetime spent looking for people in the big emptiness of the Four Corners and several futile telephone calls had taught Leaphorn that Krause would probably be off somewhere unreachable. He had tried to call him as soon as he returned to Window Rock from Santa Fe. He'd tried again yesterday before driving back from Flagstaff. By now he had the number memorized as well as on the redial button. He picked up the telephone and punched it.

"Public Health," a male voice said. "Krause."

Leaphorn identified himself. "Mrs. Vanders has asked me—"

"I know," Krause said. "She called me. Maybe she's right. To start getting worried, I mean."

"Miss Pollard's not back yet, then?"

"No," Krause said. "Miss Pollard still hasn't shown up for work. Nor has she bothered to call in or communicate in any way. But I have to tell you that's what you learn to expect from Miss Pollard. Rules were made for other people."

"Any word on the vehicle she was driving?"

"Not to me," Krause said. "And to tell the truth, I'm getting a little bit concerned myself. At first I was just sore at her. Cathy is a tough gal to work with. She's very into doing her own thing her own way, if you know what I'm saying. I just thought she'd seen something that needed doing worse than what I'd told her to do. Sort of reassigned herself, you know."

"I know," Leaphorn said, thinking back to when Jim Chee had been his assistant. Still, as much trouble as Chee had been, it had been a pleasure to see him yesterday. He was a good man and unusually bright.

"You still think that might be a possibility? That Pollard might be off working on some project of her own and just not bothering to tell anyone about it?"

"Maybe," Krause said. "It wouldn't bother her to let me stew awhile, but not this long." He'd be happy to tell Leaphorn what he knew about Pollard and her work, but not today. Today he was tied up, absolutely snowed under. With Pollard away, he was doing both their jobs. But tomorrow morning he could make some time—and the earlier the better.

Which left Leaphorn with nothing to do but wait for Chee's promised call. But Chee would be driving back to Tuba City from Flag this morning, and then he wouldn't get into his files until he dealt with whatever problems had piled up in his absence. If Chee found something interesting in the files, he'd probably call after noon. Most likely there'd be no reason to call.

Leaphorn had never been good at waiting for the telephone to ring, or for anything else. He toasted two slices of bread, applied margarine and grape jelly, and sat in his kitchen, eating and staring at the Indian Country map mounted on the wall above the table.

The map was freckled with the heads of pins— red, white, blue, black, yellow, and green, plus a variety of shapes he'd reverted to when the colors available in pinheads had been exhausted. It had been accumulating pins on his office wall since early in his career. When he retired, the fellow who took over his office suggested he might want to keep it, and he'd said he couldn't imagine why. But keep it he had, and almost every pin in it revived a memory.

The first ones (plain steel-headed seamstress pins) he'd stuck in to keep track of places and dates where people had reported seeing a missing aircraft, the problem that then had been occupying his thoughts. The red ones had been next, establishing the delivery pattern of a gasoline tanker truck that was also hauling narcotics to customers on the Checkerboard Reservation. The most common ones were black, representing witchcraft reports. Personally, Leaphorn had lost all faith in the existence of these skinwalkers in his freshman year at Arizona State, but never in the reality of the problem that belief in them causes.

He'd come home for the semester break, full of new-won college sophistication and cynicism. He'd talked Jack Greyeyes into joining him to check out a reputed home base of skinwalkers and thus prove themselves liberated from tradition. They drove south from Shiprock past Rol-Hay Rock and Table Mesa to the volcanic outcrop of ugly black basalt where, according to the whispers in their age group, skinwalkers met in an underground room to perform the hideous initiation that turned recruits into witches. It was a rainy winter night, which cut the risk that someone would see them and accuse them of being witches themselves. Now, more than four decades later, winter rains still produced memorial shivers along Leaphorn's spine.

That night remained one of Leaphorn's most vivid memories. The darkness, the cold rain soaking through his jacket, the beginnings of fear. Greyeyes had decided when they'd reached the outcrop's base that this was a crazy idea.

"I'll tell you what," Greyeyes had said. "Let's not do it, and say we did."

So Leaphorn had taken custody of the flashlight, watched Greyeyes fade into the darkness, and waited for his courage to return. It didn't. He had stood there looking up at the great jumbled hump of rock. Suddenly he had been confronted with both nerve-racking fear and the sure knowledge that what he did now would determine the kind of man he would be. He'd torn his pant leg and bruised his knee on the way up. He'd found the gaping hole the whispers had described, shone his flash into it without locating a bottom, and then climbed down far enough to see where it led. The rumors had described a carpeted room littered with the fragments of corpses. He had found a drifted collection of blown sand and last summer's tumbleweeds.

That had confirmed his skepticism about skinwalker mythology, just as his career in the Navajo

Tribal Police had confirmed his belief in what the evil skinwalkers symbolized. He'd lost any lingering doubts about that in his rookie year. He had laughed off a warning that a Navajo oil-field pumper believed two neighbors had witched his daughter, thus causing her fatal illness.

As soon as the four-day mourning period tradition decrees had ended, the pumper had killed the witches with his shotgun.

He thought about that now as he chewed his toast. Eight black pins formed a cluster in the general vicinity of that north-reaching outcrop of Black Mesa that included Yells Back Butte. Why so many there? Probably because that area had twice been the source of bubonic plague cases and once of the deadly hantavirus. Witches offer an easy explanation for unexplained illnesses. To the north, Short Mountain and the Short Mountain Wash country had attracted another cluster of black pins. Leaphorn was pretty sure that was due to John McGinnis, operator of the Short Mountain Trading Post. Not that the pins meant more witch problems around Short Mountain. They represented McGinnis's remarkable talent as a collector and broadcaster of gossip. The old man had a special love for skinwalker tales, and his Navajo customers, knowing his weakness, brought him all the skinwalker sightings and witching reports they could collect. But any sort of gossip was good enough for the old man. Thinking that, Leaphorn reached for his new edition of the Navajo Communications Company telephone directory.

The Short Mountain Trading Post number was no longer listed. He dialed the Short Mountain Chapter House. Was the trading post still operating? The woman who had picked up the telephone chuckled. "Well," she said, "I'd guess you'd say more or less."

"Is John McGinnis still there? Still alive?"

The chuckle became a laugh. "Oh, yes indeed," she said. "He's still going strong. Don't the *bilagaana* have a saying that only the good die young?"

Joe Leaphorn finished his toast, put a message on his answering machine for Chee in case he did call, and drove his pickup out of Shiprock heading northwest across the Navajo Nation. He was feeling much more cheerful.

The years that had passed since he'd visited Short Mountain hadn't changed it much— certainly not for the better. The parking area in front was still hard-packed clay, too dry and dense to encourage weeds. The old GMC truck he'd parked next to years ago still rested wheelless on blocks, slowly rusting away. The 1968 Chevy pickup parked in the shade of a juniper at the corner of the sheep pens looked like the one

McGinnis had always driven, and a faded sign nailed to the hay barn still proclaimed THIS STORE FOR SALE, INQUIRE WITHIN. But today the benches on the shady porch were empty, with drifts of trash under them. The windows looked even dustier than Leaphorn remembered. In fact, the trading post looked deserted, and the gusty breeze chasing tumbleweeds and dust past the porch added to the sense of desolation. Leaphorn had an uneasy feeling, tinged with sadness, that the woman at the chapter house was wrong. That even tough old John McGinnis had proved vulnerable to too much time and too many disappointments.

The breeze was the product of a cloud Leaphorn had been watching build up over Black Mesa for the last twenty miles. It was too early in the summer to make a serious rain likely but—as bad as the road back to the highway was—even a shower could present a problem down in Short Mountain Wash. Leaphorn climbed out of his pickup to the rumble of thunder and hurried toward the store.

John McGinnis appeared in the doorway, holding the screen door open, staring out at him with his shock of white hair blowing across his forehead and looking twenty pounds too thin for the overalls that engulfed him.

"Be damned," McGinnis said. "Guess it's true what I heard about them finally getting you off the police force. Thought I had me a customer for a while. Didn't they let you keep the uniform?"

"*Ya'eeh te'h*," Leaphorn said. "It's good to see you." And he meant it. That surprised him a little. Maybe, like McGinnis, the loneliness was beginning to get to him.

"Well, damnit, come on in so I can get this door closed and keep the dirt from blowing in," McGinnis said. "And let me get you something to wet your whistle. You Navajos act like you're born in a barn."

Leaphorn followed the old man through the musty darkness of the store, noticing that McGinnis was more stooped than he had remembered him, that he walked with a limp, that many of the shelves lining the walls were half-empty, that behind the dusty glass where McGinnis kept pawned jewelry very little was being offered, that the racks that once had displayed an array of the slightly gaudy rugs and saddle blankets that the Short Mountain weavers produced were now empty. Which will die first, Leaphorn wondered, the trading post or the trader?

McGinnis ushered him into the back room—his living room, bedroom and kitchen—and waved him into a recliner upholstered with worn red velour. He transferred ice cubes from his refrigerator into a Coca-Cola glass, filled it from a two-liter Pepsi bottle, and handed it to Leaphorn. Then he collected a bourbon bottle and a plastic measuring cup from his kitchen table, seated himself on a rocking chair across from Leaphorn, and began carefully pouring himself a drink.

"As I remember it," he said while he dribbled in the bourbon, "you don't drink hard liquor. If I'm wrong about that, you tell me and I'll get you something better than soda pop."

"This is fine," Leaphorn said.

McGinnis held the measuring cup up, examined it against the light from the dusty window, shook his head, and poured a few drops carefully back into the bottle. He inspected the level again, seemed satisfied, and took a sip.

"You want to do a little visiting first?" McGinnis asked. "Or do you want to get right down to what you came here for?"

"Either way," Leaphorn said. "I'm in no hurry. I'm retired now. Just a civilian. But you know that."

"I heard it," McGinnis said. "I'd retire myself if I could find somebody stupid enough to buy this hellhole."

"Is it keeping you pretty busy?" Leaphorn asked, trying to imagine anyone offering to buy the place. Even tougher trying to imagine McGinnis selling it if someone did. Where would the old man go? What would he do when he got there?

McGinnis ignored the question. "Well," he said, "if you came by to get some gasoline, you're out of luck. The dealers charge me extra for hauling it way out here and I have to tack a little bit on to the price to pay for that. Just offered gasoline anyway to convenience these hard cases that still live around here. But they took to getting their tanks filled up when they get to Tuba or Page, so the gas I got hauled out to make it handy for 'em just sat there and evaporated. So to hell with 'em. I don't fool with it anymore."

McGinnis had rattled that off in his scratchy whiskey voice—an explanation he'd given often enough to have it memorized. He looked at Leaphorn, seeking understanding.

"Can't say I blame you," Leaphorn said.

"Well, you oughtn't to. When the bastards would forget and let the gauge get down to empty, they'd come in, air up their tires, fill the radiator with my water, wash their windshield with my rags, and buy two gallons. Just enough to get 'em into one of them discount stations."

Leaphorn shook his head, expressing disapproval.

"And want credit for the gas," McGinnis said, and took another long, thirsty sip.

"But I noticed driving in that you still have a tank up on your loading rack. With a hand pump on it. You keep that just for your own pickup?"

McGinnis rocked a little while, considering the question. And probably wondering, Leaphorn thought, if Leaphorn had noticed that the old man's pickup was double-tanked, like most empty-country vehicles, and wouldn't need many refills.

"Well, hell," McGinnis said. "You know how folks are. Come in here with a dry tank and seventy miles to a station, you got to have something for 'em."

"I guess so," Leaphorn said.

"If you haven't got any gas to give 'em, then they just hang around and waste your time gossiping. Then they want to use your telephone to get some kinfolks to come and bring 'em a can."

He glowered at Leaphorn, took another sip of bourbon. "You ever know a Navajo to be in a hurry? You got 'em underfoot for hours. Drinking up your water and running you out of ice cubes."

McGinnis's face was slightly pink—embarrassment caused by his admission of humanity. "So finally I just quit paying the bills and the telephone company cut me off. I figured keeping a little gasoline was cheaper."

"Probably," Leaphorn said.

McGinnis was glowering at him again, making sure that Leaphorn wouldn't suspect some socially responsible purpose in this decision.

"What'd you come out here for anyway? You

just got a lot of time to waste now you're not a cop?"

"I wondered if you ever had any customers named Tijinney?"

"Tijinney?" McGinnis looked thoughtful.

"They had a place over in what used to be the Joint Use Reservation. Over by the northwest corner of Black Mesa. Right on the Navajo–Hopi border."

"I didn't know there was any of that outfit left," McGinnis said. "Sickly bunch, as I remember it. Somebody always coming in here for me to take 'em to the doctor over at Tuba or the clinic at Many Farms. And they did a lot of business with old Margaret Cigaret and some of the other shamans, getting curing ceremonials done. They was always coming in here trying to get me to donate a sheep to help feed folks at the sings."

"You remember that map I used to keep?" Leaphorn asked. "Where I'd record things I needed to remember? I looked at it this morning and I noticed I'd marked down a lot of skinwalker gossip over there where they lived. You think all that sickness would account for that?"

"Sure," McGinnis said. "But I got a feeling I know what this is leading up to. That Kinsman boy the Hopi killed, wasn't that over there on the old Tijinney grazing lease?"

"I think so," Leaphorn said.

McGinnis was holding his measuring cup up to the light, squinting at the level. He poured in another ounce or two of bourbon. "Just 'think so'?" he said. "I heard the federals had that business all locked up. Didn't that young cop that used to work with you catch the man right when he did it? Caught him right in the act, the way I heard it."

"You mean Jim Chee? Yeah, he caught a Hopi named Jano."

"So what are you working on out here?" McGinnis asked. "I know you ain't just visiting. Aren't you supposed to be retired? What're you up to? Working the other side?"

Leaphorn shrugged. "I'm just trying to understand some things."

"Well, now, is that a fact?" McGinnis said. "I was guessing you were trying to find some way to prove that Hopi boy didn't do the killing."

"Why would you think that?"

"Cowboy Dashee was in here just the other day. You remember Cowboy? Deputy with the sheriff's office?"

"Sure."

"Well, Cowboy says the Jano boy didn't do it. He says Chee got the wrong fella."

Leaphorn shrugged, thinking that Jano was probably kinfolks with Dashee, or a member of his kiva. The Hopis lived in a much smaller world than the Navajos. "Did Cowboy tell you who was the right fella?"

McGinnis had stopped rocking. He was staring at Leaphorn, looking puzzled.

"I was guessing wrong, wasn't I? Are you going to tell me what you're up to?"

"I am seeing if I can find out what happened to a young woman who worked for the Indian Health Service. She was checking on plague cases. Drove out of Tuba City more than a week ago and she still hasn't come back."

McGinnis had been rocking, holding his measuring cup in his left hand, left elbow on the rocker's arm, his forearm moving just enough to compensate for the motion—keeping the bourbon from splashing, keeping the surface level. But he wasn't watching his drink. He was staring out the dusty window. Not out of it, Leaphorn realized. McGinnis was watching a medium-sized spider working on a web between the window frame and a high shelf. He stopped rocking, pushed himself creakily out of the chair. "Look at that," he said. "The sonsabitches are slow learners."

He walked to the window, crumpled a handkerchief from his overalls pocket, chased the spider across the web with it, folded the cloth carefully around the insect, opened the window screen, and shook it out into the yard. Obviously the old man had a lot of practice capturing such insects. Leaphorn remembered once seeing McGinnis capture a wasp the same way, evicting it unharmed through the same window.

McGinnis retrieved his drink and lowered himself, groaning, back into his chair.

"Sonofabitch will be right back first time he sees the door open," he said.

"I've known people to just step on them," Leaphorn said, but he remembered his mother dealing with spiders in the same way.

"I used to do that," McGinnis said. "Even had some bug spray. But you get older, and you look at 'em up close and you get to thinking about it. You get to thinking they got a right to live, too. They don't kill me. I don't kill them. You step on a beetle, it's like a little murder."

"How about eating sheep?" Leaphorn asked.

McGinnis was rocking again, ignoring him. "Very small murders, I guess you'd have to say. But one thing leads to another."

Leaphorn sipped his Pepsi.

"Sheep? I quit eating meat a while back," McGinnis said. "But you didn't drive all the way in here to talk about my diet. You want to talk about that Health Department girl that run off with their truck."

"You hear anything about that?" Leaphorn asked.

"Woman named Cathy something or other,

wasn't it?" McGinnis said. "The Fleacatcher, the folks out here call her, because she collects the damned things. She was in here a time or two, asking questions. Wanted to get some gas once. Bought some soda pop, some crackers. Can of Spam, too. And it wasn't a truck, either, now I think of it. It was a Jeep. A black one."

"About that black Jeep. The family's offering a thousand-dollar reward to anybody who finds it."

McGinnis took another sip, savored it, stared out the window.

"That don't sound like they think she eloped."

"They don't," Leaphorn said. "They think somebody killed her. What sort of questions was she asking when she was in here?"

"About sick folks. Where they might have got the fleas on 'em to get the plague. Did they have sheepdogs? Anybody notice prairie dogs dying? Or dead squirrels? Dead kangaroo rats?" McGinnis shrugged. "Strictly business, she was. Seemed like a mighty tough lady. No time for kidding around. Hard as nails. And I noticed when she was walking around, she was looking at the floor all the time. Looking for rat droppings. And that pissed me off some. And I said, 'Missy, what are you looking for back there behind the counter? You lose something?' And she said, 'I'm looking for mice manure.'" McGinnis produced a rusty laugh and slapped the arm of his rocker. "Came right out with it without a blink and kept right on looking. Quite a lady she is."

"You heard anything about what might have happened to her?"

McGinnis laughed, took another sip of his bourbon. "Sure," he said. "It gives folks something to talk about. Heard all kinds of things. Heard she might have run off with Krause—that fellow she works with." McGinnis chuckled. "That'd be like Golda Meir running off with Yasser Arafat. Heard she might have run off with another young man who was out here with her a time or two. Some sort of student scientist, I think he was. He seemed kind of strange to me."

"Sounds like you don't think she and her boss got along."

"They was in here just twice that I remember," McGinnis said. "First time they never said a word to each other. I guess that's all right if you're stuck in the same truck all day. Second time it was snarling and snapping. Hostile-like."

"I'd heard she didn't like him," Leaphorn said.

"It was mutual. He was paying for some stuff he got, and she walked past him out the door and he said 'Bitch.'"

"Loud enough for her to hear him?"

"If she was listening."

"You think he might have knocked her on the head and dumped her somewhere?"

"I figure him for being hell on rodents and fleas, things like that. Not humans," McGinnis said. He thought about that for a moment and chuckled again. "Of course, couple of my customers figure the skinwalkers got off with her."

"What do you think of that?"

"Not much," McGinnis said. "Skinwalkers get a lot of blame around here. Sheepdog dies. Car breaks down. Kid gets the chicken pox. Roof leaks. Skinwalkers get the blame."

"I heard she had driven out toward Yells Back Butte to do some work out there," Leaphorn said. "There always seemed to be a lot of witching talk around there."

"Lot of talk about that place," McGinnis said. "Had its own legend. Old Man Tijinney was supposed to be a witch. Had a bucket of silver dollars buried somewhere. A tub full, the way some told it. When the last of that outfit died off people dug holes all around out there. Some of the city kids didn't even respect the death hogan taboo. I heard they dug in there, too."

"Find anything?"

McGinnis shook his head, sipped his drink. "You ever run into that Dr. Woody fella out there? He comes in here a time or two just about every summer. Working on some sort of a rodent research project here and there, and I think he has some sort of setup near the butte. He was in three or four weeks back to get some stuff and telling me another skinwalker story. I think it's a kind of hobby of his. Collects them. Thinks they're funny."

"Who's he get 'em from?" Leaphorn asked. It was a rare Navajo who'd pass along a skinwalker report to anyone he didn't know pretty well.

McGinnis obviously knew exactly what Leaphorn was thinking.

"Oh, he's been coming out here for years. Long enough to speak good Navajo. Comes and goes. Hires local folks to collect rodent information for him. Friendly guy."

"And he told you a fresh skinwalker story? Something that happened out near Yells Back?"

"I don't know how fresh it was," McGinnis said. "He said Old Man Saltman told him about seeing a skinwalker standing by a bunch of boulders at the bottom of the butte a little bit after sundown, and then disappearing behind them, and when he came out he turned into an owl and went flopping away like he had a broken wing."

"Turned from what into an owl?"

McGinnis looked surprised by the question. "Why, from a man. You know how it goes. Hosteen Saltman said the owl kept flopping around as if he wanted to be followed."

"Yeah," Leaphorn said. "And he didn't follow, of course. That's how the story usually goes."

McGinnis laughed. "I remember about the first or second time I saw you, I asked if you believed in skinwalkers, and you said you just believed in people who believed in 'em, and all the trouble that caused. Is that still the case?"

"Pretty much," Leaphorn said.

"Well then, let me tell you one I'll bet you haven't heard before. There's an old woman who comes in here after shearing time every spring to sell me three or four sacks of wool. Sometimes they call her Grandma Charlie, I think it is, but I believe her name is Old Lady Notah. She was in here just yesterday telling me about seeing a skinwalker."

McGinnis raised his glass in a toast to Leaphorn. "Now listen to this one. She said she was out looking after a bunch of goats she has over by Black Mesa—right on the edge of the Hopi Reservation— and she notices somebody down the slope messing around with something on the ground. Like hunting for something. Anyway, this fella disappears behind the junipers for a minute or two and then emerges, and now he's different. Now he's bigger, and all white with a big round head, and when he turned her way, his whole face flashed."

"Flashed?"

"She said like the flash thing on her daughter's little camera."

"What did the man look like when he quit being a witch?"

"She didn't stick around to see," McGinnis said. "But wait a minute. You ain't heard all of it yet. She said when this skinwalker turned around he looked like he had an elephant's trunk coming out of his back. Now how about that?"

"You're right," Leaphorn said. "That's a new one."

"And come to think of it, you can add that one to your Yells Back Butte stories. That's about where Old Lady Notah has her grazing lease."

"Well, now," Leaphorn said, "I think I might want to talk to her about that. I'd like to hear some more details."

"Me, too," McGinnis said, and laughed. "She said the skinwalker looked like a snowman."

SEVEN

THEY'D AGREED TO meet for breakfast, early because Janet had to drive south to Phoenix and Chee had to go about as far north to Tuba City. "Let's make it seven on the dot, and not by Navajo time," Janet had said.

There he was, a little before seven, waiting for her at a table in the hotel coffee shop, thinking about the night he'd walked into her apartment in Gallup. He'd been carrying flowers, a video-tape of a traditional Navajo wedding and the notion that she could explain away the way she had used him, and—

He didn't want to think about that. Not now and not ever. What could change that she'd gotten information from him and tipped off the law professor, the man she'd told Chee she hated?

Before he'd finally slept, he decided he would simply ask her if they were still engaged. "Janet," he would say. "Do you still want to marry me?" Get right to the point. But this morning, with his head still full of gloomy thoughts, he wasn't so sure. Did he really want her to say yes? He decided she probably would. She had left her high-society inside-the-Beltway life and come back to Indian Country, which said she really loved him. But that would carry with it, in some subtle way, her understanding that he would climb the ladder of success into the social strata where she felt at home.

There was another possibility. She had taken her first reservation job to escape her law professor lover. Did this return simply mean she wanted the man to pursue her again? Chee turned away from that thought and remembered how sweet it had been before she had betrayed him (or, as she saw it, before he had insulted her because of his unreasonable jealousy). He could land a federal job in Washington. Could he be happy there? He thought of himself as a drunk, worthless, dying of a destroyed liver. Was that what had killed Janet's Navajo father? Had he drowned himself in whiskey to escape Janet's ruling-caste mother?

When he'd exhausted all the dark corners that scenario offered, he turned to an alternative.

Janet had come back to him. She'd be willing to live on the Big Rez, wife of a cop, living in what her friends would rate as slum housing, where high culture was a second-run movie. In that line of thought, love overcame all. But it wouldn't. She'd yearn for the life she'd given up. He would see it. They'd be miserable.

Finally he thought of Janet as court-appointed defense attorney and of himself as arresting officer. But by the time she walked in, exactly on time, he was back to thinking of her as an Eastern social butterfly, and that thought gave this Flagstaff dining room a worn, grungy look that he'd never noticed before.

He pulled back a chair for her.

"I guess you're used to classier places in Washington," he said, and instantly wished he hadn't so carelessly touched the nerve of their disagreement.

Janet's smile wavered. She looked at him a moment, somberly, and looked away. "I'll bet the coffee is better here."

"It's always fresh anyway," he said. "Or almost always."

A teenage boy delivered two mugs and a bowl filled with single-serving-size containers labeled NON-DAIRY CREAMER.

Janet looked over her mug at him. "Jim."

Chee waited. "What?"

"Oh, nothing. I guess this is a time to talk business."

"So we take off our friend hats, and put on adversary hats?"

"Not really," Janet said. "But I'd like to know if you're absolutely certain Robert Jano killed Officer Kinsman."

"Sure I'm certain," Chee said. He felt his face flushing. "You must have read the arrest report. I was there, wasn't I? And what do you do with it if I say I'm not sure? Do you tell the jury that even the arresting officer told you that he had reasonable doubts?"

He'd tried to keep the anger out of his voice, but Janet's face told him he hadn't managed it. Another raw nerve touched.

"I'd do absolutely nothing with it," she said. "It's just that Jano swears he didn't do it. I'll be working with him. I'd like to believe him."

"Don't," Chee said. He sipped his coffee and put down the mug. It occurred to him that he hadn't noticed how it tasted. He picked up one of the containers: " 'Non-dairy creamer,' " he read. "Produced, I understand, on non-dairy farms."

Janet managed a smile. "You know what? Doesn't this episode we're having here remind you of the first time we met? Remember? In the holding room at the San Juan County Jail in Aztec. You were trying to keep me from bonding out that old man."

"And you were trying to keep me from talking to him."

"But I got him out." Janet was grinning at him now.

"But not until I got the information I wanted," Chee said.

"Okay," Janet said, still grinning. "We'll call that one a tie. Even though you had to cheat a little."

"How about our next competition," Chee said. "Remember the old alcoholic? You thought Leaphorn and I were picking on him. Until your client pleaded guilty."

"That was a sad, sad case," Janet said. She sipped her coffee. "Some things about it still bother me. Some things about this one bother me, too."

"Like what? Like the fact Jano is a Hopi and the Hopis are peaceful people? Nonviolent?"

"There's that, of course," Janet said. "But everything he told me has a sort of logic to it and a lot of it can be checked out."

"Like what? What can be checked?"

"Like, for example, he said he was going to collect an eagle his kiva needed for a ceremonial. His brothers in his religious group can confirm that. That made it a religious pilgrimage, on which no evil thoughts are allowed."

"Such as thoughts of revenge? Such as getting even with Kinsman for the prior arrest? The kind of thoughts the D.A. will want to suggest to the jury if he's going for malice, premeditation. The death penalty stuff."

"Right," she said.

"They would confirm why he was going for the eagle, and the prosecution would concede it," Chee said. "But how do you prove that deep down Jano didn't want to even the score?"

Janet shrugged.

"J. D. Mickey will probably state that in his opening. He'll say that Jano had gone onto the Navajo reservation to poach an eagle—a crime in itself. He'll say that Officer Benjamin Kinsman of the Navajo Tribal Police had previously arrested him doing the same crime last year and that Jano got off on some sort of technicality. He'll say that when he saw Kinsman was after him again, Jano was enraged. So instead of releasing the bird, getting rid of the evidence and trying to escape, he let Kinsman catch him, caught him off-guard and brained him."

"Is that the way Mickey is planning it?"

"I'm just guessing," Chee said.

"I have no doubt at all that Mickey will go for death. It would be the first one since the 1994

Congress allowed federal death penalties and there would be a media coverage circus." Janet doctored her coffee with the non-dairy creamer, tasted it. "Mickey for Congress," she intoned. "Your law-and-order candidate."

"That's the way I see it," Chee said. "But the courts would have to rule that Kinsman was a federal officer."

"People in criminal justice say he was."

Chee shrugged. "Probably."

"Which led the U.S. Department of Justice to unplug him from the various life support machines," Janet said. "So Benjamin Kinsman could hurry up and be a murder victim instead of the subject of criminal assault. Thereby simplifying the paperwork."

"Come on, Janet," Chee said. "Be fair. Ben was already dead. The machines were breathing for him, making his heart pump. Kinsman's spirit had gone away."

Janet was sipping her coffee. "You're right about one thing," she said. "This is good fresh java. Not that weird perfumed stuff the yuppie bars sell for four dollars a cup."

"What else could be checked out?" Chee asked. "In Jano's version."

Janet raised her hand. "First something else," she said. "How about that autopsy? The law requires one in homicides, sort of, but a lot of Navajos don't like the idea and sometimes they're skipped. And I heard one of the docs saying something about organ donations?"

"Kinsman was a Mormon. So were his parents. He'd had a donor card registered," Chee said, studying her as he said it. "But you already knew that. You were changing the subject."

"I'm the defense attorney," she said. "You think my client is guilty. I've got to be careful what I tell you."

Chee nodded. "But if there's something that can be checked out that I'm missing, something that could help his case, then I ought to know about it. I'm not going to go out there and destroy the evidence. Don't you—"

He had started to say: "Don't you trust me?" But she would have said she did. And then she would have returned the question, and he had no idea how he could answer it.

She was leaning forward, elbows on table, chin resting on clasped hands, waiting for him to finish.

"End of statement," he said. "Sure, I think he's guilty. I was there. Had I been a little faster, I would have stopped it."

"Cowboy doesn't think he's guilty."

"Cowboy? Cowboy Dashee?"

"Yes," Janet said. "Your old friend, Deputy Sheriff Cowboy Dashee. He told me Jano is his cousin. He's known him since childhood. They were playmates. Close friends. Cowboy told me that thinking Robert Jano would kill somebody with a rock is like thinking Mother Teresa would strangle the Pope."

"Really?"

"That's what he said. His exact words, in fact."

"How come you got in touch with Cowboy?"

"I didn't. He called the D.A.'s office. Asked who'd be assigned to handle Jano's defense. They told him a new hire would be assigned to it, and he left a message for whoever that would be to give him a call. It was me, so I called him."

"Well, hell," Chee said. "How come he didn't contact me?"

"I don't have to explain that, do I? He was afraid you'd think he was trying—"

"Sure," Chee said. "Of course."

Janet looked sympathetic. "That makes it worse for you, doesn't it? I know you guys go way back."

"Yeah, we do," Chee said. "Cowboy's about as good a friend as I ever had."

"Well, he's a cop, too. He'll understand."

"He's also a Hopi," Chee said. "And some wise man once told us that blood's thicker than water." He sighed. "What did Cowboy tell you?"

"He said Jano had caught his eagle. He was coming home with it. He heard noises. He checked. He found the officer on the ground, head bleeding."

Chee shook his head. "I know. That's the statement he gave us. When he finally decided to talk about it."

"It could be true."

"Sure," Chee said. "It could be true. But how about the slash on his forearm, and his blood mixed with Ben's? And no blood on the eagle? And where's the perpetrator, if it wasn't Jano? Ben Kinsman didn't hit himself on the head with that rock. It wasn't suicide."

"The eagle flew away," Janet said. "And don't be sarcastic."

That stopped Chee cold. He sat for a long moment, just staring at her.

She looked puzzled. "What?"

"He told you the eagle flew away?"

"That's right. When he caught it, Jano was under some brush or something," she said. "A blind, I guess, with something on a cord for bait. He tried to grab the eagle by the legs and just got one of them, and it slashed him on the arm and he released it."

"Janet," Chee said. "The eagle didn't fly away. It was in a wire cage just about eight or ten feet from where Jano was standing over Kinsman."

Janet put down her coffee cup.

Chee frowned. "He told you it got away? But he knew we had it. Why would he tell you that?"

She shrugged. Looked down at her hands.

"And it didn't have any blood on its feathers. At least, I didn't see any. I'm sure the lab would check for it.

"If you think I'm lying, look." He held out his hand, displaying the still healing slash on its side. "I picked up the cage to move it. That's where its talon caught me. Ripped the skin."

Janet's face was flushed. "You didn't have to show me anything," she said. "I didn't think you were lying. I'll ask Jano about it. Maybe I misunderstood. I must have."

Chee saw Janet was embarrassed. "I'll bet I know what happened," he said. "Jano didn't want to talk about the eagle because it got too close to violating kiva secrecy rules. I think it would become a symbolic messenger to God, to the spirit world. Its role would be sacred. He just couldn't talk about it, so he said he turned it loose."

"Maybe so," she said.

"I'll bet he just wanted to divert you. To talk about something besides a touchy religious subject."

Janet's expression told him she doubted that.

"I'll ask him about it," Janet repeated. "I really haven't had much chance to talk to him yet. Just a few minutes. I just got here."

"But he told you he didn't kill Kinsman. Did he tell you who did?"

"Well," Janet said, and hesitated. "You know, Jim, I have to be careful talking about this. Let me just say that I guess whoever it was who had hit Officer Kinsman with the rock must have heard Jano coming and went away. Jano said it started raining about the time you got there. By the time you had him handcuffed in the patrol car, and called in for help, and tried to make Kinsman comfortable, any tracks would have been washed away."

Chee didn't comment on that. He had to be careful, too.

"Don't you think so? Or did you find other tracks?"

"You mean other than Jano's?"

"Of course. Did you have a chance to look for any before it started raining?"

Chee considered the question, why she had asked it and whether she already knew the answer.

"You want some more coffee?"

"Okay," Janet said.

Chee signaled the waiter, thinking about what he was about to do. It was fair, if her effort to get him to state that he hadn't looked for other tracks was fair.

"Janet, Jano told you how he got those deep

slashes on his forearm. Did he mention exactly when he got scratched?"

The boy brought the coffee, refilled their cups, asked if they were ready to order breakfast.

"Give us another minute," Chee said.

"When?" Janet said. "Isn't that obvious? It would have been either while he was catching the eagle or when he was putting it in the cage. Or somewhere in between. I didn't quiz him about it."

"But did he say? Specifically when?"

"You mean in relation to what?" she asked, grinning at him. "Come on, Jim. Say it. The police lab people have told you that Jano's blood is mixed with Kinsman's on Kinsman's shirt. The lab is probably doing some of their new molecular magic to tell them if Jano's blood had been exposed to the air longer than Kinsman's, and how much longer, and all that."

"Can they do that now?" he asked, wishing he hadn't been pressing her on this, making her angry for no reason. "They probably would if they could, because the official, formal theory of the crime will be that Jano struggled with Kinsman and got his arm slashed on Kinsman's belt buckle."

"Can they do it? I don't know. Probably. But how can you get cut on a belt buckle?"

"Kinsman liked to bend the rules when he could. Put a feather in his uniform hat, that sort of thing. He put a fancy buckle on his belt to see how long it would be before I told him to take it off. Anyway, that's why the timing seems to be important."

"Well, go ahead then. Ask me. Just exactly to the minute, when did Jano get his arm slashed?"

"Okay," Chee said. "Exactly, precisely when?"

"Ha!" Janet said. "You're treading on client confidentiality."

"Whaddaya mean?"

"You know what I mean. I see J. D. Mickey with a new hundred-dollar haircut and an Italian silk suit addressing the jury. 'Ladies and gentlemen. The defendant's blood was found mixed with the blood of the victim on Officer Kinsman's uniform.' And then he gets into all the blood chemistry stuff." Janet raised her hand, dropped her voice—providing a poor imitation of Mickey's courtroom dramatics. " 'But! But! He told an officer of this court that he suffered the cut later. After he had moved Officer Kinsman.' "

"So I guess you're not going to tell me," Chee said.

"Right," Janet said. She put down her menu, studied him. Her expression was somber. "A little while ago, I might have."

Chee let his expression ask the question.

"How can I trust you when you don't trust me?"

Chee waited.

She shook her head. "I'm not just a shyster trying for a reputation with some sort of cheap acquittal," she said. "I really want to know if Robert Jano is innocent. I want to know what happened."

She put down her menu and stared at him, inviting a response.

"I understand that," Chee said.

"I respect—" she began. Her voice tightened. She paused, looked away from him. "When I asked you about the tracks, I wasn't trying to trick you," she said. "I asked because I think if somebody else had been there and left any traces you would have found them. That is, if anybody in the world could have found them. And if there weren't any, then maybe I'm wrong and maybe Robert Jano did kill your officer, and maybe I should be trying to talk him into a plea bargain. So I ask you, but you don't trust me, so you change the subject."

Chee had put down his menu to listen to this. Now he picked it up, opened it. "And now, once again, I think we should change the subject. How were things in Washington?"

"I'm really not going to have time for break-fast." She put down her menu, said, "Thanks for the coffee," and walked out.

EIGHT

"**THERE'S JUST ONE** thing I can tell you and feel absolutely certain about it," said Richard Krause without looking up from the box full of assorted stuff he was picking through. "Cathy Pollard didn't just run off with our Jeep. Something happened to her. But don't ask me what."

Leaphorn nodded. "That's what my client believes," he said. My client. It was the first time he'd used that term, and he didn't like the sound of it. Was this what he was making of himself? A private investigator?

Krause was probably in his late forties, Leaphorn guessed, big-boned, lean and gristly, probably an athlete in college, with a shock of blondish hair just showing signs of gray. He was sitting on a high stool behind a table in a faded green work shirt, dividing his attention between Leaphorn and stacks of transparent Ziploc bags that seemed to contain small dead insects—fleas or lice. Or maybe ticks.

"I guess you're working for her family," Krause said. He opened another bag, extracted a flea, and put it on a slide, which he placed in a binocular microscope. "Do they have any theories?"

"Ideas float around," Leaphorn said, asking himself if the ethics of private investigators, presuming they had them, allowed one to reveal the identity of clients. He'd deal with that when circumstances required. "The obvious ones. A sex crime. A nervous breakdown. A rejected boyfriend. Things like that."

Krause adjusted the microscope's focus, stared into the lenses, grunted and removed the slide. In its former existence this temporary lab had been a low-down-payment double-wide mobile home, and the heat of the summer sun radiated through its aluminum roof. The swamp-cooler fan roared away at its highest setting, mixing damp air into the dry heat. The rows of specimen jars on the shelf behind Krause were sweating. So was Krause. So was Leaphorn.

"I really doubt there's a boyfriend involved in this," he said. "She didn't seem to have one. Never talked about it anyway." He transferred the flea into another Ziploc bag, wrote something on an adhesive tag, and stuck it in place. "Of course, there could be a jilted one floating around somewhere in the past. That wouldn't be the sort of thing Cathy would have chatted about, even if she chatted. Which she didn't do much."

The cluttered, makeshift laboratory was reminding Leaphorn of his student career at Arizona State, which in those long-ago days required a mix of natural science courses even if your major was anthropology. Then he realized it wasn't as much what he was seeing as what he was smelling—those tissue-preserving, soap-defying chemicals that drove the scent of death deep into the pores of even the cleanest students.

"Cathy was a very serious lady. Focused. Just talked about business," Krause was saying. "She had a thing about bubonic plague. Thought it was downright criminal that we protect the middle-class urbanites from these communicable diseases and let the vectors do their thing out here in the boondocks where nobody gets killed except the working class. Cathy sounded like one of those old-fashioned Marxists sometimes."

"Tell me about the Jeep," Leaphorn said.

Krause stopped what he'd been doing, stared at Leaphorn, frowning. "The Jeep? What's to tell?"

"If there's foul play involved in this, the truck will probably be how the case gets broken."

Krause shook his head. Laughed. "It was just a black Jeep. They all look alike."

"It's harder to dispose of a vehicle," Leaphorn said.

"Than a body?" Krause said. "Sure. I see what you mean. Well, actually it was a pretty fancy model. We heard it was one of those seized by the DEA guys in a drug bust and turned over to the Health Department. Had a white pinstripe. Very hi-fi radio with special speakers. Telephone installed. The cowboy model. No top. Roll bars. Winch on the front. Tow-chain hooks and a trailer hitch on the back. I think it was three years old, but you know they don't change those models much. I drove it myself some until Cathy got it away from me."

"How'd that happen?"

"What Cathy wanted, Cathy got." He shrugged. "Actually, she had a good argument for it. Spent more time out in the bad country while I was doing the paperwork in here."

"I'm trying to get the word around that there's a reward out for whoever finds that vehicle. A thousand dollars."

Krause raised his eyebrows. "The family sounds serious then," he said, grinning. "What if she just drives in here and parks it? Can I call in and collect?"

"Probably not," Leaphorn said. "But I'd appreciate the call."

"I'll be happy to let you know."

"How about a man named Victor Hammar?" Leaphorn asked. "I'm told they knew each other. You wouldn't put him in the boyfriend category?"

Krause looked surprised. "Hammar? I don't think so." He shook his head, grinning.

"One of the theories has it that Hammar was in love with her. The way it's told, she didn't share the sentiment, but she couldn't get rid of him."

"Naw," Krause said. "I don't think so. Matter of fact, she invited him out here a while back. He's working on his doctorate in vertebrate biology. He's interested in what we're doing."

"Just in what you're doing? Not in the woman who's doing it?"

"Oh, they're friends," Krause said. "And he probably feels those glandular urges. Young male, you know. And he likes her, but I think that was because she sort of gave him a little mothering when he was new in the country. He has a sort of funny accent. No friends in the department, I'll bet. From what I've seen of him, probably not many friends anywhere else either. So along comes Cathy. She's like a lot of these kids who grow up rich. They like doing good for the working-class losers. So she helped him along.

Makes 'em feel less guilty about being part of the parasitic privileged class."

"When you think about it, though," Leaphorn said, "what you described is sort of typical of these stalker homicides. You know, the kind-hearted girl takes pity on the poor nerd and he thinks it's love."

"I guess you could ask him. He's out here again and said he was coming in to get copies of some of our mortality statistics."

"Mortality?"

"In fact, he's late," Krause said, looking at his watch. "Yeah, mortality. Die-offs among mammal communities in plague outbreaks, rabbit fever, hantavirus, that sort of thing. How many kangaroo rats survive compared with ground squirrels, pack rats, prairie dogs, so forth. But my point is, it's the data that brings him out, not Cathy. Take today, for example. He knows Cathy's not here, but he's coming anyway."

"He knew she was missing?"

"He called a couple of days after she didn't show up. Wanted to talk to her."

Leaphorn considered this.

"How well do you remember that conversation?"

Krause looked surprised, frowned. "What do you mean?"

"You know: 'he said,' and 'I said,' and 'he said.' That sort of thing. How did he react?"

Krause laughed. "You're hard to convince, aren't you?"

"Just curious."

"Well, first he asked whether we'd wrapped up the work on the plague cases. I said no, we still didn't know where the last one got it. I told him Cathy was still working on that one. Then he asked if we'd found any live kangaroo rats up around the Disbah place. That's one of the places where a hantavirus case had turned up. I told him we hadn't."

Krause tore off a sheet from a roll of paper towels and swabbed the sheen of perspiration from his forehead. "Let's see now. Then he said he had some time and thought he'd come out and maybe go along with Cathy if she was still chasing down prairie dogs and plague fleas. He wanted to ask her if she'd mind. I said she wasn't here. He said when'll she be back. So I told him about her not coming to work. Couple of days I guess it was by then."

Leaphorn waited. Krause shook his head. Went back to sorting through his bags. Now the chemical smell reminded Leaphorn of the Indian Health Service Hospital at Gallup, of the gurney rolling down the hallway carrying Emma away from him. Of the doctor explaining— He drew a deep breath, wanting to finish this. Wanting out of this laboratory.

"She didn't tell you she was taking off?"

"Just left a note. Said she was going back up to Yells Back to collect some fleas."

"Nothing else?"

Krause shook his head.

"Could I see the note?"

"If I can find it. It probably went in the waste-basket but I'll look for it."

"How did Hammar react to what you told him?"

"I don't know. I think he said something like, whaddaya mean? Where did she go? What did she tell you? Where'd she leave the truck? That sort of thing. Then he seemed worried. What did the police say? Was anybody looking for her? So forth."

Leaphorn considered. That response seemed normal. Or well rehearsed.

There was the sound of tires crunching over gravel, a car door slamming.

"That's probably Hammar," Krause said. "Ask him yourself."

NINE

ABOUT A MONTH into his first semester at Arizona State, Leaphorn had overcome the tendency of young Navajos to think that all white people look alike. But the fact was that Victor Hammar looked a lot like a bigger, less sun-baked weightlifter version of Richard Krause. At second glance Leaphorn noticed Hammar was also several years younger, his eyes a paler shade of blue, his ears a bit flatter to his skull, and—since cops are conditioned to look for "identifying marks"—a tiny scar beside his chin had defied sunburning and remained white.

Hammar showed less interest in Leaphorn. He shook hands, displayed irregular teeth with a perfunctory smile, and got down to business.

"Is she back yet?" he asked Krause. "Have you heard anything from her?"

"Neither one," Krause said.

Hammar issued a violent non-English epithet. A German curse, Leaphorn guessed. He sat on a stool across from Leaphorn, shook his head, and swore again—this time in English.

"Yeah," Krause said. "It's worrying me, too."

"And the police," Hammar said. "What are they doing? Nothing, I think. What do they tell you?"

"Nothing," Krause said. "I think they put the Jeep on the list to be watched for and—"

"Nothing!" Hammar said. "How could that be?"

"She's a full-grown woman," Krause said. "There's no evidence of any crime, except maybe for getting off with our vehicle. I guess—"

"Nonsense! Nonsense! Of course something has happened to her. She's been gone too long. Something happened to her."

Leaphorn cleared his throat. "Do you have any theories about that?"

Hammar stared at Leaphorn. "What?"

Krause said, "Mr. Leaphorn here is a retired policeman. He's trying to find Catherine."

Hammar was still staring. "Retired policeman?"

Leaphorn nodded, thinking Hammar would have no idea of what he knew and what he didn't and trying to decide how he would lead into this.

"Do you remember where you were July eighth? Were you here in Tuba then?"

"No," Hammar said, still staring.

Leaphorn waited.

"I'd already gone back. Back to the university."

"You're on a faculty somewhere?"

"I am just a graduate assistant. At Arizona State. I had lectures that day. Introduction to the laboratory for freshmen." Hammar grimaced. "Introduction to Biology. Awful course. Stupid students. And why are you asking me these questions? Do you—"

"Because I was asked to help find the woman," Leaphorn said, thereby violating his rule and Navajo courtesy by interrupting a speaker. But he wanted to cut off any questions from Hammar. "I will just collect a little more information and be out of here so you gentlemen can get back to your work. I wonder if Miss Pollard might have left any papers in the office here. If she did, they might be helpful."

"Papers?" Krause said. "Well, she had sort of a ledger and she kept her field notes in that. Is that what you mean?"

"Probably," Leaphorn said.

"Her aunt called me from Santa Fe yesterday and told me you'd come by," Krause said, shuffling through material stacked on a desk in the corner of the room. "I think her name is Vanders. Something like that. Cathy was planning to visit her last weekend. I thought maybe that's where she'd gone."

"You're working for old Mrs. Vanders," Hammar said, still staring at Leaphorn.

"Here's the sort of stuff that might be useful," Krause said, handing Leaphorn an accordion file containing a jumble of papers. "She's going to need it if she comes back."

"When she gets back," Hammar said. "When."

Leaphorn flipped through the papers, noticing that most of the entries Catherine had made were in a small irregular scribble, hard to read and even harder for a layman to interpret. Like his own notes, they were a shorthand that communicated only to her.

"Fort C," Leaphorn said. "What's that?"

"Centers for Disease Control," Krause said. "The feds who run the lab at Fort Collins."

"IHS. That's Indian Health Service?"

"Right," Krause said. "Actually, that's who we're working for here, but technically for the Arizona health people. Part of the big, complicated team."

Leaphorn had skipped to the back.

"Lots of references to A. Nez," he said.

"Anderson Nez. One of the three fatalities in the last outbreak. Mr. Nez was the last one, and the only one we haven't found the source for," Krause said.

"And who's this Woody?"

"Ah," said Hammar. "That jerk!"

"That's Albert Woody," Krause said. "Al. He's into cell biology, but I guess you'd call him an immunologist. Or a pharmacologist. Microbiologist. Or maybe a—I don't know." Krause chuckled. "What's his title, Hammar? He's closer to your field than mine."

"He's a damned jerk," Hammar said. "He has a grant from the Institute of Allergy and Immunology, but they say he also works for Merck, or Squibb, or one of the other pharmaceutical firms. Or maybe for all of them."

"Hammar doesn't like him," Krause said. "Hammar was trapping rodents somewhere or other this summer and Woody accused him of interfering with one of his own projects. He yelled at you, didn't he?"

"I should have kicked his butt," Hammar said.

"He's on this plague project, too?"

"No. No. Not really. He's been working out here for years, since we had an outbreak in the nineteen-eighties. He's studying how some hosts of vectors—like prairie dogs, or field mice, and so forth—can be infected by bacteria or viruses and stay alive while others of the same species are killed. For example, plague comes along and wipes out about a billion rodents, and you've got empty burrows and nothing but bones for a hundred miles. But here and there you find a colony still alive. They carry it, but it didn't kill them.

They're sort of reservoir colonies. They breed, renew the rodent population, and then the plague spreads again. Probably from them, too. But nobody really knows for sure how it works."

"It's the same with snowshoe rabbits in the north of Finland," Hammar said. "And in your Arctic Alaska. Different bacteria but the same business. It's a seven-year cycle with that, regular as a clock. Everywhere rabbits, then the fever sweeps through and nothing but dead rabbits and it takes seven years to build back up and then the fever comes and wipes them out again."

"And the drug companies are paying Woody?"

"Wasting their money," Hammar said. He walked to the door, opened it, and stood looking out.

"It's more like they're looking for the Golden Fleece," Krause said. "I just have a sort of hazy idea of what Woody's doing, but I think he's trying to pin down what happens inside a mammal so that it can live with a pathogen that kills its kinfolks. If he learns that, maybe it's just a little step toward understanding intercellular chemistry. Or maybe it's worth a mega-trillion dollars."

Leaphorn let that hang while he sorted through what he remembered of Organic Chemistry 211 and Biology 331 from his own college days. That was vague now, but he recalled what the surgeon who'd operated on Emma's brain tumor had told him as if it were yesterday. He could still see the man and hear the anger in his voice. It was just a simple staph infection, he'd said, and a few years ago a dozen different antibiotics would have killed the bacteria. But not now. "Now the microbes are winning the war," he'd said. And Emma's small body, under the sheet on the gurney rolling down the hallway, was the proof of that.

"Well, maybe that's exaggerating," Krause said. "Maybe it would be just a few hundred billion."

"You're talking about a way to make better antibiotics?" Leaphorn said. "That's what Woody's after?"

"Not exactly. More likely he'd like to find the way a mammal's immune system is being adjusted so that it can kill the microbe. It would probably be more like a vaccine."

Leaphorn looked up from the journal. "Miss Pollard seems to connect him to Nez," he said. "The note says: 'Check Woody on Nez.' Wonder what that would mean."

"I wouldn't know," Krause said.

"Maybe Nez was that guy Woody had working for him," Hammar said. "Sort of a smallish fellow, with his hair cut real short. He'd put out traps for Woody and help him take blood samples from the animals. Things like that."

"Maybe so," Krause said. "I know that over

the years Woody has located a bunch of prairie dog colonies that seem to resist the plague. And he was also collecting kangaroo rats, field mice, and so forth. The sort of rodents that spread the hantavirus. Cathy said he's been working with one near Yells Back Butte. That might be why Cathy was going up there. If Nez had been working for Woody, maybe she was going up there to see if he knew where Nez was when he got infected."

"Could Mr. Nez have been bitten up there?" Leaphorn asked. "I understand there'd been a couple of plague victims from that area in the past."

"I don't think so," Krause said. "She had pretty well pinned down where Nez had been during the period he was infected. It was mostly up south of here. Between Tuba and Page."

Krause had been sorting slides while he talked. Now he looked up at Leaphorn. "You know much about bacteria?"

"Just the basic stuff. Freshman-level biology."

"Well, with plague, the flea just puts a tiny bit in your bloodstream, and then it usually takes five or six days, sometimes longer, for the bacteria to multiply enough so you start showing any symptoms, usually a fever. Or maybe if you get bitten by a bunch of fleas, or they're loaded with some really virulent stuff, then it's quicker. So you skip back a few days from when the fever showed up and find out where the victim's been from that date to maybe a week earlier. When you know that, then you start checking those places for dead mammals and infected fleas."

Hammar was still looking out the door. He said: "Poor Mr. Nez. Killed by a flea. Too bad the flea didn't bite Al Woody."

TEN

LEAPHORN BLAMED IT on being lonely—this bad habit he'd developed of talking too much. And now he was paying the price. Instead of waiting until he'd arrived at Louisa Bourebonette's little house in Flagstaff to tell her of his adventures, the empty silence in his Tuba City motel room had provoked him into babbling away on the telephone. He'd told her about his visit with John McGinnis and his talk with Krause. He had given her a thumbnail sketch of Hammar and asked if she could think of an easy, make-no-waves way to check on his alibi.

"Can't you just call the police in Tempe and have them do it? I thought that's what was done."

"If I was still a cop I could, providing we had any evidence a crime had been committed and some reason to believe Mr. Hammar was a suspect in this crime."

"Lieutenant Chee would do it."

"If he would, that would take care of problem one. We'd still have problems two and three," Leaphorn said. "How is Chee going to explain to the Tempe police why he wants them to poke into the life of a citizen when there's not even a crime to suspect him of committing?"

"Yeah," Louisa said. "I see it. Academics can be touchy about things like that. I'll handle it myself."

Which left Leaphorn merely breathing into the phone for a moment or two. Then he said: "What?"

"Hammar was supposed to be teaching a lab class July eighth, isn't that what he said? So I have a friend over in our biology department who knows people in biology down at ASU. He calls somebody in his good-old-boy network down at Tempe and they ask around and if Mr. Hammar cut his lab class that day—or got somebody to handle it—then we know it. That sound okay?"

"That sounds great," Leaphorn said. It would also have been a great place to end the conversation, just to tell Louisa he'd be there for dinner tonight and say good-bye. But, alas, he kept on talking.

He told her about Dr. Woody and his project. Even though Louisa's field was ethnology and, even worse, mythology—on the extreme opposite end of the academic spectrum from microbiology— Louisa had heard of Woody. She said the fellow she'd ask to make the call to Tempe for her sometimes worked with the man, doing blood and tissue studies in his microbiology lab at the NAU.

Thus the restful evening Leaphorn had yearned for with Louisa had turned into a threesome with Professor Michael Perez invited to join them.

"He's one of the brighter ones," Louisa had said, thereby separating him from a good many of the hard science faculty, whom she found too narrow for her taste. "He'll be interested in what you're doing, and maybe he can tell you something helpful."

Leaphorn doubted that. In fact, he was wondering if he would ever learn anything helpful about Catherine Pollard. He'd classified what McGinnis had told him as no higher than interesting, and yesterday had left him wondering why he was wasting so much energy on what seemed more and more like a hopeless cause. He'd spent weary hours locating the sheep camp where Anderson Nez resided during the grazing months. As expected, he found the Navajo taboo against talking about the dead adding to the usual taciturnity of rural folks dealing with a citified stranger. Except for a teenager who remembered Catherine Pollard coming by earlier collecting fleas off their sheepdogs, checking rodent burrows and quizzing everyone about where Nez might have been, he learned just about nothing at the camp beyond confirming what Hammar had told him. Yes indeed, Nez had worked part-time for several summers helping Dr. Woody catch rodents.

He arrived at Louisa's house just before sunset with the high dry-weather ice crystals dusted across the stratosphere reflecting red. The spot where he usually parked his pickup in her narrow driveway was occupied by a weather-beaten Saab sedan. Its owner was standing beside Louisa in the doorway as Leaphorn came up the steps—a lanky man with a narrow face and a narrow white goatee whose bright blue eyes were inspecting Leaphorn with undisguised curiosity.

"Joe," Louisa said. "This is Mike Perez, who'll tell us both more about molecular biology than we want to know."

They shook hands.

"Or about bacteria, or virology," Perez said, grinning. "We don't understand the virus end of it yet, but that doesn't keep us from pretending we do."

Louisa had presumed that Leaphorn, being Navajo, enjoyed mutton so the entrée was lamb chops. Having been raised a sheep-camp Navajo, Leaphorn was both thoroughly tired of mutton and far too polite to say so. He ate his lamb chop with green mint jelly and listened to Professor Perez discuss Woody's work with rodents. Two or three questions early in the meal had established that Perez seemed to know absolutely nothing that would connect him to Catherine Pollard. But he knew an awful lot about the career and personality of Dr. Albert Woody.

"Mike thinks Woody's going to be one of the great ones," Louisa said. "Nobel Prize winner, books written about him. The Man Who Saved Humanity. A giant of medical science. That sort of thing."

Perez looked embarrassed by that. "Louisa tends to exaggerate. It's an occupational hazard of mythologists, you know," he said. "Hercules wasn't really any stronger than Gorgeous George, and Medusa just had her hair done in cornrows, and Paul Bunyan's blue ox was really brown. But I do think that Woody has a shot at it. Maybe one chance in a hundred. But that's better odds than Speed Ball lottery."

Louisa offered Leaphorn another chop. "Everyone in the hard sciences is making the headlines these days," she said. "It's 'breakthrough of the month' season. If it isn't a new way to clone toe-jam fungus, it's rediscovering life on Mars."

"I saw something about that life on Mars business," Leaphorn said. "It sounded like that molecules-in-the-asteroid discovery back in the sixties. Didn't the geologists discredit that?"

Perez nodded. "This one is a NASA publicity ploy. They'd been having their usual run of fiascoes and blunders, so they dug out an asteroid with the proper minerals in it and conned the reporters again. New generation of science writers, nobody remembered the old story, and it looked better on TV than the footage of astronauts demonstrating their bigger bubblegum bubbles, and that other sophomoric stuff they're always bragging about."

Louisa laughed. "Mike resents NASA because it siphons federal research money away from his microbiology research. It must have some purpose."

Perez looked slightly offended. "I don't resent our Clowns in Space program. It provides entertainment. But what Woody's working on is dead serious."

"Like recording the blood pressure of prairie dogs," Louisa said.

Leaphorn watched her pass Perez the bowl of boiled new potatoes. He had decided to drop out of this conversation and be a spectator.

Perez took a small potato. Looked at Louisa thoughtfully. Took another one.

"I just read a paper this morning from one of the microbiologists at NIH," Perez said, pausing to sample the potato. "NIH." He grinned at Louisa. "For you mythologists, that's the National Institutes of Health."

Louisa tried to let that pass but didn't manage it. "Not affiliated with the UN then," she said. "For you biologists, that's United Period Nations."

Perez laughed. "Okay," he said. "Peace be with us all. My point is, this guy was reporting dreadful stuff. For example, remember cholera? Virtually wiped out back in the sixties. Well, there were almost a hundred thousand new cases in South America alone in the past two years. And TB, the old 'white plague,' which we finally eliminated about 1970. Well, now the world death rate from that is up to three million per annum again—and the pathogen is a DR mycobacterium."

Louisa gave Leaphorn a wry look. "I listen to this guy a lot and learn his jargon. He's trying to say the TB germ has become drug-resistant."

"What we'd call the perpetrator," Leaphorn said.

"Great subject for dinner conversation," Louisa said. "Cholera and TB."

"More cheerful, though, than telling you about the summer-session papers I've been grading,"

Perez said. "But I'd like to hear from Mr. Leaphorn about this vanished biologist he's looking for."

"There's not much to tell," Leaphorn said. "She's a vector control person for the Indian Health Service, or maybe it's the Arizona Health Department. They sort of operate together. She's been working out of Tuba City. About two weeks ago she drove out in the morning to check on rodent burrows and didn't come back."

He stopped, waiting for Perez to ask the standard questions about boyfriend, stalker, nervous breakdown, job stress, et cetera.

"I'd guess that's why Louisa wanted me to find out whether the Hammar boy was teaching his lab on July eighth," Perez said. "Was that the day?"

Leaphorn nodded.

"Mike Devente handles those lab programs," Perez said. "He said Hammar was sick. Had food poisoning or something."

"Sick," Leaphorn said.

Perez laughed. "Or called in sick, anyway. With teaching assistants, sometimes there's a difference."

Perez sampled his second potato, said: "Is he a suspect?"

"He might be if we had a crime," Leaphorn said. "All we have is a woman who drove off in an Indian Health Service vehicle and didn't come back."

"Louisa said this Pollard lady was checking sources for this latest *Yersinia pestis* outbreak. Is that why you are interested in Woody?"

Leaphorn shook his head. "I never heard of him before today. But they're both interested in prairie dogs, pack rats and so forth and in the same territory. Not many people are, so maybe their paths crossed. Maybe he saw her somewhere. Maybe she told him where she was going."

Perez looked thoughtful. "Yeah," he said.

"They're working in the same field, so he'd probably know about her," Leaphorn said. "But in such a big country it's not likely they'd meet, and if they did, why is she going to tell a virtual stranger that she's going to run off with a government vehicle?"

"Mutual interests, though," Perez said. "They cut pretty deep. How often do you find someone who wants to talk to you about fleas on prairie dogs? And Woody is a downright fanatic about his work. Run him into another human with any knowledge of infectious diseases, immunology, any of that, and he's going to tell 'em a lot more about it than they'll want to know. He's obsessed by it. He thinks the bacteria are going to eliminate mammals unless we do something about it. And if they don't get us, the viruses will. He feels this need to warn everybody about it. Jeremiah complex."

"I can sympathize with that," Leaphorn said. "I'm always talking about what's wrong with the War on Drugs. Until I notice everybody is yawning."

"Same problem with me," Perez said. "I'll bet you're not very interested in discussing molecular mineral transmission through cell walls."

"Only if you explained it so I could understand it," Leaphorn said. He wished he hadn't mentioned Woody to Louisa, wished she hadn't invited Perez, wished they could just be having a relaxing evening together. "And first I guess you'd have to explain why I should care about it."

It was the wrong thing to say, inspiring Dr. Perez to defend pure science and orate on the need to collect knowledge merely for the sake of knowledge. Leaphorn nibbled at the second chop. He down-rated his character for lacking the courage to refuse it. He examined his semi-hostile reaction to Perez. It had begun when he saw the Saab parked where he liked to park in Louisa's driveway and worsened when he saw the man standing beside her in the doorway, grinning at him. And it clicked up another notch when he noticed that Perez seemed to be looking upon him as a rival. Perez was jealous, he concluded. But then what about Joe Leaphorn? Was

Joe Leaphorn jealous? It was an unsettling thought, and he took another bite of the lamb chop to drive it away.

Perez had completed his account of how pure science had led to the discovery of penicillin and the whole arsenal of antibiotics, which had pretty well wiped out infectious diseases. Now he digressed into how stupid misuse of those drugs had turned victory into defeat and how the killer bugs were mutating furiously into all sorts of new forms.

"Mom brings her kid in with a runny nose. The doc knows a virus is causing it, and antibiotics won't touch the virus, but the kid is crying, and Mom wants a prescription, so he gives her his pet antibiotic and tells Mama to give it to the kid for eight days. And then two days later, the immune system deals with the virus, and she stops the medicine. But two days of the antibiotic"—Perez paused, took a long sip from his wineglass, wiped his mustache—"has slaughtered all the bacteria in the kid's bloodstream except—" Perez paused again, waved his hand. "Except the few freaks who happened to be resistant to the drug. So, with the competition wiped out, these freaks multiply like crazy, and the kid is full of drug-resistant bacteria. And then—"

"And then it's time for dessert," Louisa said. "How about some ice cream? Or brownies?"

"Or maybe both," Perez said. "Anyway, just a few years ago about ninety-nine-point-nine percent of *Staphylococcus aureus* was killed by penicillin. Now it's down to about four percent. Only one of the other antibiotics works on the stuff now, and sometimes it doesn't work."

Louisa's voice came from the kitchen. "Enough! Enough! No more doomsday talk." She emerged, carrying dessert. "And now thirty percent of the people who die in hospitals die of something they didn't have when they came in." She laughed. "Or is it forty percent? I've heard this lecture before, but mythologists aren't good with numbers."

"It's about thirty percent," Perez said, looking miffed. A bowl of ice cream and two brownies later, Perez pleaded the need to finish grading papers and rolled his Saab out of Leaphorn's place in the driveway.

"An interesting man," Leaphorn said, stacking saucers on plates, and cutlery atop that, and heading for the kitchen.

"Have a seat," Louisa said. "I can take care of the cleanup."

"Widowers get awfully good at this. I want to demonstrate my skills." Which he did, until he noticed Louisa rearranging the plates he'd put into the washer.

"Wrong way?" he asked.

"Well," she said, "if you put them in with the

food side facing inward, then the hot water spray hits that. It gets 'em cleaner."

So Leaphorn sat and wondered if Perez had actually been jealous of him and what that might imply, and tried to think of a way to bring up the subject. He drew a blank. A few moments later the clattering in the kitchen stopped. Louisa emerged and sat on the sofa across from him.

"Wonderful dinner," Leaphorn said. "Thank you."

She nodded. "Michael really is an interesting man," she said. "He was way too talky tonight, but that was because I told him you were interested in what Professor Woody was doing." She shrugged. "He was just trying to be helpful."

"I sort of got the feeling he didn't care too much for me."

"That was jealousy. He was showing off a little bit. The male territorial imperative at work."

Leaphorn had not the slightest idea how to react to that. He opened his mouth, took a breath, said "Aah," and closed it.

"We go way back. Old friends."

"Aah," Leaphorn said again: "Friends." He had left the question off the sound of that, but it didn't fool Louisa.

"He wanted to marry me once, long ago," Louisa said. "I told him I'd tried getting married once when I was young and I hadn't cared much for it."

Leaphorn considered this. Now was one of those times when you wished you hadn't quit smoking. Lighting up a cigarette gave you time for thought. "You never told me you'd been married," he said.

"There really wasn't any reason to," she said.

"I guess not," he said. "But I'm interested."

She laughed. "I really ought to tell you it's none of your business. But I think I'll put on a pot of coffee and decide what I'm going to say."

When she came back with two steaming cups, she handed one to Leaphorn with a broad smile.

"I decided I'm glad you asked," she said, sat down, and told him about it. They had both been graduate students, and he was big, handsome, and sort of out of it and always needed help with his classes. She'd thought that was charming at the time, and the charm had lasted about a year.

"It took me that long to understand that he'd been looking for a second mother. You know, somebody to take care of him."

"Lots of men like that," Leaphorn said, and since he couldn't think of anything to add to that, he switched the subject over to Catherine Pollard and his meeting with Mrs. Vanders.

"I wondered why you decided to take that on," she said. "It sounds hopeless to me."

"It probably is," Leaphorn said. "I'm going to give it a couple more days and if it still looks hopeless, I'll call the lady and tell her I failed." He finished his coffee and stood. "It's eighty miles back to Tuba City—actually eighty-two to my motel—and I've got to get going."

"You're too tired to make that drive," she said. "Stay here. Get some sleep. Drive it in the morning."

"Um," Leaphorn said. "Well, I wanted to try to find this Woody and see if he can tell me anything."

"He'll keep," Louisa said. "It won't take any longer to drive it in the morning."

"Stay here?"

"Why not? Use the guest bedroom. I have a nine-thirty lecture. But if you want a real early start there's an alarm clock on the desk in there."

"Well," Leaphorn said, digesting this, and recognizing how tired he was, and the nature of friendship. "Yes. Well, thank you."

"There's some sleeping stuff in the chest. Nightgowns and so forth in the top drawer and pajamas in the bottom one."

"Men's?"

"Men's, women's, what have you. Guests can't be too particular about borrowed pajamas."

Louisa, taking their empty cups into the kitchen, stopped in the doorway.

"I'm still wondering why you took the job," she said. "It surprises me."

"Me, too," Leaphorn said. "But I'd been thinking about that Navajo policeman killed up near Yells Back Butte, and it turns out Catherine Pollard disappeared the same day, and she was supposed to be going to check on rodent burrows about the same place."

"Ah," Louisa said, smiling. "And if I remember what you've told me, Joe Leaphorn never could believe in coincidence."

She stood holding the cups, studying him. "You know, Joe, if I didn't have to work tomorrow I'd invite myself along. I'd like to meet this Woody fellow."

"You'd be welcome," Leaphorn said.

And more than welcome. He'd been dreading tomorrow, doing his duty, keeping a promise he'd made for no particular reason to an old woman he didn't even know without any real hope of learning anything useful.

Louisa still hadn't moved from the doorway.

"Would I be?"

"It would make my day," Leaphorn said.

ELEVEN

A HIGH-PITCHED METHODICAL whimpering sound intruded into Joe Leaphorn's dream and jerked him abruptly awake. It came from a strange-looking white alarm clock on a desk beside his bed, which was also strange—soft and warm and smelling of soap and sunshine. His eyes finally focused and he saw a ceiling as white as his own, but lacking the pattern of plaster cracks he had memorized through untold hours of insomnia.

Leaphorn pushed himself into a sitting position, fully awake, with his short-term memories flooding back. He was in Louisa Bourebonette's guest bedroom. He fumbled with the alarm clock, hoping to shut off the whimpering before it awakened her. But obviously it was too late for that. He smelled coffee brewing and bacon frying—the almost forgotten aromas of contentment. He stretched, yawned, settled back against the pillow. The crisp, fresh sheets reminded him of Emma. Everything did. The morning breeze ruffled the curtains beside his head. Emma, too, always left their windows open to the outside air until Window Rock's bitter winter made it impractical. The curtains, too. He had teased her about that. "I didn't see window curtains in your mother's hogan, Emma," he'd said. And she rewarded him with her tolerant smile and reminded him he'd moved her out of the hogan, and Navajos must remain in harmony with houses that needed curtains. That was one of the things he loved about her. One of the many. As numerous as the stars of a high country midnight.

He'd persuaded Emma that she should marry him two days before he was to take the Graduate General Examination for his degree at Arizona State. The degree was in anthropology, but the dreaded GGE covered the spectrum of the humanities and he'd been brushing up on his weak points—which had led him into a quick scan of Shakespeare's "most likely to be asked about on GGE" plays and hence to Othello's discourse about Desdemona. He still remembered the passage, although he wasn't sure he had it quite right: "She loved me for the dangers I had passed, and I loved her that she did pity them."

"Leaphorn, are you up? If you're not, your eggs are going to be overhard."

"I'm up," Leaphorn said, and got up, grabbed his clothes and hurried into the bathroom. The point Othello was trying to make, he thought, was that he loved Desdemona because she loved him. Which sounded simple enough, but actually was a very complicated concept.

Louisa's guest bathroom was equipped with a guest toothbrush, and Leaphorn, being blessed with the Indian's sparse and slow-growing beard, didn't miss a razor. ("No whiskers is proof," his grandfather had told him, "that Navajos are evolved further from the apes than those hairy white men.")

Despite the threat, Louisa had actually delayed cracking the breakfast eggs until he appeared in the kitchen doorway.

"I hope you meant it when you said you'd be happy to have me along today," she said as they started breakfast. "If you did, I can come."

Leaphorn was buttering his toast. He'd already noticed that Professor Bourebonette was not wearing the formal skirt and blouse that were her teaching attire. She was clad in jeans and a long-sleeved denim shirt.

"I meant it," he said. "But it'll be boring, like about ninety-nine percent of this kind of work. I was just going to see if I could find this Woody, find out if he'd seen Catherine Pollard and if he could tell me anything helpful. Then I was going to drive back to Window Rock and call Mrs. Vanders, report no progress and—"

"Sounds all right," she said.

Leaphorn put down his fork. "How about your class?"

It wasn't really the question he wanted to ask. He wanted to know what her plans were when the day's duties were done. Did she expect him to bring her back to Flagstaff? Did she intend to stay in Tuba City? Or accompany him home to Window Rock? And if so, what then?

"All I have today is one meeting of my ethnology course," Louisa said. "I'd already scheduled David Esoni to do his lecture on Zuni teaching stories. I think you met him."

"He's the professor from Zuni? I thought he taught chemistry."

Louisa nodded. "He does. And every year I get him to talk to my entry-level class about Zuni mythology. And culture in general. I called him this morning. The class expects him and he said he could introduce himself."

Leaphorn nodded. Cleared his throat, trying to phrase the question. He didn't need to.

"I'll drop off when we get to Tuba. I want to

see Jim Peshlakai—he teaches the traditional cultural stuff at Grey Hills High School there. He's going to set up interviews for me with a bunch of his students from other tribes. Then he's coming down to Flag tonight for some work in the library. I'll ride back with him."

"Oh," Leaphorn said. "Good."

Louisa smiled. "I thought you'd say that," she said. "I'll fix a thermos of coffee. And a little snack, just in case."

So nothing remained but to check his telephone answering service. He dialed the number and the code. Two calls. The first was from Mrs. Vanders. She still had heard nothing from Catherine. Did he have anything to tell her?

The second was from Cowboy Dashee. Would Mr. Leaphorn please call him as soon as possible. He left his number.

Leaphorn hung up and listened to the noises Louisa was causing in the kitchen while he stared at the telephone, getting Cowboy Dashee properly placed. He was a cop. He was a Hopi. A friend of Jim Chee. A Coconino County deputy sheriff now, Leaphorn remembered. What would Dashee want to talk about? Why try to guess? Leaphorn dialed the number.

"Cameron Police Department," a woman's voice said. "How may I be of service?"

"This is Joe Leaphorn. I just had a call from Deputy Sheriff Dashee. He left this number."

"Oh, yes," the woman said. "Just a moment. I'll see if he's still here."

Clicking. Silence. Then: "Lieutenant Leaphorn?"

"Yes," Leaphorn said. "But it's mister now. I got your message. What's up?"

Dashee cleared his throat. "Well," he said. "It's just that I need some advice." Another pause.

"Sure," Leaphorn said. "It's free and you know what they say about free advice being worth what it costs you."

"Well," Dashee said. "I have a problem I don't know how to handle."

"You want to tell me about it?"

Another clearing of throat. "Could I meet you someplace where we could talk? It's kind of touchy. And complicated."

"I'm calling from Flag and just getting ready to drive up to Tuba City. I'll be coming through Cameron in maybe an hour."

"Fine," Dashee said, and suggested a coffee shop beside Highway 89.

"I'll have an NAU professor with me," Leaphorn said. "Will that be a problem?"

A long pause. "No, sir," Dashee said. "I don't think so."

But by the time they'd reached Cameron and

pulled up beside the patrol car with the Con-
onino County Sheriff's Department markings,
Louisa had decided she should wait in the car.

"Don't be silly," she said. "Of course he'd say it
would be no problem to have me listening in.
What else could he say when he's asking you for
a favor." She opened her purse and extracted a
paperback and showed it to Leaphorn. *"Execution
Eve,"* she said. "You ought to read it. The son of a
former Kentucky prison warden remembering
the murder case that turned his dad against the
death penalty."

"Oh, come on in. Dashee won't mind."

"This book's more interesting," she said, "and
he would mind."

And of course she was right. When they parked,
Leaphorn had seen Deputy Sheriff Albert "Cowboy" Dashee sitting in a booth beside the window looking out at them, his expression glum.
Now, as he sat across from Dashee, watching
him order coffee, Leaphorn was remembering
that this Hopi had struck him as a man full of
good humor. A happy man. There was no sign of
that this morning.

"I'll get right to the point," Dashee said. "I
need to talk to you about Jim Chee."

"About Chee?" This wasn't what Leaphorn had
expected. In fact, he'd had no idea what to expect. Something about the Hopi killing the Na-

vajo policeman, perhaps. "You two are old friends, aren't you?"

"For a long, long time," Dashee said. "That makes this harder to deal with."

Leaphorn nodded.

"Jim always considered you a friend, too," Dashee said. He grinned ruefully. "Even when he was sore at you."

Leaphorn nodded again. "Which was fairly often."

"The thing is, Jim got the wrong man in this Benjamin Kinsman homicide. Robert Jano didn't do it."

"He didn't?"

"No. Robert wouldn't kill anyone."

"Who did?"

"I don't know," Dashee said. "But I grew up with Robert Jano. I know you hear this all the time, but—" He threw up his hands.

"I know people myself who I just can't believe would ever kill anyone—no matter what. But sometimes something snaps, and they do it. Temporary insanity."

"You'd have to know him. If you did, you'd never believe it. He was always gentle, even when we were kids trying to be tough. Robert never seemed to really lose his temper. He liked everybody. Even the bastards."

Leaphorn could see Dashee was hating this.

He'd pushed his uniform cap back on his head. His face was flushed. His forehead was beaded with perspiration.

"I'm retired, you know," Leaphorn said. "So all I get is the secondhand gossip. But what I hear is that Chee caught the man red-handed. Jano was supposed to be leaning over Kinsman, blood all over him. Some of the blood was Jano's. Some of the blood was Kinsman's. Was that about it?"

Dashee sighed, rubbed his hand across his face. "That's the way it must have looked to Jim."

"You talked to Jim?"

Dashee shook his head. "That's the advice I wanted. How do I go about that? You know how he is. Kinsman was one of his people. Somebody kills him. He must feel pretty strong about that. And I'm a cop, too. It's not my case. And being a Hopi. The kind of anger that's grown up between us and you Navajos." He threw up his hands again. "It's such a damned complicated situation. I want him to know it's not just sentimental bullshit. How can I approach him?"

"Yeah," Leaphorn said, thinking that everything Dashee had said did indeed sound like sentimental bullshit. "I understand your problem."

The coffee arrived, reminding Leaphorn of Louisa waiting outside. But she had the thermos they'd brought and she would understand. Just as Emma always understood. He sipped the coffee without noticing anything, except that it was hot.

"Did they let you talk to Jano?"

Dashee nodded.

"How'd you manage that?"

"I know his lawyer," Dashee said. "Janet Pete."

Leaphorn grunted, shook his head. "I was afraid of that," he said. "I saw her at the hospital the day Kinsman died. The prosecution bunch was gathering and she showed up, too. I'd heard she's been appointed as a federal defender."

"That's it," Dashee said. "She'll do a good job for him, but it sure as hell won't make dealing with Jim any easier."

"They were about to get married once, I think," Leaphorn said. "And then she went back to Washington. Is that on again?"

"I hope not," Dashee said. "She's a city gal. Jim's always going to be a sheep-camp Navajo. But whatever, it's going to make him touchy as hell, being on opposite sides of this. He'll be hard to deal with."

"But Chee was always reasonable," Leaphorn said. "If it was me, I'd just go and lay it out for him. Just make the best case you can."

"You think it will do any good?"

"I doubt it," Leaphorn said. "Not unless you give him some sort of evidence. How could it? If what I hear at Window Rock is right, Jano had a motive. Revenge as well as avoiding arrest. Kinsman had already nailed him before for poaching an eagle. He got off light then, but this would be a second offense. More important, I understand there was no other possible suspect. Besides, even if you persuade Chee he's wrong, what can he do about it now?"

Dashee hadn't touched his coffee. He leaned across the table. "Find the person who actually killed Kinsman," Dashee said. "I want to ask him to do that. Or help me do it."

"But as I understand the situation, only Jano and Kinsman were there, until Chee came along answering Kinsman's call for some backup."

"There was a woman up there," Dashee said. "A woman named Catherine Pollard. Maybe other people."

Leaphorn, caught in the process of raising his cup for another sip, said, "Ah," and put down the cup. He stared at Dashee for a moment. "How do you know that?"

"I've been asking around," Dashee said, and produced a bitter laugh. "Something Jim should be doing." He shook his head. "He's a good man and a good cop. I'm asking you how I can get him moving. If he doesn't, I think Jano could get the death penalty. And one day Jim's going to know they gassed the wrong man. And then you might as well kill him, too. Chee would never get over that."

"I know something about Catherine Pollard," Leaphorn said.

"I know," Dashee said. "I heard."

"If she was there—and I understand that's where she was supposed to be going that day—how could she fit into this? Except, of course, as a potential witness."

"I'd like to give Jim another theory of the crime," Dashee said. "Ask him to look at it for a while as a substitute for 'Jano kills Kinsman to avoid arrest.' It goes like this: Pollard goes up to Yells Back Butte to do her thing. Kinsman is up there looking for Jano, or maybe he's looking for Pollard. One way, he runs across her. The other way, he finds her. Just a couple of nights earlier, Kinsman was in a bistro off the interstate east of Flag, and he saw Pollard and tried to take her away from the guy she was with. A fight started. An Arizona highway patrolman broke it up."

Leaphorn turned the cup in his hand, considering this. No reason to ask Dashee how he knew this. Cop gossip travels fast.

Dashee was watching him, looking anxious. "What do you think?" he said. "Kinsman has a reputation as a woman-chaser. He's attracted and now he's angry, too. Or maybe he thinks she'll file a complaint and get him suspended." He shrugged. "They struggle. She whacks him on the head with a rock. Then she hears Jano coming and flees the scene. Does that sound plausible?"

"A lot would depend on whether you have a witness who would testify they saw her there. Do you? I mean, beyond that being where she told her boss she'd be working that day?"

"I got it from Old Lady Notah. She keeps a bunch of goats up there. She remembers seeing a Jeep driving up that dirt road past the butte about daylight that morning. I understand Pollard was driving a Jeep." Dashee looked slightly abashed. "Just circumstantial evidence. She couldn't identify the driver. Not even the gender."

"Still, it was probably Pollard," Leaphorn said.

"And I understand the Jeep is still missing. And so is Pollard."

"Right again."

"And you've been offering a thousand-dollar reward for anyone who can find it."

"True," Leaphorn said. "But if Pollard did it, and Pollard was fleeing the scene, why didn't Chee see her? Remember, he got there just a few minutes after it happened. Kinsman's blood was still fresh. There's just that one narrow dirt road into there, and Chee was driving up it. Why didn't he—"

Dashee held up his hand. "I don't know, and

neither do you. But don't you think it could have happened?"

Leaphorn nodded. "Possibly."

"I don't want to get out of line with this, or sound offensive, but let me add something else to my theory of the crime. Let's say that Pollard got out of there, got to a telephone, called somebody and told them her troubles and asked for help. Let's say whoever it was told her where to hide and they'd cover her trail for her."

Leaphorn asked: "Like who and how?" But he knew the answer.

"Who? I'd say somebody in her family. Probably her daddy, I'd say. How? By giving the impression that she's been abducted. Been murdered."

"And they do that by hiring a retired policeman to go looking for her," Leaphorn said.

"Somebody respected by all the cops," Dashee said.

TWELVE

THE ROCK UPON which Chee had so carelessly put his weight tumbled down the slope, bounced into space, struck an obtruding ledge, touched off a clattering avalanche of stone and dirt and disappeared amid the weeds far below. Chee shifted his body carefully to his right, exhaled a huge breath and stood for a moment, leaning against the cliff and letting his heartbeat slow a little. He was just below the tabletop of Yells Back Butte, high on the saddle that connected it with Black Mesa. It wasn't a difficult climb for a young man in Chee's excellent physical shape, and not particularly dangerous if one kept focused on what he was doing. Chee hadn't. He'd been thinking of Janet Pete, facing the fact that he was wasting his day off just because she'd implied he hadn't done a proper job of checking the Kinsman crime scene.

Now, with both feet firmly placed and his shoulder leaning into the cliff wall, he looked down at where the boulder had made its plunge and thought about that chronic problem of the Navajo Tribal Police—lack of backup. Had he not caught himself, he'd be down there in the weeds with broken bones and multiple abrasions and about sixty miles from help. He was thinking of that as he scrambled up the last fifty feet of talus and crawled over the rim. Kinsman would be alive if he hadn't been alone. The story was the same for the two officers killed in the Kayenta district. A huge territory, never enough officers for backup, never enough budget for efficient communications, never what you needed to get the job done. Maybe Janet had been right. He'd take the FBI examination, or accept the offer he'd had from the BIA law-and-order people. Or maybe, if all else failed, consider signing on with the Drug Enforcement Agency.

But now, standing on the flat stone roof of Yells Back Butte, he looked westward and saw the immense sky, the line of thunderheads building over the Coconino Rim, the sunlight reflecting off the Vermillion Cliffs below the Utah border, and the towering cauliflower shape of the storm already delivering a rain blessing upon the San Francisco Peaks, the Sacred Mountain marking the western margin of his people's holy land. Chee closed his eyes against that, remembering Janet's beauty, her wit, her intelligence. But other memories crowded in: the dreary skies of Washington, the swarms of young men entombed in three-piece suits and subdued by whatever neckties today's fashion demanded; remembering the clamor, the sirens, the smell of the traffic, the layers upon layers of social phoniness. A faint breeze stirred Chee's hair and brought him the smell of juniper and sage, and a cluttering sound from far overhead that reminded him of why he was here.

At first glance he thought the raptor was a red-tailed hawk, but when it banked to repeat its inspection of this intruder Chee saw it was a golden eagle. It was the fourth one he'd seen today— a good year for eagles and a good place to find them—patrolling the mesa rimrock where rodents flourished. He watched this one circle, gray-white against the dark blue sky, until it satisfied its curiosity and drifted eastward over Black Mesa. When it turned, he noticed a gap in its fan of tail feathers. Probably an old one. Tail feathers aren't lost to molting.

Even with Janet's directions, it took Chee half an hour to find Jano's blind. The Hopi had roofed a crack in the butte's rimrock with a network of dead sage branches and covered that with foliage cut from nearby brush. Much of that was broken and scattered now. Chee climbed into the crack, squatted, and examined the place, reconstructing Jano's strategy.

He would have first assured himself that the eagle he wanted routinely patrolled this place. He would have probably come in the evening to prepare his blind—or more likely to repair one members of his kiva had been using for centuries. If he'd changed anything noticeable, he would have waited a few days until the eagle had become accustomed to this variation in his landscape. That done, Jano would have returned early on the morning he was fated to kill Ben Kinsman. He would have brought a rabbit with him, tied a cord to the rabbit's leg and put it atop the blind's roof. Then he would have waited, watching through the cracks for the eagle to appear. Since the eyes of raptors detect motion far better than any radar, he would have made sure the rabbit moved when the proper moment came. When the eagle seized it with its talons, he'd pull the rabbit downward, throw his coat over the bird to overpower it, and push it into the cage he'd brought.

Chee checked the ground around him, looking for any proof that Jano had been there. He didn't expect to find anything, and he didn't.

The rock where Jano must have sat while he waited for his eagle was worn smooth. Anyone might have sat there that day, or no one. He found not a trace of the bloodstains Jano might have left here had the eagle gashed him as he caught it. The rain might have washed blood away, but it would have left a trace in the grainy granite. He climbed out of the crack, bringing with him only a bedraggled eagle feather from the sandy floor of the blind and a cigarette butt that looked like it had weathered much more than last week's shower. The feather was from the body—not one of the strong wingtip or tail feathers valued for ceremonial objects. And neither the feather nor the butt showed any sign of bloodstains. He tossed them back into the blind.

Chee spent another hour or so making an equally fruitless check around the butte. He came across another blind a half mile down the rim, and several places where stones had been stacked with little painted prayer sticks placed among them and feathers tied to nearby sage branches. Clearly the Hopis considered this butte part of their spiritual homeland, and it probably had been since their first clans arrived about the twelfth century. The federal government's decision to add it to the Navajo Reservation hadn't changed that, and never would. The thought made him feel like a trespasser on his own reservation and did nothing good for Chee's mood. It was time to say to hell with this and go home.

The desk work required of an acting lieutenant had not helped the muscle tone in Jim Chee's legs, nor his lungs. He was tired. He stood at the rim, looking across the saddle, dreading the long climb down. An eagle soared over Black Mesa and the shape of another was outlined against the clouds far to the south over the San Francisco Peaks. This was eagle country and always had been. When the first Hopi clans founded their villages on the First Mesa, the elders had assigned eagle-collecting territory just as they'd assigned cornfields and springs. And when the Navajos came along a couple of hundred years later they, too, soon learned that one came to Black Mesa when one's medicine bundle required eagle feathers.

Chee took out his binoculars and tried to locate the bird he'd seen against the cloud. It was gone. He found the one hunting over the mesa and focused on it—thinking it might be the one he'd watched earlier. It wasn't. This one had a complete fan of tail feathers. He swung the binoculars downward, focused on the place where he'd found Jano beside Ben Kinsman's dying body and tried to re-create how that tragedy must have happened.

Jano might not have seen Kinsman below,

because Kinsman would have concealed himself. But looking down from here, he could hardly have missed noticing Kinsman's patrol car where he'd left it down the arroyo. Jano had been arrested once for poaching an eagle. He would have been nervous, and careful.

So why climb down to be captured? Probably because he had no choice. But why not just release the eagle, hide the cage, climb down and tell the cop he was up here meditating and saying his prayers? Jano's faded red pickup had been parked below the low point of the saddle and Kinsman had left his patrol car near the arroyo maybe a half mile away. Even without binoculars, Jano would have seen that Kinsman had his escape route blocked.

Chee scanned the valley again, picking up the ruins of what must have been the tumbled stones that once formed the walls of the Tijinney hogan, its sheep pens and its fallen brush arbor. Beyond the hogan site, a glint of reflected sunlight caught his eye. He focused on the spot. The side mirror of some sort of van parked in a cluster of junipers. What would that be doing up here? Two of last spring's plague victims had come from this quadrant of the reservation. The van might be Arizona Health Department people collecting rodents and checking fleas. He remembered Leaphorn had told him the woman he was looking for had come up this way working on a plague case.

On the opposite side of the saddle, away from the van, the Tijinney "death hogan" and the murder site, motion caught Chee's peripheral vision. He focused on it. A black-and-white goat grazing on a bush. And not just one. He counted seven, but there might be seventeen or seventy scattered through that rough area.

While counting them, he found the track. Actually, two tracks, probably formed by the vehicle of whomever held this grazing lease and drove in now and then to see about his flock.

It was not something even a sheep-camp Navajo would dignify by calling a road, but as Chee traced the track back toward the access road through his binoculars, he realized its importance. Jano did have a way out—a way to avoid capture without giving up his eagle. He could have slipped down the other side of the saddle, invisible to the officer waiting to arrest him. He could have left the eagle in some safe place, made the easy climb over the low point of the saddle with nothing to incriminate him. Then he could have recovered his pickup truck, driven back to the gravel road, followed it a mile or two back toward Tuba City, and then circled back on this goatherd's track to recover his captive bird.

Jano would have known about this track. These

were his eagle-catching grounds. He could have escaped easily. Instead he chose the path that led him directly to where Kinsman was waiting.

Chee started his descent carefully, remembering the dislodged stone that had almost sent him tumbling down the slope. It had been a bad day so far. He'd climbed the saddle thinking that Jano was a man who had killed in what probably had been a frantic effort to avoid arrest and then made up unlikely lies to save himself from prison. At the foot of the saddle, Chee stood for a moment to catch his breath. He glanced at his watch. He'd locate the van now, find out if whoever was with it had been here on the fateful day and—if they had been—whether they'd seen anything. If they hadn't, that, too, could be useful as a sort of negative evidence.

When he'd climbed Yells Back Butte he had nursed a vague, ambiguous hope that maybe he could find something to suggest Jano wasn't lying, that Jano wouldn't have to face the death penalty or (worse, in Chee's opinion) life in prison. To be honest, he had wanted to discover something that would restore his prestige in the eyes of Janet Pete. But now he knew that the murder of Benjamin Kinsman had been a deliberate, premeditated, and savage act of revenge.

THIRTEEN

THE VAN WAS parked on the sandy bed of a shallow wash, partly shaded by a cluster of junipers and screened by a growth of four-winged saltbush. No one was visible, but what looked like an oversized air-conditioning unit was purring away on its roof. Chee stood on the fold-down step beside its door and rapped on the metal, then rapped again, and—harder this time—once again. No response. He tried the doorknob. Locked. He leaned his ear against the door and listened. Nothing at first, except the vibrations from the air conditioner, then a faint, rhythmic sound.

Chee stepped back from the van and inspected it. It had a custom-made body mounted on a heavy GMC truck chassis with dual rear wheels. It looked expensive, fairly new and—judging from the dents and abrasions—heavily (or carelessly) used in rough country. Except for the lack of a door, nothing was different on the driver's side. Built against the rear was a fold-down metal ladder to provide access to the roof and a rack, which now held a dirt bike, a folding table and two chairs, a five-gallon gasoline can, a pick, a shovel, and an assortment of rodent traps and cages. There were no windows on the rear and the only side windows were high on the wall. Placed high, Chee guessed, to allow more space for storage cabinets.

He knocked again, rattled the knob, shouted, received no response, put his ear against the door again. This time he heard another faint sound. Something scratching. A tiny squeak, like chalk on a blackboard.

Chee folded down the access ladder, climbed onto the roof, dropped to his stomach, and secured a firm grip on the air-conditioner engine mount. Then he squirmed over the edge and leaned down to look into the high windows. All he saw was darkness and a streak of light reflecting from a white surface.

"Ho, there," a voice shouted. "Whatcha doing?"

Chee jerked his head up. He looked down into a face staring up at him, expression quizzical, bright blue eyes, dark, sun-peeled face, tufts of gray hair protruding from under a dark blue cap that bore the legend SQUIBB. The man carried what looked like a shoebox containing what seemed to be a dead prairie dog inside a plastic sack.

"Is that your car I saw back there?" the man asked. "The Navajo Tribal Police car?"

"Yeah," Chee said, trying to scramble to his feet without further loss of dignity. He pointed down to the roof under his boots. "I heard something in there," he stammered. "Thought I did, anyway. Something squeaking. And I couldn't raise anyone, so—"

"Probably one of the rodents," the man said. He put down the shoebox, extracted a key ring from a pocket and unlocked the doors. "Come on down. How about a drink of something?"

Chee scrambled down the ladder. The man under the Squibb cap was holding the door open for him. Cold air rushed out.

"My name's Chee," he said, extending a hand. "With the Navajo Tribal Police. I guess you're with the Arizona Health Department."

"No," the man said. "I'm Al Woody. I'm working on a research project up here. For the National Institutes of Health, Indian Health Service, so forth. But come on in."

Inside Chee turned down a beer and accepted a glass of water. Woody opened the door of a built-in floor-to-ceiling refrigerator and brought out a bottle white with frost. He scraped away the ice crystals and showed Chee a Dewar's scotch label.

"Antifreeze," he said, laughing, and began pouring himself a drink. "But once I was preserving some tissue and turned the fridge down so low that even the whiskey froze up on me."

Chee sipped his water, noticing it was stale and had a slightly unpleasant taste. He searched his brain for a proper apology for trying to peek into the man's window. He decided there wasn't one. He'd just forget it and let Woody think whatever he wanted to think.

"I'm doing some back-checking on a homicide case we had up here," Chee said. "It was July eighth. One of our officers was killed. Hit on the head with a rock. You probably heard about it on the radio or saw it in the paper. We're trying to find any witnesses we might have overlooked."

"I heard about that," Woody said. "But the man down at the trading post told me you'd caught the killer right in the act."

"Who told you?"

"That grouchy old man at the Short Mountain Trading Post," Woody said, frowning. "I think his name was Mac something. Sounded Scotch. Did he have it wrong?"

"About as close as you can get," Chee said. "The smoking gun was a bloody rock."

"The old man said it was a Hopi and the cop

had arrested the same guy before," Woody said, looking pensive. Then he nodded, understanding it. "But out here you'd get Hopis on the jury. So you're trying not to leave them any grounds for reasonable doubts."

"Yeah," Chee said. "I guess that about sums it up. Were you working up here that day? If you were, did you see anybody? Or anything? Or hear anything?"

"July eighth, was it?" He punched buttons on his digital watch. "That would make it a Friday," he said, and frowned, thinking about it. "I drove down to Flagstaff, but I think that was Wednesday. I think I was up here Tuesday early, and then I drove over to Third Mesa. That's one of the prairie dog colonies I'm watching. Over there by Bacavi. That and some kangaroo rats."

"It rained that day," Chee said. "Thundershower. Little bit of hail."

Woody nodded. "Yeah, I remember," he said. "I'd stopped at the Hopi Cultural Center to get some coffee, and you could see a lot of lightning over that side of Black Mesa and southwest over the San Francisco Peaks, and it looked like it was pouring down at Yells Back Butte. I was feeling glad I got down that road before it got muddy."

"Did you see anybody when you were driving out? Meet anyone coming in?"

Woody had been unzipping the plastic bag

while he talked, and a puff of escaping air added another unpleasant aroma to the room. Now he pulled out the prairie dog, stiff with rigor mortis, and laid it carefully on the tabletop. He stared at it, felt its neck, groin area and under the front legs. He looked thoughtful. Then he shook his head, dismissing some troublesome notion.

"Going out?" he said. "I think I saw that old lady that herds her goats over on the other side of the butte. I think that was Tuesday I saw her. And then, when I was turning out onto the gravel, I remember seeing a car coming from the Tuba City direction."

"Was it a police car?"

Woody looked up from the prairie dog. "It might have been. It was too far away to tell. But, you know, he never did pass me. Maybe he turned in toward the butte. Maybe that was your policeman. Or maybe the Hopi."

"Possibly," Chee said. "About when was it?"

"Morning. Fairly early."

Woody reclosed the bag, shook it vigorously, reopened it, and poured its contents onto a white plastic sheet on the table.

"Fleas," he said. He selected stainless-steel tweezers from a tray on a lab table, picked up a flea and showed it to Chee. "Now, if I'm lucky, the blood in these fleas is laced with *Yersinia pestis* and"—Woody poked the prairie dog with the tweezers—"so is the blood of our friend here. And if I'm very lucky, it will be *Yersinia X*, the new, modified, recently evolved fast-acting stuff that kills mammals much quicker than the old stuff." He redeposited the flea among its brethren on the plastic, grinned at Chee. "Then, if fortune continues to smile on me, the autopsy I'm about to do on this dog here will confirm what not finding any swollen glands suggests. That this fellow here didn't die of bubonic plague. He died of something old-fashioned."

Chee frowned, not quite understanding Woody's excitement. "So he died of what?"

"That's not the question. Could be old age, any of those ills that beset elderly mammals. Doesn't matter. The question is, why didn't the plague kill him?"

"But that's nothing new, is it? Haven't you guys known for years that when the plague comes through, it always leaves behind a colony here and there that's immune or something? And then the stuff spreads again, from them? I thought—"

Woody had no patience for this. "Sure, sure, sure," he said. "Reservoir colonies. Host colonies. They've been studied for years. How come their immune system blocks the bacteria? If it kills the bacteria, how come the toxin released doesn't kill the dog? If our friend here just has the original version of *Pasteurella pestis*, as we used to call it, then he just gives us another chance to poke around in the blind alley. But if he has—"

It had been a hard and disappointing day for Chee, and this interruption rankled him. He interrupted Woody:

"If he has developed immunity to this new fast-acting germ, you can compare—"

"Germ!" Woody said, laughing. "I don't hear that good old word much these days. But yes. It gives us something to check against. Here's what we know about the blood chemistry of the dogs who survived the old plague." He suggested a big box with his hands. "Now we know this modified bacteria is also killing most of those survivors. We want to know the difference in the chemistry of those who survived the new stuff."

Chee nodded.

"You understand that?"

Chee grunted. He'd taken six hours of biology at the University of New Mexico to help meet the science requirement for his degree in anthropology. The teacher had been a full professor, an international authority on spiders who had made no effort to hide his boredom with basic undergraduate courses nor his disdain for the ignorance of his students. He'd sounded a lot like Woody.

"That's easy enough to understand," Chee

said. "So when you solve the puzzle, you de-
velop a vaccine and save untold billions of prairie dogs from the plague."

Woody had done something to the flea that
produced a brownish fluid and put a bit of it into
a petri dish and a drop on a glass slide. He looked
up. His face, already unnaturally flushed, was
now even redder.

"You think it's funny?" he said. "Well, you're
not the only one who does. A lot of the experts at
the NIH do, too. And at Squibb. And the *New En-
gland Journal of Medicine.* And the American Pharmaceutical Association. The same damn fools
who thought we won the microbe war with penicillin and the streptomycin drugs."

Woody slammed his fist on the countertop, his
voice rising. "So they misused them, and misused
them, and kept on misusing them until they'd
evolved whole new variations of drug-resistant
bacteria. And now, by God, we're burying the
dead! By the tens of thousands. Count Africa and
Asia and its millions. And these damn fools sit on
their hands and watch it get worse."

Chee was no stranger to anger barely under
control. He'd seen it while breaking up bar fights,
in domestic disputes, in various other ugly forms.
But Woody's rage had a sort of fierce, focused in-
tensity that was new to him.

"I didn't mean to sound flippant," Chee said.

"I'm just not familiar with the implications of this sort of research."

Woody took a sip of his Dewar's, his face flushed. He shook his head, studied Chee, recognized repentance.

"Sorry I'm so damned touchy about this," he said, and laughed. "I think it's because I'm scared. All the little beasties we had beaten ten years ago are back and meaner than ever. TB is an epidemic again. So is malaria. So is cholera. We had the staph bacteria whipped with nine different antibiotics. Now none of 'em work on some of it. And then there's the same story with viruses. Viruses. They're what makes this most important. You know that Influenza A, that Swine Flu that came out of nowhere in 1918 and killed maybe forty million people in just a few months. That's more than were killed in four years of war. Viruses scare me even more than bacteria."

Chee raised his eyebrows.

"Because nothing stops them except your immune system. You don't cure a viral sickness. You try to prevent it with a vaccine. That's to prepare your immune system to deal with it if it shows up."

"Yeah," Chee said. "Like polio."

"Like polio. Like some forms of influenza. Like

a lot of things," Woody said. He refilled his whiskey glass. "Are you familiar with the Bible?"

"I've read it," Chee said.

"Remember what the prophet says in the Book of Chronicles? 'We are powerless against this terrible multitude that will come against us.'"

Chee wasn't sure how to take this. "Do you read that as an Old Testament prophet warning us against viruses?"

"As it stands now, they are a terrible multitude and we are damn near powerless against them," Woody said. "Not as well prepared as some of these rodents are anyway. Some of these prairie dogs here somehow have had their immune systems modified to deal with this evolved bacteria. And some of the kangaroo rats have learned to live with the hantavirus. We have to find out how."

Woody's discourse had restored his good temper. He grinned at Chee. "We don't want the rodents outlasting the humans."

Chee nodded. He slid off the stool, picked up his hat. "I'll let you get back to work. Thanks for the time. And the information."

"I just had a thought," Woody said. "The Indian Health Service has had people up here the last several weeks working through this area. Doing the vector control cleanup on that plague outbreak. You might ask them if they had anyone out there on that day."

"They did," Chee said. "I was just going to get into that. One of their people was supposed to be checking on rodents around here the day Kinsman was killed. I was going to ask you if you'd seen her. And then I was going to be on my way."

"A woman? Did she notice anything helpful?"

"Nobody even knows for sure if she got here. She's missing," Chee said. "So is the vehicle she was driving."

"Missing?" Woody said, startled. "Really? You think there could be some connection with the attack on your policeman?"

"I don't see how there could be," Chee said. "But I'd like to talk to her. I understand she's a sturdy-looking brunette, about thirty, named Catherine Pollard."

"I've seen some of those Arizona public health people here and there. That sounds like one of them," Woody said. "But I don't know her name."

"You remember the last time you saw her? And where she was?"

"Nice-looking woman, was she?" Woody said, and glanced up at Chee, not wanting to give the wrong impression. "I don't mean pretty, but good bone structure." He laughed. "Looked like she might have been an athlete."

"She was around here?"

"I think it was over at Red Lake that I saw her. Filling the gas tank on a Health Service Jeep, if that's the right woman. She asked me about the van, if I was the man doing rodent research on the reservation. She asked me to let them know if I saw any dead rodents. Let her know if I saw anything that suggested the plague was killing the rodents."

He pushed himself up from the cot. "By golly, I think she gave me a card with a phone number on it." He sorted through a box labeled OUT on his desk, said "Ah," and read: "'Catherine Pollard, Vector Control Specialist, Communicable Disease Division, Arizona Department of Public Health.'"

He handed the card to Chee, grinned, and said: "Bingo."

"Thanks," Chee said. It didn't sound like bingo to him.

"And, hey," Woody added. "If the time's important you can check on it. When I drove up there was a Navajo Tribal Police car there and she was talking to the driver. Another woman." Woody grinned. "That one you really could call cute. Had her hair in a bun and the uniform on, but she was what we used to call a dish."

"Thanks again," Chee said. "That would be Officer Manuelito. I'll ask her."

But he wouldn't. The timing didn't matter,

and if he asked Bernie Manuelito about it, he'd have to ask her why she hadn't reported that Kinsman had been hitting on her. That was a can of worms he didn't want to dig into. Claire Dineyahze, who as secretary in Chee's little division, always knew such things, had already told him. "She doesn't want to cause you any trouble," Claire had said. Chee had asked her why not, and Claire had given him one of those female "you moron" looks and said: "Don't you know?"

FOURTEEN

AS THEY DROVE northward out of Cameron, Leaphorn explained to Louisa what was troubling Cowboy Dashee.

"I can see his problem," she said, after spending a while staring out the windshield. "Partly professional ethics, partly male pride, partly family loyalty, partly because he feels Chee is going to think he's trying to use their friendship for a personal reason. Is that about it? Have you decided what you're going to do about it?"

Leaphorn had pretty much decided, but he wanted to give it some more thought. He skipped past the question.

"It's all of that, I guess. But it's even more complicated. And why don't you pour us some coffee while we're thinking about it."

"Didn't you just drink about two cups in

there?" Louisa asked. But she reached back and extracted her thermos from the lunch sack.

"It was pretty weak," Leaphorn said. "Besides, I believe the caffeine helps my mind work. Didn't I read that somewhere?"

"Maybe in a comic book," she said. But she poured a cup and handed it to him. "What's the more complicated part that I'm missing?"

"Another friend of Cowboy Dashee's is Janet Pete. She's been assigned as Jano's public defender. Janet and Chee were engaged to be married a while back and then they had a falling-out."

"Ouch," Louisa said, and grimaced. "That does complicate matters some."

"There's more," Leaphorn said, and sipped his coffee.

"It's starting to sound like a soap opera," Louisa said. "Don't tell me that the deputy sheriff was the third party in a love triangle."

"No. It wasn't that."

He took another sip, gestured out of the windshield at the cumulus clouds, white and puffy, drifting on the west wind away from the San Francisco Peaks. "That's our sacred mountain of the west, you know, made by First Man himself, but—"

"He built it with earth brought up from the Fourth World in the usual version of the myth,"

Louisa said. "But if it 'wasn't that,' then what was it?"

"I was going to tell you that in the stories told out here on the west side of the reservation, some of the clans also call it 'Mother of Clouds.'" He pointed through the windshield. "You can see why. When there's any humidity, the west winds hit the slopes, rise, the moisture cools with altitude, the clouds form, and the wind drifts them, one after another, out over the desert. Like a cat having a litter of kittens."

Louisa was smiling at him. "Mr. Leaphorn, am I to conclude that you don't want to tell me what it was with Miss Pete and Jim Chee if it wasn't another man?"

"I'd just be passing along gossip. That's all I have. Just guesswork and gossip."

"You don't start something like that with someone and just leave it hanging. Not if you're going to be trapped in the front seat with them all day. They'll nag you. They'll get mad and surly."

"Well, then," Leaphorn said, "maybe I better make up some sort of a story."

"Do it."

Leaphorn sipped coffee, handed her the empty cup.

"Miss Pete's half Navajo. On the paternal side. Her dad's dead and her mother's a socialite rich lady. Ivy League type. Janet came out here to work for DNA after quitting a job with some big Washington law firm, which handled tribal legal work. Now we get to the gossipy part."

"Good," Louisa said.

"The way the gossips tell it, she and one of the big-shot lawyers were very good friends, and she quit the job because they had a breakup, and she was very, very, very angry with the guy. She was sort of his protégée from way back when he was a professor and she was his law student."

Leaphorn stopped talking and glanced at Louisa. He found himself thinking how much he had come to like this woman. How comfortable he felt with her. How much more pleasant this drive was because she was there on the seat beside him.

"You enjoying this so far?"

"So far, so good," she said. "But I wonder if it's going to have a happy ending."

"I don't know," Leaphorn said. "I doubt it. But anyway. Out here, she and Jim meet because she's defending Navajo suspects and he's arresting them. They get to be friends and—"

Leaphorn paused, gave Louisa a doubtful look. "Now this is about fifthhand. Pure hearsay. Anyway, the gossips had it that what Miss Pete had told Chee about her ex-boss and boyfriend had Jim hating the guy, too. You know, thinking he was a real gold-plated manipulative jerk who had simply used Janet. Understand?"

"Sure," Louisa said. "Probably true, too."

"Understand, it's just gossip."

"Get on with it," Louisa said.

"So Chee tells her some of the information he's learned in a case he's working on. It involved a client of her old Washington law firm and her old boyfriend. So she passes it along to her old boyfriend. Jim figures she's betrayed him. She figures he's being unreasonable, that she was just being friendly and helpful. No harm done, she says. Chee's just being jealous. They have an angry row. She moves back to Washington with no more talk of marriage."

"Oh," Louisa said. "And now she's back."

"It's all just gossip," Leaphorn said. "And you didn't get any of it from me."

"Okay," Louisa said, and shook her head. "Poor Mr. Dashee. What did you tell him?"

"I told him I'd talk to Jim the first chance I get. Probably today." He made a face. "That won't be so easy either, talking to Chee. I'm his ex-boss and he's sort of touchy with me. And, after all, it's none of my business."

"Well, it shouldn't be."

Leaphorn took his eyes off the road long enough to study her expression. "What do you mean by that?"

"You should have just told Mrs. Vanders you were too busy. Or something like that."

Leaphorn let that pass.

"You're retired, you know. The golden years. Now's the time to travel, do all those things you wanted to do."

"That's true," Leaphorn said. "I could trot down to the senior center and play—whatever they do down there."

"You're not too old to get into golf."

"I already did that," Leaphorn said. "At a federal law-enforcement seminar in Phoenix. The feds stay at those three-hundred-dollar-a-night resort places with the big golf courses. I went out with some FBI agents and knocked the ball in all eighteen holes. It wasn't hard, but once you've done it, I don't know why you'd want to do it again."

"You think you're going to like this being a private detective any better?"

Leaphorn smiled at her. "I think it may be a lot harder to get the hang of than golf," he said. "Even the FBI agents mastered golf. They don't have much luck at detecting."

"You know, Joe, I have a feeling that Mr. Dashee might be right about what Pollard's aunt has in mind. I think the old lady might not really want you to find her niece."

"You may be right about that," Leaphorn said. "But still, that would make it a lot more interesting than knocking a golf ball around. Why don't we find Chee and see what he thinks."

They spent the rest of the drive to Tuba City with Louisa plowing through Catherine Pollard's hodgepodge of papers.

Leaphorn had already gone through them once, quickly. Pollard wrote fast, producing a tiny, erratic script in which all vowels looked about the same, and an h might be a k, or an l, or perhaps another of her many uncrossed t's. This unintended code was made worse by a personal shorthand, full of abbreviations and cryptic symbols. Not knowing what he was looking for, he'd found nothing helpful.

Now Louisa read and he listened, amazed. "How can you decipher that woman's handwriting?" he said. "Or are you just guessing at it?"

"Schoolteacher skill," Louisa said. "Most students give you computer printouts for the long papers these days, but in olden times you got a lot of practice plowing through bad penmanship. Repetition develops skill." She went slowly through the papers, translating.

The first fatal case this spring had been a middle-aged woman named Nellie Hale, who lived north of the Kaibito chapter house and who had died in the hospital at Farmington the morning of May 19, ten days after being admitted. Pollard's notes were mostly information collected from family and friends about where Nellie Hale had been during the first weeks of May and the last few days of April. They reported checks made around the Hale hogan, the examination of a prairie dog town near Navajo National Monument where the victim had visited her mother (the dogs had fleas but neither fleas nor dogs had the plague), and the discovery of a deserted colony at the edge of the Hale grazing permit. Fleas collected from the burrows were carrying the plague. The burrows were dusted with poison and the case of Nellie Hale put on the back burner.

That brought them to Anderson Nez. Pollard's notes showed the date he died as June 30 in the hospital at Flagstaff, with "date of admission?" followed by "find out!" She had filled the rest of the page with data accumulated from quizzing family and friends about where his prior travels had taken him. This showed he left home on May 24 en route to Encino, California, to visit his brother. He had returned on June 22. Here Louisa paused.

"I can't make this out," she said, pointing.

He looked at the page. "It's 'i g h,'" he said. "I think I'd figure out that's short for 'in good health.' Notice she underlined it. I wonder why?"

"Double underlines," Louisa said, and resumed reading. Anderson Nez had left the next afternoon for the Goldtooth area and "job with Woody," according to Pollard's notes. "Did you notice he was working for Dr. Woody?" Louisa asked. Then she looked embarrassed. "Of course you did."

"Sort of ironic, isn't it?"

"Very," Louisa said. "Did you notice those dates? She was looking for sources of infection starting back three weeks or so before the dates of the deaths. Is that how long it takes for the bacteria to kill you?"

"I think that's the usual time range that's been established, and I guess that explains why she underlined the 'i g h.' In good health on the twenty-second. Dead on the thirtieth," Leaphorn said. "Anything more about Nez?"

"Not on this page," she said. "And I haven't found any mention of that third case you mentioned."

"That was a boy over in New Mexico," Leaphorn said. "They wouldn't handle that here."

They rolled past the Hopi outpost village of Moenkopi and into Tuba City and parked on the packed-dirt lot of the Navajo Tribal Police station. There Leaphorn found Sergeant Dick Roanhorse and Trixie Dodge, old friends from his days in the department, but not Jim Chee. Roanhorse

told him Chee had headed out early for the Kinsman homicide crime scene and hadn't called in.
He took Leaphorn into the radio room and asked
the young man in the dispatcher's chair to try
to get Chee on the radio. Then it was nostalgia
time.

"You remember when old Captain Largo was
out here, and the trouble he had with you?"
Trixie asked.

"I'm trying to forget that," Leaphorn said. "I
hope none of you people are giving Lieutenant
Chee that kind of headache."

"Not that kind. But he's got one," Roanhorse
said, and winked.

"Well, now," Trixie said. "If you mean Bernie
Manuelito, I wouldn't call that trouble."

"You would if you were her supervisor," Roanhorse said, and noticed Leaphorn's uncompre-
hending look. "Bernie has what we used to call a
crush on the lieutenant, and I guess he's more or
less engaged to this woman lawyer, and everybody around here knows it. So he has to walk on
eggs all the time."

"Yeah," Leaphorn said. "I'd call that a problem." He remembered now that when the word
came on the grapevine at Window Rock that
Chee was transferred from Shiprock to Tuba,
people thought that was ironic. When he asked
why, the answer was that when Officer Manuel-

ito heard Chee was going to marry Janet Pete, she'd gotten herself transferred to Tuba to get away from him.

The dispatcher came to the door. "Lieutenant Chee said he'd be waiting for you," the young man said. "You take U.S. 264 seven miles south from the 160 junction, then turn right on the dirt road that connects there, and then about twenty miles down the dirt. There's a track that connects there leading back toward Black Mesa. Lieutenant Chee said he'll be parked there."

"Okay," Leaphorn said, thinking that would be the old road across the Moenkopi Plateau to Goldtooth, where nobody lived anymore, and on into the empty northwestern edge of the Hopi reservation to Dinnebito Wash and Garces Mesa. It was a drive you didn't start without a full tank of gasoline and air in your spare tire. Maybe it was better now. "Thank you."

"You think you can find it?"

Sergeant Roanhorse laughed and whacked Leaphorn on the back. "How soon they forget you," he said.

But Trixie hadn't exhausted the unrequited romance business as yet. "Bernie's been worried all week about whether she should invite him to a *kinaalda* her family's having for one of her cousins. She invited everybody else but would it be, you know, pushy or something if she invited the boss? Or would he feel hurt if she didn't? Can't make up her mind."

"Is that why she's been so hard to get along with the last day or two?" Roanhorse asked.

"What do you think?" she said. And grinned at him.

FIFTEEN

ACTING LIEUTENANT JIM Chee sat on a sandstone slab in the shade of a juniper awaiting the arrival of Joe Leaphorn, Former Boss, Former Mentor, and, as far as Chee was concerned, Perpetual Legendary Lieutenant. He admired Leaphorn, he respected him, he even sort of liked him. But for some reason, an impending meeting with the man had always made him feel uneasy and incompetent. He'd thought he'd get over that when Leaphorn was no longer his supervisor. Alas, he hadn't.

This afternoon he didn't need a Leaphorn conversation to make him feel like a rookie. He'd learned very little prowling around Yells Back, mostly negative, reinforcing what he already knew. Jano had hit Ben Kinsman on the head with a rock. He'd found no trace of blood at the blind where Jano had caught the bird to suggest that Jano's arm had been slashed by the eagle's talons. Nor had he turned up any evidence that he was overlooking any possible witnesses to the crime. He reconsidered what Dr. Woody had told him. Woody had recalled seeing a car coming from the north as he emerged from the track that led toward Yells Back Butte. Possibly it had been Kinsman en route to meet his destiny. Possibly it was the person who had killed Kinsman following him. Or possibly Woody's memory was faulty, or Woody was lying for some reason Chee couldn't fathom. Whatever the case, Chee had this uneasy feeling that he was missing something and that Leaphorn, in his gentle way, would point it out.

Well, now he'd find out. The cloud of dust coming down the road from the north would be the Legendary Lieutenant. Chee got up, put on his hat, and walked down the hill to where his patrol car had been baking in the sun beside the road. The pickup pulled up beside it and two people emerged—Leaphorn and a stocky woman wearing a straw hat, jeans, and a man's shirt.

"Louisa," Leaphorn said. "This is Lieutenant Chee. I think you met him in Window Rock. Jim, Professor Bourebonette."

"Yes," Chee said as they shook hands, "it's good to see you again." But it wasn't. Not now. He just wanted to know why Leaphorn was looking for him. He didn't want any complications.

"I hope this isn't causing you any inconvenience," Leaphorn said. "I told Dineyahze we'd just wait there at the station if you were coming in."

"No problem," Chee said, and stood there waiting for Leaphorn to get on with it.

"I'm still trying to find Catherine Pollard," Leaphorn said. "I wondered if you've turned up anything."

"Nothing helpful," Chee said.

"She wasn't here the day Kinsman was attacked?"

"Nope. At least, she wasn't until later in the day," Chee said. "I don't have to tell you how long it takes to get an ambulance into a place like this. By the time the criminalistics team got its photographs and all that, it was late afternoon. But she could have shown up after that."

Leaphorn was waiting for him to add something. But what could he add?

"Oh," Chee said. "Of course, she could have gotten here earlier."

That seemed to be what Leaphorn wanted him to think. The Legendary Lieutenant nodded.

"I ran into Cowboy Dashee at Cameron today," Leaphorn said. "He'd heard I was looking for Pollard. Knew about the reward we were offering for the Jeep she was driving. He told me a woman who keeps some goats up here had seen a Jeep going up that old road to the Tijinney place before sunrise that morning. He asked me to pass it along to you. In case it might be useful."

"He did?"

Leaphorn nodded. "Yeah. He said you had a tough one with this Kinsman homicide. He said he wished he could help you."

"Jano is his cousin," Chee said. "I think they were childhood buddies. Cowboy thinks I've got the wrong man. Or so I hear."

"Well, anyway, he thought you might want to talk to the woman. He told me they call her Old Lady Notah," Leaphorn said.

"Old Lady Notah," Chee said. "I think I saw some of her goats up there by the butte today. I'll go talk to her."

"Might be wasting your time," Leaphorn said.

"Or might not be," Chee said. He looked back toward the butte. "And, hey," he added. "Would you tell Cowboy I said thanks?"

"Sure," Leaphorn said.

Chee was still looking away from Leaphorn. "Did Cowboy have any other tips?"

"Well, he has his own theory of the crime."

Chee turned. "Like what?"

"Like Catherine Pollard did it."

Chee frowned, thinking about it. "Had he worked out the motive? The opportunity? All that?"

"More or less," Leaphorn said. "He has her coming up here on her vector control job. She runs into Kinsman, he makes a move on her. She resists. They struggle. She bangs him on the head and flees the scene." Leaphorn gave Chee a while to consider that. Then he said: "But then why didn't you see her driving out while you were driving in?"

"That's what I was thinking. And if she's on the run, why did her family—" He stopped, looking abashed.

Leaphorn grinned. "If Cowboy is guessing right, the family hired me to look for her thinking that would make it look like she'd been abducted. Or killed or something like that."

"That doesn't make sense," Chee said.

"Well, it sort of does, actually," Leaphorn said. "The lady who hired me struck me as a mighty shrewd woman. I told her I didn't see how I could be of any help. She didn't seem to care."

Chee nodded. "Yeah, I guess so. I can see it."

"Except how did she get the Jeep out of here? The TV commercials make them look like they can drive up cliffs, but they can't."

"There's a way, though," Chee said. "There's

another way in here if you don't mind doing a little scrambling. An old trail comes up the other side of Yells Back toward Black Mesa. I think the lady with the goats might use it. You could drive the Jeep up there, park it, climb over the saddle, do your deed, and then climb back over the saddle and drive out on the goat path."

Chee stopped. "There's trouble with that, though."

"You mean she wouldn't do that unless she knew in advance that she was going to need an escape route?"

"Exactly," Chee said. "How could she have known that?"

Louisa had been listening, looking thoughtful. Now she said: "Do you professionals object if an amateur butts in?"

"Be our guest," Leaphorn said.

"I find myself wondering just why Pollard was coming up here anyway," Louisa said. She looked at Leaphorn. "Didn't you tell me she was looking for the place where Nez was infected? Where the flea bit him?"

"Right," Leaphorn said, looking puzzled.

"And isn't the period between infection and death—I mean in cases where treatment doesn't effect a cure—doesn't that range just a couple of weeks?" Louisa made one of those modifying gestures with her hands. "I mean, usually. Statistically. Often enough so that when vector control people are looking for the source, they're looking for places the victim had been during that period. And what Miss Pollard was writing in her notes suggested that she was always trying to find out where the victim was in that period before their death."

"Ah," Leaphorn said. "I see."

Chee, whose interest in plague and vector control people who hunted it extended back only a few minutes, had little idea what any of this was about.

He said: "You mean she knew Nez couldn't have been around Yells Back in that time frame? How would—?"

"Pollard's notes show where he was. They show—" She stopped in midsentence. "Just a minute. I don't want to be wrong about this. The book's in the car."

She found it on the dashboard, extracted it, leaned against the fender, and flipped through the pages.

"Here," she said. "Under her Anderson Nez heading. It shows that he was visiting his brother in Encino, California. He came home to his mother's hogan four miles southwest of Copper Mine Trading Post on June twenty-third. The next afternoon, he left to go to his job with Woody near Goldtooth."

"June twenty-fourth?" Leaphorn said thoughtfully. "Right?"

"And six days later he dies in the hospital at Flag." She checked back in the notes. "Actually more like five days. Pollard says in here somewhere he died just after midnight."

"Wow," Leaphorn said. "Are we sure he died of plague?"

"Slow down," Jim Chee said. "Explain this date business to me."

Louisa shook her head, looking doubtful. "I guess the point is that Pollard knows a lot more about plague than we do. So she would have known that Nez didn't get his infected flea up here. Plague doesn't kill that fast. So she didn't have any reason to come up here flea hunting when she did."

"That's the question," Leaphorn said. "If that wasn't her reason, what was? Or did she tell Krause she was coming, and not come? Or did Krause lie about it?"

Louisa was reading from another section of the notebook. She held up her hand.

"Pollard must have been thinking something was funny. She went back out to the Nez place near Copper Mine Mesa. Rechecking.

"'Mom says Nez dug postholes, stretched

sheep fencing to expand pens. Family dogs wearing flea collars and sans fleas. No cats. No prairie dog towns in vicinity. No history of rats or rat sign found. Nez drove to Page with mother, buying groceries. No headache. No fever.'" She closed the notebook, shrugged.

"That's it?" Chee asked.

"There's a marginal note for her to check sources at Encino," Louisa said. "I guess to see if he was sick when he was there."

Chee said, "But she told her boss she was coming up to Yells Back to check for fleas here. Or at least he says she did. I think I've met that guy." He looked at Leaphorn. "Big, raw-boned guy named Krause?"

"That's him."

"What else did she tell him?"

"Krause said she came by early that day before he got to work. He didn't see her. She just left him a note," Leaphorn said. "I didn't see it, but Krause said that she just reported she was going up to Yells Back to collect fleas."

"By the way," Chee asked, "with Pollard missing, as well as the Jeep she was driving, how did you get her notebook?"

"I guess we should call it a journal," Leaphorn said. "It was with a folder full of stuff her aunt's lawyer collected from her motel room in Tuba. It looks like she took the notes she jotted down in the field and converted them into sort of a report when she got home with her comments."

"Like a diary?" Chee asked.

"Not really," Leaphorn said. "There's nothing very personal or private in it."

"That was the last entry about Nez?" Chee asked.

"No," Louisa said. She flipped back through the pages.

" 'July 6. Krause says he heard Dr. Woody checked Nez into the hospital. Krause not answering his telephone. Will get to Flag mañana and see what I can learn.'

" 'July 7. Can't believe what I heard at Flag today. Somebody is lying. Yells Back Butte mañana, collect fleas, find out.' "

Louisa shut the notebook. "That's it. The final entry."

SIXTEEN

"IT'S FUNNY," LEAPHORN said, "how you can look at something a half dozen times and not see it."

Louisa waited for him to explain that, decided he didn't intend to and said, "Like what?"

"Like what Catherine Pollard wrote in that journal," Leaphorn said. "I should have noticed the pattern. The incubation period of that bacteria. I should have wondered why she would be coming up here."

They were jolting up the rocky tracks that had once given the Tijinney family access to the world outside the shadow of Yells Back Butte and Black Mesa. Over Black Mesa afternoon clouds were forming, hinting that the rainy season might finally begin.

"How?" Louisa said. "Did you know when Mr. Nez died?"

"I could have found out," Leaphorn said. "That would have been as easy as making a telephone call."

"Oh, knock it off," Louisa said; "I've noticed males have this practice of entertaining themselves with self-flagellation. Mea culpa, mea culpa, mea maxima culpa. We females find that habit tiresome."

Leaphorn considered that awhile. Grinned.

"You mean like Jim Chee blaming himself for not getting up here quick enough to keep Kinsman from getting himself hit on the head."

"Exactly."

"Okay," Leaphorn said. "You're right. I guess I couldn't have known."

"On the other hand, you shouldn't get too complacent," Louisa said. "I hope you noticed that I figured it out pretty quick."

He laughed. "I noticed it. It took me a while to deal with that. Then two thoughts occurred. You could translate Pollard's scribbles and I couldn't, and you were paying attention while Professor Perez was educating us about pathogenic bacteria last night and I was just sitting there letting my mind wander. I decided that you just have a much higher tolerance for boredom than I do."

"Academics have to be boredom-invulnerable," Louisa said. "Otherwise we'd walk out of faculty meetings, and if you do that, you don't get tenure. You have to go get real jobs."

Leaphorn shifted into second and followed the established tire tracks through the arroyo where Chee had left his car that fatal day. They ran out of old tracks on the little hump of high ground that overlooked what was left of the old Tijinney place. Leaphorn stopped and turned off the ignition, and they sat looking down on the abandoned homestead.

"Mr. Chee said Woody had his van parked over closer to the butte," Louisa said. "Over there where all those junipers are growing by the arroyo."

"I remember," Leaphorn said. "I just wanted to take a look." He waved at the ruined hogan, its door missing, its roof fallen, its north wall tumbled. Beyond it stood the remains of a brush arbor, a sheep pen formed of stacked stones, two stone pylons that once would have supported timbers on which water storage barrels had rested. "Sad," he said.

"Some people would call it picturesque."

"People who don't understand how much work went into building all that. And trying to make a living here."

"I know," Louisa said. "I was a farm girl myself. Lots of work, but Iowa had rich black dirt.

And enough rain. And indoor plumbing. Electricity. All that."

"Old Man McGinnis told me kids had vandalized this place. It looks like it."

"Not Navajo kids, I'll bet," she said. "Isn't it a death hogan?"

"I think the old lady died in it," Leaphorn said. "You notice the north wall's partly knocked down."

"The traditional way to take out the body, isn't it? North, the direction of evil."

Leaphorn nodded. "But McGinnis was complaining that a lot of young Navajos, not just the city ones, don't respect the old ways these days. They ignore the taboos, if they ever heard of them. He thinks some of them tore into this place, looking for stuff they could sell. He said they even dug this deep hole where the fire pit was. Apparently they thought something valuable was buried there."

Louisa shook her head. "I wouldn't think there would be anything very valuable left in that hogan. And I don't see any sign of a big deep hole."

Leaphorn chuckled. "I don't either. But then McGinnis never certifies the accuracy. He just passes along the gossip. And as for the value, he said they were looking for ceremonial stuff. When that hogan was built, the owner probably had a place in the wall beside the door where he kept his medicine bundle. Minerals from the sacred mountains. That sort of thing. Some collectors will pay big money for some of that material, and the older it is the better."

"I guess so," Louisa said. "Collecting antiques is not my thing."

Leaphorn smiled at her. "You collect everybody's antique stories. Even ours. That's how I met you, remember. One of your sources was in jail."

"Collect them and preserve them," she said. "Remember when you were telling me about how First Man and First Woman found the baby White Shell Girl on Huerfano Mesa and you had it all wrong?"

"I had it exactly right," Leaphorn said. "That's the version we hold to in my Red Forehead Clan. That makes it correct. The other clans have it wrong. And you know what, I'm going to take a closer look at that hogan. Let's see if McGinnis knew what he was talking about."

She walked down the slope with him. There was nothing left of the hogan building but the circle of stacked stone that formed a wall around the hard-packed earth of the floor, and the ponderosa poles and shreds of tar paper that had formed its collapsed roof.

"There was a hole there once," Louisa said. "Mostly filled in, though."

They were in cloud shadow now, and the thunderhead over the mesa made a rumbling noise. They climbed the slope back to the truck.

"I wonder what they found?"

"In the hole?" Leaphorn said. "I'd guess nothing. I never heard of a Navajo burying anything under his hogan fire pit. But of course McGinnis had an answer for that. He said Old Man Tijinney was a silversmith. Had a lard bucket full of silver dollars."

"Sounds more logical than ceremonial things," Louisa said.

"Until you ask why bury a bucket when there's a million places you could hide it. And hoarding wealth isn't part of the Navajo Way anyway. There're always kinfolks who need it."

She laughed. "You tell McGinnis that?"

"Yeah, and he said, 'You're supposed to be the goddamn detective. You figure it out.' So I figured out there wasn't any bucket. You notice I never came up here with my pick and shovel to check it out."

"I don't know," she said. "You're the tidiest man I ever knew. Just the kind of looter who'd push the dirt back in the hole."

They found Dr. Albert Woody's van just where Chee had said it would be. Woody was standing in the doorway watching them park. To Leaphorn's surprise, he looked delighted to see them.

"Two visitors on the same day," he said as they got out of the truck. "I've never been this popular."

"We won't take much of your time," Leaphorn said. "This is Dr. Louisa Bourebonette, I'm Joe Leaphorn and I presume you must be Dr. Albert Woody."

"Exactly," Woody said. "And glad to meet you. What can I do for you?"

"We're trying to locate a woman named Catherine Pollard. She's a vector control specialist with the Arizona Health Department, and—"

"Oh, yes," Woody said. "I met her over near Red Lake some time ago. She was looking for sick rodents and infected fleas. Looking for the source of a plague case. In a way we're in the same line of work."

He looked very excited, Leaphorn thought. Wired. Ready to burst. As if he were high on amphetamines.

"Have you seen her around here?"

"No," Woody said. "Just over at the Thriftway station. We were both buying gasoline. She noticed my van and introduced herself."

"She's working out of that temporary laboratory in Tuba City," Leaphorn said. "On the morning of July eighth she left a note for her boss saying she was coming up here to collect rodents."

"There was a Navajo Tribal policeman up here talking to me this morning," Woody said. "He asked me about her, too. Come in and let me give you something cold to drink."

"We didn't intend to take a lot of your time," Leaphorn said.

"Come in. Come in. I've just had something great happen. I need somebody to tell it to. And Dr. Bourebonette, what is your specialty?"

"I'm not a physician," Louisa said. "I'm a cultural anthropologist at Northern Arizona University. I believe you know Dr. Perez there."

"Perez?" Woody said. "Oh, yes. In the lab. He's done some work for me."

"He's a great fan of yours," Louisa said. "In fact, you're his nominee for the next Nobel Prize in medicine."

Woody laughed. "Only if I'm guessing right about the internal working of rodents. And only if somebody in the National Center for Emerging Viruses doesn't get it first. But I'm forgetting my manners. Come in. Come in. I want to show you something."

Woody was twisting his hands together, grinning broadly, as they went past him through the doorway.

It was almost cold inside, the air damp and clammy and smelling of animals, formaldehyde, and an array of other chemicals that linger forever in memory. The sound was another mixture—the motor of the air-conditioner engine on the roof, the whir of fans, the scrabbling feet of rodents locked away somewhere out of sight. Woody seated Louisa in a swivel chair near his desk, motioned Leaphorn to a stool beside a white plastic working surface, and leaned his lanky body against the door of what Leaphorn presumed was a floor-to-ceiling refrigerator.

"I've got some good news to share with Dr. Perez," he said. "You can tell him we've found the key to the dragon's cave."

Leaphorn shifted his gaze from Woody to Louisa. Obviously she didn't understand that any better than he did.

"Will he know what that means?" she asked. "He understands you're hunting for a solution to drug-resistant pathogens. Do you mean you've found it?"

Woody looked slightly abashed.

"Something to drink," he said, "and then I'll try to explain myself." He opened the refrigerator door, fished out an ice bucket, extracted three stainless steel cups from an overhead cabinet and a squat brown bottle, which he displayed. "I only have scotch."

Louisa nodded. Leaphorn said he'd settle for water.

Woody talked while he fixed their drinks.

"Bacteria, like about everything alive, split themselves into genera. Call it families. Here we're dealing with the *Enterobacteriaceae* family. One branch of that is *Pasteurellaceae*, and a branch of that is *Yersinia pestis*—the organism that causes bubonic plague. Another branch is *Neisseria gonorrhoeae*, which causes the famous venereal disease. These days, gonorrhea is hard to treat because—" Woody paused, sipping his scotch.

"Wait," he said. "Let me skip back a little. Some of these bacteria, gonorrhea for example, contain a little plasmid with a gene in it that codes for the formation of an enzyme that destroys penicillin. That means you can't treat the disease with any of those penicillin drugs. You see?"

"Sure," Louisa said. "Remember, I'm a friend of Professor Perez. I get a lot of this sort of information."

"We now understand that DNA can be transferred between bacteria—especially between bacteria in the same family."

"Kissing cousins," Louisa said. "Like incest."

"Well, I guess," Woody said. "I hadn't thought of it like that."

Leaphorn had been sampling his ice water, which had the ice cube flavor plus staleness, plus an odd taste that matched the aroma of the van's air supply. He put down the cup.

Leaphorn had been doing some reading. He

said: "I guess we're talking about a mixture of plague and gonorrhea—which would make the plague microbe resistant to tetracycline and chloramphenicol. Is that about right?"

"About right," Woody said. "And possibly several other antibiotic formulations. But that's not the point. That's not what's important."

"It sounds important to me," Louisa said.

"Well, yes. It makes it terribly lethal if one is infected. But what we have here is still a blood-to-blood transmission. It requires a vector—such as a flea—to spread it from one mammal to another. If this evolution converted it directly into an aerobic form—a pneumonic plague spread by coughing or just breathing the same air—we'd have cause for panic."

"No panic then?"

Woody laughed. "Actually, the epidemic trackers might even be happier with this form. If a disease kills its victims fast enough, they don't have time to spread it."

Louisa's expression suggested she took no cheer from this. "What is important then?"

Woody opened the door of a bottom cabinet, extracted a wire cage, and displayed it. A tag with the name CHARLEY printed on it was tied to the wire. Inside was a plump brown prairie dog, apparently dead.

"Charley, this fellow here, and his kith and

kin in the prairie dog town where I trapped him, are full of plague bacteria—both the old form and the new. Yet he's alive and well, and so are his relatives."

"He looks dead," Louisa said.

"He's asleep," Woody said. "I took some blood and tissue samples. He's still recovering from the chloroform."

"There's more to it than this," Leaphorn said. "You've known for years that when the plague sweeps through it leaves behind a few towns where the bacteria doesn't kill the animals. Host colonies. Or plague reservoirs. Isn't that what they're called?"

"Exactly," Woody said. "And we've studied them for years without finding out what happens in the one prairie dog's immune system to keep it alive while a million others are dying." He stopped, sipped scotch, watched them over the rim of his cup, eyes intense.

"Now we have the key." He tapped the cage with his finger. "We inject this fellow's blood into a mammal that has resisted the standard infection and study the immune reaction. We inject it into a normal mammal and make the same study. See what's happening to white blood cell production, cell walls, so forth. All sorts of new possibilities are open."

"And what you learn from the rodent immune system applies to the human system."

"That's been the basis of medical research for generations," Woody said. He put down his cup. "If it doesn't work this time, we can quit worrying about global warming, asteroids on collision courses, nuclear war, all those minor threats. The tiny little beasties have neutralized our defenses. They'll get us first."

"That sounds extreme," Louisa said. "After all, the world has had these sweeping epidemics before. Humanity survived."

"Before fast mass transportation," Woody said. "In the old days a disease killed everybody in an area, then died out because there was nobody left to pass it around. Now airlines can have it spread planetwide before the Centers for Disease Control knows it's happening."

That produced a moment of thoughtful silence, which Woody ended after mixing another drink.

"Let me show you what had me so excited when you drove up," he said after Louisa declined a refill. He pointed to the larger of his two microscopes. Louisa looked first.

"Notice the clusters of ovoid cells, very regular shapes. Those are the *Yersinia*. See the rounder ones? They're darker because they take the dye differently. They look a lot like what you find in a gonorrhea victim. But not quite. They also have some of the *Yersinia* characteristics."

"You couldn't prove it by me," Louisa said. "When I look into one of these things, I always think I'm seeing my eyelashes."

Leaphorn took his turn. He saw the bacteria and what he guessed were blood cells. Like Louisa, they told him nothing except that he was wasting time. He had come up here to find out what had happened to Catherine Pollard.

"Very interesting," Leaphorn said. "But we're taking too much of your time. About two or three more questions and we'll go. I guess Lieutenant Chee told you that Miss Pollard was trying to find the source of Mr. Nez's infection. Did Nez work for you?"

"Yes. Part-time for several years. He'd put out the traps, and check them, and collect the rodents. Take care of all such things."

"I understand you checked him into the hospital. Did you tell the people there where Nez was infected?"

"I didn't know."

"Not even a general idea?"

"Not even that," Woody said. "He'd been in several places. Here and there. Fleas get into people's clothing. You carry them around. You're not sure when you get bit."

Leaphorn weighed that against his own experience. He had been bitten by fleas more than once. Not very painful, but something you noticed.

"When did you notice he was sick?"

"It would have been the evening before I checked him in. He had driven in that morning to do some things, and after we ate our supper he said he had a headache. No other symptoms and no temperature, but you don't take chances in this business. I gave him a dose of doxycycline. Next morning, he still had a headache, and he was also running a temp. It was a hundred and three. I took him right to the hospital."

"How long does it usually take between the infected flea bite and those sort of symptoms?"

"Usually about four or five days. The longest I know of is sixteen days."

"What was the shortest?"

Woody thought. "I've been told of a two-day case, but I have my doubts. I think an earlier flea bite caused that one." He paused. "Here," he said. "Let me show you another slide."

He opened a filing case, pulled out a box of slides, selected one and inserted it into the microscope.

"Take a look at this."

Leaphorn looked. He saw the ovoid cells of the plague bacteria and the rounder specimens of the evolved bacteria. Only the blood cells looked different.

"It looks almost the same," he said.

"You have a good eye," Woody said. "It is almost the same. But this slide is from a blood sample I took from Nez when I took his temperature."

"Oh," Leaphorn said.

"Two things are important here. From the onset of the fever to death was less than three days. That's far too short a time for the standard *Yersinia* bacteria to kill. And the second—" Woody paused for effect, grinning at Leaphorn.

"Charley is still alive," he said.

SEVENTEEN

IT HAD TAKEN Acting Lieutenant Jim Chee about a year to learn the three ways of getting things done in the Navajo Tribal Police. Number one was the official system. The word, neatly typed on an official form, worked its way up through the prescribed channels to the correct level, and then down again to the working cops. In number two, the midlevel bureaucrat whom Chee had now become telephone friends at the Window Rock headquarters and the various substations, explained what he needed done, and either called in IOUs or asked for a favor.

Chee learned quickly that number three was the fastest. There, one outlined the problem to the proper woman in the office and asked her for help. If the asker had earned the askee's respect, she would get the really savvy folks at work on the project—the female network.

Since racing back to his Tuba City office from his meeting with the Legendary Lieutenant Leaphorn, Chee was using all three systems to make sure that if Catherine Pollard's missing Jeep could be found, it would be found in a hurry. Until it was—in fact, until Pollard herself was found—Chee knew he wouldn't have a comfortable moment. He'd be haunted by the thought that he might be hanging Jano for a crime he hadn't committed. Jano had done it, of course. He'd seen him do it. Or practically had, and there was no alternative. But what had been an open-and-shut case in his mind now had a crack in it. He had to close it.

Therefore, when he walked into the Tuba City station, he went directly to the office of Mrs. Dineyahze and explained to her how important it was to find the vehicle. "All right," she said, "I'll call around. Get some people off their rear ends."

"I'd appreciate it," Chee said. He didn't explain to Mrs. Dineyahze what should be done, which was one of the reasons she liked him.

He hadn't noticed that Officer Bernadette Manuelito had come through the open door of the secretary's office and was standing behind him.

She said, "Can I help?" which was exactly what Bernie often said. Nor did how she looked surprise him, which was shirt wrinkled, hair sort of disheveled, lipstick slightly askew and—despite all that—very feminine and very pretty.

Chee looked at his watch. "Thanks, but you're off-duty now, Bernie. And tomorrow's your day off."

He didn't think that would have much effect, since Bernie did pretty much what she wanted to do. But he could hear the telephone clamoring for attention in his office, and so was the stack of paperwork he'd abandoned this morning. He headed for the door.

"Lieutenant," Bernie said. "My family is having a *kinaalda* starting next Saturday for Emily— that's my cousin. Over at Burnt Water. You'd be welcome."

"Golly, Bernie, I'd like to. But I don't think I can get away from here."

Bernie looked downcast. "Okay," she said.

The telephone call was to remind him not to be late for a coordination meeting with people from the BIA Law and Order staff, the Coconino County Sheriff's Office, the Arizona Highway Patrol, the FBI and the Drug Enforcement Agency. While he listened, he could overhear Mrs. Dineyahze discussing the impending puberty ceremonial with Bernie—Mrs. D. sounding cheerful, Ms. Manuelito sounding sad. As for Chee, he felt repentant. He hated hurting Bernie's feelings.

When he returned from the coordination meeting about sundown, his IN basket held a report from Mrs. Dineyahze with a note clipped to it. The report assured him that the right people in the state police and highway patrols of Arizona, New Mexico, Utah, and Colorado now had all the needed data on the missing Jeep. More important, they knew why it was needed. A brother cop had been killed. Finding that Jeep was part of the investigation. The same information had gone to police departments in reservation border towns and to sheriff's offices in relevant county seats.

Chee leaned back in his chair, feeling better. If that Jeep was rolling down a highway anywhere in the Four Corners there was a fair chance it would be spotted. If a city cop saw it parked somewhere, there was a good chance the license plate would be checked. He unclipped the note, which was handwritten. By Mrs. Dineyahze's standards, untyped meant unofficial.

"Lt. Chee: Bernie called the Arizona State motor pool and got all the specifications on the Jeep. It had been impounded in a drug bust and had a lot of fancy add-ons, which are listed below. Also note battery and tire types, rims, other things that Bernie thought might turn up at pawnshops, etc. She relayed the list to shops in Gallup, Flag, Farmington, etc., and also called Thriftway people in Phoenix and asked them to ask their stores on reservation to be alert." This was signed "C. Dineyahze."

Far below this signature, which made it not only unofficial but off the record, Mrs. Dineyahze had scrawled:

"Bernie is a good girl."

Chee already knew that. He liked her. He admired her. He thought she was a very neat lady. But he also knew that Bernadette Manuelito had a crush on him, and almost everybody else in the extended family of the Navajo Tribal Police seemed to know it, too. That made Bernie a pain in the neck. In fact, that was how Chee, who wasn't very good at understanding women, had come to notice Bernie had her eye on him. He'd started being kidded about it.

But there was no time to think of that now. Nor about her idea—which was smart. If the Jeep had been abandoned somewhere on the Big Rez or in the border country, the odds were fairly good that it would be stripped—especially since it had been loaded with expensive, easily stolen stuff. Now he was hungry and tired. None of the frozen dinners awaiting him in the little refrigerator in his trailer home had any appeal for him tonight. He'd go by the Kentucky Fried Chicken place, pick up a dinner with biscuits and gravy, go home, dine, kick back, finish *Meridian*, the Norman Zollinger novel he was reading, and get some sleep.

He was finishing a thigh and the second biscuit when the phone rang.

"You said to call you if anything turned up on the Jeep," the dispatcher said.

"Like what?"

"Like a guy came into the filling station at Cedar Ridge last Monday and tried to sell the clerk a radio and tape player. It was the same brand that was in that Jeep."

"They have an identification?"

"The clerk said it was a kid from a family named Pooacha. They have a place over on Shinume Wash."

"Okay," Chee said. "Thanks." He looked at his watch. It would have to wait until morning.

By midafternoon the next day the Jeep was found. If you discount driving about two hundred miles back and forth, and some of it over roads far too primitive even to be listed as primitive on Chee's AAA Indian Country road map, the whole project proved to be remarkably easy.

Since Officer Manuelito had provided the idea that made it possible, and had the day off anyway, Chee could think of no way to discourage

Bernie from coming along. In fact, he didn't even try. He enjoyed her company when she had her mind on business instead of on him. They drove first to the Cedar Ridge trading post, talked to the clerk there, learned the would-be radio salesman was a young man named Tommy Tsi, and got directions to the Pooacha place, where he lived. They took the dusty washboard gravel of Navajo Route 6110 westward to Blue Moon Bench, turned south on the even rougher Route 6120 along Bekihatso Wash, and found the track that wandered through the rocks and saltbush to the Pooacha establishment.

At this intersection a cracked old boot was stuck atop the post beside the cattle guard.

"Well, good," said Bernie, pointing to the boot. "Somebody's home."

"Somebody is," Chee agreed, "unless the last one out forgot to take the boot down. And in my experience, when the road's as bad as this one, the somebody who's there isn't the one you're looking for."

But Tommy Tsi, a very young Pooacha son-in-law, was home—and very nervous when he noticed the uniform Chee was wearing and the Navajo Tribal Police decal on his car. No, he didn't still have the radio and tape player. It belonged to a friend who had asked him to try to sell it for him. The friend had reclaimed it, Tsi said, rubbing his hand uneasily over a very sparse mustache as he spoke.

"Give us the friend's name," Chee said. "Where can we locate him?"

"His name?" Tommy Tsi said. And thought a while. "Well, he's not exactly a close friend. I met him in Flag. I think they call him Shorty. Or something like that."

"And how were you going to get his money back to him when you sold his stuff?"

"Well," Tommy Tsi said. And hesitated again. "I'm not sure."

"That's a shame," Bernie said. "If you could find him we want you to tell him we're not much interested in the radio stuff. We want to find the Jeep. If he can show us where the Jeep is, then he gets to collect the reward."

"Reward? For the Jeep?"

"A thousand bucks," Bernie said. "Twenty fifty-dollar bills. The family of the woman who was driving the Jeep put it up."

"Really," Tsi said. "A thousand bucks."

"For finding the Jeep. That's what this guy did, you know. Found an abandoned vehicle. No law against that, is there?"

"Right," Tommy Tsi agreed, nodding and looking much more cheerful.

"If he told you where the Jeep is, then you could take us there. We could arrange for you to get the money. Then if you can find him again, you could share it with him."

"Yes," Tsi said. "Let me get my hat."

"Tell you what," Chee said. "Bring the radio stuff along, too. We might need that for fingerprints."

"Mine?" Tsi looked startled.

"We know yours are on it," Chee said. "We're thinking of whoever drove it where you found it."

And so they had jolted back down 6120, to 6110, to Cedar Ridge, and thence southward on the pavement past Tuba City and through Moenkopi, and back onto the dusty road past the abandoned Goldtooth trading post, and then a left turn over a cattle guard onto dirt tracks that led up the slope of Ward Terrace. Where the track crossed a shallow wash, Tommy Tsi said, "Here," and pointed down it.

The Jeep had been left mid-wash around a bend some fifty yards downstream. They left Tsi in the car and walked along the edge of the streambed, careful not to mar any tracks that might still be there. There was no sign of foot traffic up the sand. Much of the Jeep's tire marks had already been erased by the pickup Tsi had been driving, and the wind had softened the edges of what few remained. But enough had survived to add one bit of information. Bernie noticed it, too.

"That little rainstorm came through just after you found Ben, didn't it?" And she pointed to a protected place where the Jeep tires had left their imprint in sand that obviously had been damp.

"How far is this from where that happened?"

"I'd say maybe twenty miles as the crow flies," Chee said. "And no rain since. I think that tells us a little something."

The Jeep itself told them little else. They stood back from it, examining the ground. The sand around the driver's side had been churned, presumably by Tsi's boots, as he got in and out looking for something easy to loot, and while he pried out the radio.

From the passenger's door, one could step directly onto the stony slope of the arroyo bank. If the occupant had left that way, it made tracking this many days later virtually hopeless.

"What's that stuff in the backseat?" Bernie asked. "I guess the equipment for the job."

"I see some traps," Chee said. "And cages. That canister is probably for poison they blow into burrows to kill the fleas."

He took out his pocketknife, used it to depress the button to open the passenger-side door, then used it to swing the door open.

"Looks like nothing much here," Bernie said, "unless we find something in the litter bag."

Chee wasn't ready to concede that. Leaphorn had once told him that you're more likely to find something if you're not looking for anything in particular. "Just keep an open mind and see what you see," Leaphorn liked to say. Now Chee saw a dark stain on the leather upholstery on the Jeep's passenger seat.

He pointed at it.

"Oh," Bernie said, and made a wry face.

The stain streaked downward, almost black.

"I'd guess dried blood," Chee said. "Let's get the crime scene people out here."

EIGHTEEN

"DID YOU NOTICE his face when he said that?"
Leaphorn asked. "Said 'Mr. Nez is dead. Charley
is still alive.' The damn prairie dog is still alive.
Like it was the best news possible."

"I don't think I've ever seen you really angry
before," Louisa said.

"I try not to let things get to me," Leaphorn
said. "You really can't if you're a cop. But that
was a little too damn coldhearted for me."

"I've seen a few of the real superbrains act
like that before," she said. "He was making a
point, of course. The dog's immune system had
modified to deal with the new bacteria forms,
and nothing mattered except the research. No
such luck with Nez. So now he thinks he'll have
a whole prairie dog colony full of test subjects.
So it's Nez that died but the rodent lived. Hip,

hip, hooray. And aren't you driving too fast for this road?"

Leaphorn slowed a little, enough so the following breeze engulfed them in dust but not enough to stop the jolting the car was taking. "Weren't you going to have dinner with Mr. Peshlakai and set up interviews with some students? I don't want you to miss that and we're running late."

"Mr. Peshlakai and I always operate on Navajo time," she said. "No such thing as late. We meet when I get there and he gets there. What's got you in such a rush?"

"I'm going on back down to Flag," Leaphorn said. "I want to go to the hospital and talk to the people there and try to find out what Pollard learned that made her so angry."

"You mean that 'Somebody is lying' note in her journal?"

"Yeah. That seemed to explain why she was going back up to Yells Back Butte. To find out for herself."

"Lying about what?" Louisa said, mostly to herself.

"I'd guess she meant about where Nez picked up his lethal flea. That was her job, and from what I've heard, she took it very seriously." He shook his head. "But who knows? I don't. This is getting hard to calculate."

Louisa nodded.

"Find out for herself?" Leaphorn repeated. "And how does she do that? We know she drove up to Yells Back bright and early either to talk to Woody about where he had Nez working on the day the flea got onto him. Or maybe to collect some rodents or fleas from around there for herself. But she didn't go talk to Woody. Or so he tells us. And if she collected fleas she sure must have done it fast, because she drove right out again."

"Any idea now where she drove?"

"Well, she didn't go back to her motel room to pack up for a trip. Her stuff was still there. And none of the people there had seen her."

"Which doesn't sound good."

"We've got to find that Jeep," Leaphorn said. "And meanwhile I'll try to find out who she talked to at the hospital. It could be helpful."

They jolted off the gravel onto Navajo Route 3 and skirted past Moenkopi to U.S. Highway 160 and Tuba City.

"Where do I drop you?"

"At the filling station right here," Louisa said, "but just long enough to use the telephone. I'm going to call Peshlakai and cancel. Tell him I'll get with him later."

Leaphorn stared at her.

"This is getting too interesting," she said. "I don't want to quit now."

It was after nine when they got back to Flag. They stopped for a fast snack at Bob's Burgers and decided to check at the hospital on the chance a doctor who knew something about the Nez case might be working the night shift.

The doctor proved to be a young woman who had completed intern training at Toledo in March and was doing her residency duties at the Flagstaff hospital in a deal with the Indian Health Service—paying off her federal medical school loan.

"I don't think I ever saw Mr. Nez," she said. "Dr. Howe probably handled him in the Intensive Care Unit. Or maybe the nurse on that floor would know something helpful. Tonight it would be Shirley Ahkeah."

Shirley Ahkeah remembered Mr. Nez very well. She also remember Dr. Woody. Even better, she remembered Catherine Pollard.

"Poor Mr. Nez," she said. "Except for Dr. Howe, it didn't seem like the others cared about him after he was dead."

"I'm not sure I know what you mean," Leaphorn said.

"Forget it," she said. "It wasn't fair to say it. After all, it was Dr. Woody who checked him in.

And Miss Pollard was just doing her job—trying to find out where he picked up the infected flea. Did she ever find out?"

"We don't know," Leaphorn said. "The morning after she left here she left a note for her boss. It just said that she was driving up to where Dr. Woody had his mobile laboratory and checking for plague carriers around there. Dr. Woody tells us she never arrived at his lab. She didn't go back to her office or to the motel where she was staying. Nobody has seen her since."

Shirley's face registered a mixture of shock and surprise.

"You mean—has something happened to her?"

"We don't know," Leaphorn said. "Her office reported her disappearance to the police. And the vehicle she was driving is missing, too."

"You think I was the last one to talk to her? Nobody has seen her since she left here?"

"We don't know. No one that we can locate. Did she say anything to you about where she was going? Anything that would give us a hint of what was going on with her?"

Shirley shook her head. "Nothing that you don't already know. All she talked about here was Mr. Nez. She wanted to know how he'd been infected. Where and when."

"Did you tell her?"

"Dr. Delano told her we didn't know for sure.

That Nez had a high fever and fully developed plague symptoms—the black splotches under the skin where the capillaries have failed, and the swollen glands—he already had all that when we got him up here in Intensive Care, and they brought him right up. She asked Delano a lot of questions, and he told her that Dr. Woody had said that Nez had been bitten by the flea the evening before he brought him in. And she said that wasn't what Dr. Woody had told her, and Delano—"

"Wait a second," Louisa said. "She had already talked to Woody about Nez?"

Shirley chuckled. "Apparently. She said something about a lying sonofabitch. And Delano, he's sort of touchy and he seemed to think that Miss Pollard was accusing him of lying. So then she said something to make it clear she had meant Woody. And Delano said he wasn't certifying what Woody had told him, because he didn't think it was true either. He said Nez couldn't possibly have developed a fever that high and the other plague symptoms so quickly."

Shirley shrugged. End of explanation.

Leaphorn frowned, digesting this. He said: "Do you think Dr. Delano could have misunderstood him? About when Nez was infected?"

"I don't see how," Shirley said. She pointed. "They were standing right there and I heard it all myself. Delano had told Woody that Nez had died sometime after midnight. And Woody said he wanted to know just exactly when Nez died. Exactly. He said the flea had bitten Nez on the inside of his thigh the evening before he brought him in. Woody was very emphatic about the time. He told Delano he'd left a list of symptoms and so forth that he wanted timed and charted as the disease developed. He wanted an autopsy scheduled and he wanted to be there when it was done."

"Was it done?"

"So I hear," Shirley said. "Nurses aren't included in the circuit of information at that level, but the word gets around."

Louisa chuckled at that. "Hospitals and universities. About the same story."

"What did you hear?" Leaphorn asked.

"Mostly that Woody had more or less tried to take over the procedure, and the pathologist was sore as hell. Otherwise, I guess it was just a finding of another death from bubonic plague. And Woody had a lot of tissue and some of the organs preserved."

Neither Leaphorn nor Louisa had much to say on their way back to his truck. Settled in their seats, Louisa said they were probably lucky Delano hadn't been there. "He might have known a little more, but he probably wouldn't have told us much. Professional dignity involved, you know."

"Yeah," Leaphorn said, and started the engine.

"You're not very talkative," Louisa said. "Did that answer any questions for you?"

"Well, now we know for sure who Miss Pollard thought had been lying to her," Leaphorn said. "And of course that raises the next question."

"Which is why would Woody lie to her? And for that matter, he must have lied to us, too."

"Exactly," Leaphorn said.

"We should go up there again and confront him with it. See what he says."

"Not yet," Leaphorn said. "I think he'd just insist he wasn't lying. He'd come up with some sort of explanation. Or he'd tell me to bug off. Quit wasting his time."

"I guess he could, couldn't he."

"We're just two nosy civilians," Leaphorn said, wondering if that sounded as sad as it felt.

"So what are you going to do?"

"I'm going to call Chee in the morning. See if anything new has turned up on Pollard or her Jeep. And then I'll return Mrs. Vanders's call and tell her what little we know. And then I want to go see Krause."

"And see if he knows more than he's told you?"

"I didn't know what questions to ask," Leaphorn said. "And I'd like to get a look at that note Pollard left for him."

Louisa's expression asked him why.

Leaphorn laughed. "Because I spent too many years being a cop, and I can't get over it. I ask him to see the note, so what happens? Possibility A. He finds a reason not to show it to me. That makes me wonder why not."

"Oh," Louisa said. "You think he might, ah, be involved?"

"I don't think that now, but I might if he refused to let me see the note. But on to possibility B. He shows me the note. The handwriting obviously doesn't match her script in the journal. That raises all sorts of possibilities. Or C. He hands me the note, and it has information on it that he didn't think was important enough to mention. Possibility C is the best bet. Even that's unlikely, but it doesn't cost anything to try."

"Are you going to invite me along again?"

"I'm counting on it, Louisa. Instead of the job just being a grind, you make it fun."

She sighed. "I can't go tomorrow. I'm chairing a committee meeting, and it's my project and my committee."

"I'll miss you," Leaphorn said. And he knew he would.

NINETEEN

CHEE HAD STARED at the telephone with distaste, dreading this call. Then he picked it up, took a deep breath and dialed Janet Pete's office at the federal building in Phoenix. Ms. Pete was not in. Did he want her voice mail? He didn't. Where could he reach her? Was this matter urgent?

"Yes," Chee said. Janet might not agree, but it was urgent for him. He couldn't focus on anything else until the genie that Cowboy's "Pollard did it" theory had released was securely back in the bottle. Chee's "yes" earned him a number in Flagstaff, which proved to be the telephone on a desk in a multiple-users' office assigned to public defenders in the courthouse at Flagstaff.

The very familiar voice of many happy memories said: "Hello, Janet Pete."

"Jim Chee," he said. "Do you have some time to talk, or should I call you back?"

Brief silence. "I have time." The voice was even softer now, or was it his imagination? "Is this about business?"

"Alas, it's business," Chee said. "I've heard Cowboy Dashee's theory of what happened to Kinsman and we've been checking on it. I need to talk to your client. Is he still being held there at Flag? And would you be willing to get me in to talk to him?"

"Yes, on the first one," Janet said. "He's still there because I couldn't get bail for him. Mickey opposed it and I think that's stupid. Where could Jano hide?"

"It is stupid," Chee agreed. "But Mickey wants to go for the death penalty, I guess. If he didn't fight bond, even for a Hopi who sure as hell isn't going to run, then you could use it to prove even the U.S. attorney didn't really believe Jano is dangerous."

Even as he was finishing the sentence, Chee was wondering why he always seemed to begin conversations with Janet like this—as if he were trying to start a fight. The silence at the other end of the line suggested she was having the same thought.

"What do you want to talk to Mr. Jano about?"

"I understand he saw the Jeep Ms. Pollard was driving."

"He saw a Jeep. Have you picked her up yet?"

More adversarial than "Have you found her?" Chee closed his eyes, remembering how it had been once.

"We haven't located her," he said.

"It may not be easy," Janet said. "She's had a long time to hide, and I understand she has plenty of money to make that easy."

"We didn't make the connection until—" He stopped. He wasn't going to apologize. None was needed. Janet had worked as a defense attorney long enough to know how the police operated. How they couldn't possibly investigate every time someone drove off without telling anyone where they were going. Why explain what she already knew?

"Look, Jim," she said. "I'm the man's defense attorney. Unless you can let me see how he—how justice would benefit by letting you cross-examine him, then I can't do it. Tell me what good it would do him."

Chee sighed. "We found the Jeep," he said. "The passenger-side seat was smeared with dried blood. There's evidence it was abandoned within an hour or so after Jano—after Kinsman was hit on the head."

Silence. Then Janet said: "Blood. Whose was it? But you haven't had time for any lab work yet, I guess. Is Jano a suspect in this, too?"

"I don't see how he could be. I know exactly where he was when the Jeep was being abandoned."

"Where was it?"

"About twenty miles southwest. Down an arroyo."

"You think Jano might have seen something, or heard something, that would help you find Catherine Pollard?"

"I think he might have. Slim chance, but we don't have anything else to go on. Not now, anyway. Maybe we will when the crime scene crew and the lab people finish with the Jeep."

"Okay then," Janet said. "You know the rules. I'm there, and if I cut off the questions, that ends it. You want to do it today?"

"Fair enough," Chee said. "And the sooner the better. I'll leave Tuba City as soon as I hang up."

"I'll meet you at the jail," she said. "And, Jim, let's try not to make each other mad all the time." She didn't wait for a response.

Janet was waiting in the interrogation room— a small dingy space with two barred windows looking out at nothing. She was sitting across a battered wooden table from Robert Jano. She talked quietly. Jano listened intently. Glanced up as Chee appeared in the doorway. Examined Chee with mild, polite curiosity. Chee nodded to him, suddenly aware that when he had caught Jano with his hands still red with Kinsman's blood he hadn't—in his shock and rage—really studied the man. He studied him now. This handsome, polite young killer whom Chee was trying to give a place in history. The first man strapped into a gas chamber under the new federal reservation death sentence law.

Chee nodded to Janet, said: "Thanks."

"You two have met," Janet said, with no sign that she appreciated the irony of that. They nodded. Jano smiled, then seemed embarrassed that he had.

"Have a seat," Janet said, "and I'll go over the rules. Mr. Chee here will ask a question. And, Robert, you won't answer it until I say it's okay. All right?"

Jano nodded. Chee looked at Janet, who returned the look with no trace of warmth. She'd learned a lot, he thought, since he'd first met her in the interrogation room at the San Juan County Jail in Aztec. Many happy times ago.

"Okay," Chee said. He looked at Jano. "That morning I arrested you, did you see a young woman anywhere around there?"

"I saw—" he began, but Janet interrupted.

"Just a moment," she said, and took a tape

recorder from her purse, put it on the table, set up a microphone and switched it on. "Okay," she said.

"I saw a black Jeep," Jano said. "I didn't see who was driving it."

"When did you see it, and where were you?"

Jano looked at Janet. She nodded.

"I had climbed the butte and was walking along the rim to where I have a blind for catching eagles. I looked down and saw a black Jeep parked on that rise near the abandoned hogan."

"No one was in it?"

Jano glanced at Janet. She nodded.

"No."

"Did you see Officer Kinsman's car driving in?"

Jano glanced at Janet.

"What's the purpose of that question?"

"I want to find out if the Jeep was still there when Kinsman arrived."

Janet thought about it. "Okay."

"I saw him coming in, yes. And the Jeep was still there."

Chee looked at Janet. "So," he said, "if Pollard was the Jeep driver, she was in the vicinity when Kinsman was killed."

"Injured," Janet said. "But yes, she was."

"I intend to ask your client to just re-create

what he saw and heard and did that morning," Chee said.

She thought. "Go ahead. We'll see."

Jano said he arrived about dawn, parked his pickup, unloaded his eagle cage with the rabbit in it that he'd brought along as bait and climbed the saddle to the rim of the butte. He heard an engine sound, watched and saw the Jeep arriving, but he couldn't see who got out of it because of where it had been parked. He had settled himself into the blind and put the rabbit, secured with a cord on the brush, on top of it. Then he had waited about an hour. The eagle came circling over, in its hunting pattern. It saw the rabbit, dived, and caught it. He had caught the eagle by one leg and its tail. It had slashed his forearm with its other talon. "Then I turned the eagle loose and—"

"Just a second," Chee said. "You had the eagle in the cage when I arrested you. The cage was beside the rocks, just a few feet away. Remember?"

"That was the second eagle," Jano said.

"You're saying you caught an eagle, released it and then caught a second one?"

"Yes," Jano said.

"Will you tell me why you released the first one?"

Jano looked at Janet.

"No, he won't," she said.

"He'll be asked at the trial," Chee said.

"If it goes to trial, he will say his reason involves religious beliefs that he is not free to discuss outside his kiva. He may say that two of its tail feathers were pulled out in the struggle, eliminating its ritual use. And then, if I have to do it, I will call in an authority on the Hopi religion who will also explain why a eagle thus stained by bloody violence could not be used in the role assigned to it in this religious ceremonial."

"Okay," Chee said. "Please continue, Mr. Jano. What happened next?"

"I took the rabbit and walked maybe two miles down the rim of the butte to where another eagle has its hunting ground, got into the blind there and waited. Then the eagle you saw came for the rabbit and I caught it."

Jano stopped, looked at Chee as if waiting for an argument and then went on.

"This time I was more careful." He smiled and displayed his forearm. "No injury this time."

Jano said he had seen the Navajo Tribal Police car driving up the trail while he was carrying the eagle down the saddle toward his truck. He said he'd hidden behind an outcrop of rock for a while, hoping the policeman would leave, and then had crept down the rest of the way, thinking he had not been seen.

"Then I heard a loud voice. I think it was the policeman. I heard him several times. And then—"

Chee held up his hand. "Hold it there. Did you hear a response from the person he was talking to?"

"I just heard that one voice," Jano said.

"A man's voice?"

"Yes. It sounded like he was giving orders to someone."

"Orders? What do you mean?"

"Yelling. Like he was arresting someone. You know. Ordering them around."

"Could you tell where the voices were coming from?"

"Just one voice," Jano said. "From about over where I found Mr. Kinsman."

"I want you to skip back a little," Chee said. "When you were climbing down the saddle, was the Jeep still parked where you first saw it parked?"

Jano nodded, then looked at the microphone and said: "Yes, the Jeep was still there."

"Okay. Then what did you do when you heard the voice?"

"I hid behind a juniper for a while, just listening. I could hear what sounded like walking. You know, boots on rocky ground and sort of coming in my direction. Then I heard a voice saying something. And then I heard a sort of a thumping sound."

Jano paused, looking at Chee. "I think it might have been Mr. Kinsman being hit on the head with something. And then there was a clatter."

Jano paused again, pursed his lips, seemed to be remembering the moment.

"Then what?" Chee asked.

"I just waited there behind the juniper. And after it was silent a while, I went to look. And there was Mr. Kinsman on the ground, with the blood running out of his head." He shrugged. "Then you walked up and pointed your gun at me."

"Did you recognize Kinsman?"

Janet Pete said: "Hold it. Hold it." She frowned at Chee. "What are you trying to do, Jim? Establish malice?"

"The D.A. will establish that Kinsman had arrested Mr. Jano before," Chee said. "I wasn't trying anything tricky."

"Maybe not," she said. "But this looks like a good place to cut this off."

"Just one more question," Chee said. "Did you see anyone else when you were there? Anyone at all? Or anything? Going in, or coming out, or anything?"

"I saw a bunch of goats over on the other side of the saddle," Jano said. "Lot of trees over there. I couldn't tell for sure. But maybe there was somebody with them."

"Okay," Janet said. "Mr. Jano and I have some things to talk about. Good-bye, Jim."

Chee stood, took a step toward the door, turned back. "Just one more thing," he said. "I found a blind at the rim of Yells Back where you may have caught an eagle." He described the location and the blind. "Is that right?"

Jano looked at Janet, who looked at Chee. She nodded.

"Yes," Jano said.

"The first eagle, or the second one?"

"The second one."

"Where did you catch the first eagle?"

Jano didn't glance at Janet this time for permission to answer. He sat, eyes on Chee, looking thoughtful.

He won't tell me, Chee thought, because there was only one eagle, or he won't tell me because he isn't willing to reveal the location of another of his kiva's hidden hunting blinds.

Janet cleared her throat, rose. "I'm going to cut this off," she said. "I think—"

Jano held up a hand. "Stand there on the rim at the top of the saddle. Look directly at Humphrey's Peak in the San Franciscos. Walk straight toward it. About two miles you come to the rim again. It's a place there where a slab tilted down and left a gap."

"Thank you," Chee said.

Jano smiled at him. "I think you know eagles," he said.

TWENTY

LEAPHORN AWOKE IN a silent house, with the early sun shining on his face. He had built their house in Window Rock with their bedroom window facing the rising sun because that pleased Emma. Therefore, both the sun and the emptiness were familiar. Louisa had left a note on the kitchen table, which began: "Push ON button on the coffee maker," and went on to outline the availability of various foods for breakfast and concluded on a more personal note.

"I have errands to run before class. Good hunting. Please call and let me know what luck you're having. I enjoyed yesterday. A LOT. Louisa."

Leaphorn pushed the ON button, dropped bread into the toaster, got out a plate, cup, knife and the butter dish. Then he went to the telephone, began dialing Mrs. Vanders's number in Santa Fe, then hung up. First he would call Chee. Perhaps that would give him something to tell Mrs. Vanders besides that he had nothing at all to tell her.

"He hasn't arrived yet, Lieutenant Leaphorn," the station secretary said. "Do you want his home number?"

"It's 'Just call me mister' now," Leaphorn said. "And thanks, but I have it."

"Wait a minute. Here he comes now."

Leaphorn waited.

"I was just going to call you," Chee said. "We found the Jeep." He gave Leaphorn the details.

"You said the tire tracks showed the sand was still wet when it got there?"

"Right."

"So it got there after Kinsman was hit."

"Right again. And probably not long after. It wasn't a very wet rain."

"I guess it's too early to have anything much from the crime lab about prints or—" Leaphorn paused. "Look, Lieutenant, I keep forgetting that I'm a civilian now. Just say no comment or something if I'm overstepping."

Chee laughed. "Mr. Leaphorn," he said. "I'm afraid you're always going to be Lieutenant to me. And they said they found a lot of prints everywhere matching the guy who stole the radio. But there was no old latent stuff in the obvious places. The steering wheel, gearshift knob, door handles—all those places had been wiped. Very thoroughly."

"I don't like the sound of that," Leaphorn said.

"No," Chee said. "Either she's on the run and wanted to leave the impression she'd been abducted, or she actually was taken by someone who didn't want to be identified. Take your pick."

"Probably number two if I had to guess. But who knows? And I guess it's way too early to know anything about the blood," Leaphorn said.

"Way too early."

"Is there any chance you could find any samples of Pollard's blood anywhere? Was she a blood bank donor? Or was she scheduled for any surgery that she'd stockpile blood for?"

"That was one reason I was about to call you," Chee said. "We can get next of kin and so forth from her employer, but it would be quicker to call that woman who hired you. Was it Vanders?"

Leaphorn provided the name, address and telephone number.

"I'm going to call her right now and tell her the Jeep was found and to expect a call from you," Leaphorn added. "Anything you've told me that you want withheld?"

A moment of silence while Chee considered.

"Nothing I can think of," he said. "You know any reason we should?"

Leaphorn didn't. He called Mrs. Vanders.

"Give me a moment to get ready for this," she said. "People who call early in the morning usually have bad news."

"It might be," Leaphorn said. "The Jeep she was driving has been located. It had been abandoned in an arroyo about twenty miles from where she said she was going. There was no sign of an accident. But some dried blood was found on the passenger-side seat. The police don't know yet how long the blood was there, whether it was hers or where it came from."

"Blood," Mrs. Vanders said. "Oh, my."

"Dried," Leaphorn said. "Perhaps from an old injury, an old cut. Do you remember if she ever told you of hurting herself? Or of anyone being hurt in that vehicle?"

"Oh," she said. "I don't think so. I can't remember. I just can't make my mind work."

"It's too early to worry," Leaphorn said. "She may be perfectly all right." This was not the time to tell her the Jeep had been wiped clean of fingerprints. He asked her if Catherine might have been a blood bank donor, if she had scheduled any surgery for which she would have stockpiled blood. Mrs. Vanders didn't remember. She didn't think so.

"You'll be getting a call this morning from the officer investigating the case," Leaphorn told her. "A Lieutenant Jim Chee. He'll tell you if anything new has developed."

"Yes," Mrs. Vanders said. "I'm afraid something terrible has happened. She was such a headstrong girl."

"I'm going now to talk to Mr. Krause," Leaphorn said. "Maybe he can tell us something."

Richard Krause was not in his temporary laboratory at Tuba City, but a note was thumbtacked to the door: "Out mouse hunting. Back tomorrow. Reachable through Kaibito Chapter House."

Leaphorn topped off his gasoline tank and headed northeast—twenty miles of pavement on U.S. 160 and then another twenty on the washboard gravel of Navajo Route 21. Only three pickups rested in the Chapter House parking lot, and none of them belonged to the Indian Health Service. Discouraging news.

But inside Leaphorn found Mrs. Gracie Nakaidineh in charge of things. Mrs. Nakaidineh remembered him from his days patrolling out of Tuba City long, long ago. And he remembered Gracie as one of those women who always do what needs to be done and know what needs to be known.

"Ah," Gracie said after they had gotten through

the greeting ritual common to all old-timers, "you mean you're looking for the Mouse Man."

"Right," Leaphorn said. "He left a note on his door saying he could be contacted here."

"He said if anyone needed to find him, he'd be catching mice along Kaibito Creek. He said he'd be about where it runs into Chaol Canyon."

That meant leaving washboard gravel and taking Navajo Route 6330, which was graded dirt circling up onto the Rainbow Plateau for twenty-six bumpy empty miles. Leaphorn avoided much of that journey. About eight miles out, he spotted an Indian Health Service pickup parked in a growth of willows. He pulled off onto the shoulder, got out his binoculars and tried to make out enough of the symbol painted on its dusty, brush-obscured door to determine whether it was the Indian Health Service or something else. Failing that, he scanned the area for Krause.

A figure, clad head to foot in some sort of shiny white coverall, was moving through the brush toward the truck, carrying plastic sacks in both hands. Krause? Leaphorn couldn't even tell whether it was a man or woman. Whoever was wearing the astronaut's suit stopped beside the truck and began removing shiny metal boxes from the sacks, placing them in a row in the shade behind the vehicle. That done, he took one of the boxes to the truck bed, put it into another plastic sack, sprayed something from a can into the bag, and then began arranging a row of flat square pans on the tailgate.

It must be Krause on his mouse-hunting expedition, and now he was performing whatever magic biologists perform with mice. He was working with his back to Leaphorn, revealing a curving black tube that extended from a black box low on his back upward into the back of his hood. Here was what Mrs. Notah had seen behind the screen of junipers at Yells Back Butte. The witch who looked part snowman and part elephant.

As that thought occurred to Leaphorn, Krause turned, and as he took the box from the sack, sunlight reflected off the transparent face shield— completing Mrs. Notah's description of her skinwalker. He turned to watch Leaphorn approaching.

Leaphorn restarted the engine and rolled his truck down the slope. He parked, got out, slammed the door noisily behind him.

Krause spun around, yelling something and pointing to a hand-lettered sign on the pickup: IF YOU CAN READ THIS YOU'RE TOO DAMNED CLOSE.

Leaphorn stopped. He shouted: "I need to talk to you."

Krause nodded. He held up a circled thumb and finger, and then a single finger, noted that Leaphorn understood the signals, and turned back to his work—which involved holding a small rodent in one hand over a white enamel tray and running a comb through its fur with the other. That job done, he held up the tiny form of a mouse, dangling it by its long tail, for Leaphorn to see. He dropped the animal into another of the traps, peeled off a pair of latex gloves, disposed of them in a bright red canister beside the truck. He walked toward Leaphorn, pushing back his hood.

"Hantavirus," he said, grinning at Leaphorn. "Which we used to call, in our days of cultural insensitivity, the Navajo Flu."

"A name which we didn't like any better than the American Legion liked your name for Legionnaire's disease."

"So now we give both of them their dignified Greek titles, and everybody is happy," Krause said. "And anyway, what I was doing was separating the fleas from the fur of a *Peromyscus*, actually a *Peromyscus maniculatus*, and ninety-nine-point-nine chances out of a hundred, when we test both fleas and mammal, the tests will show I have murdered a perfectly healthy deer mouse who never hosted a virus in his life. But we won't know until we get the lab work done."

"Are you finished here now?" Leaphorn asked. "Do you have time for some questions?"

"Some," Krause said. He turned and waved at the row of metal boxes in the shade. "But before I can peel off this uniform—which is officially called a Positive Air Purifying Respirator suit, or PAPR, in vector controller slang—I've got to finish with the mice in those traps. Separate the fleas and then it's slice and dice for the poor little deer mice."

"I have plenty of time," Leaphorn said. "I'll just watch you work."

"From a distance, though. It's probably safe. As far as we know, hantavirus spreads aerobically. In other words, it's carried in the mouse urine, and when that dries, it's in the dust people breathe. The trouble is, if it infects you, there's no way to cure it."

"I'll stay back," Leaphorn said. "And I'll hold my questions until you get out of that suit. I'll bet you're cooking."

"Better cooked than dead," Krause said. "And it's not as bad as it looks. The air blowing into the hood keeps your head cool. Stick your hand close here and feel it."

"I'll take your word for it," Leaphorn said.

He watched while Krause emptied the box traps one at a time, combed the fleas out of the fur into individual bags and then extracted the pertinent internal organs. He put those in bottles and the corpses into the disposal canister. He peeled off the PAPR and dropped it into the same can.

"Runs the budget up," he said. "When we're hunting plague, we don't use the PAPRS when we're just trapping. And after we've done the slice-and-dice work, we save 'em for reuse, unless we slosh prairie dog innards on them. But with hantavirus you don't take any chances. But what can I tell you that might be useful?"

"Well, first let me tell you that we found the Jeep Miss Pollard was driving. It had been left in an arroyo down that road that leads past Goldtooth."

"Well, at least she was going in the direction she told me she was going," Krause said, grinning. "No note left for me about taking an early vacation or anything like that?"

"Only a little smear of blood," Leaphorn said.

Krause's grin vanished.

"Oh, shit," he said. "Blood. Her blood?" He shook his head. "From the very first, I've been taking for granted that one day she'd either call or just walk in, probably without even explaining anything until I asked her. You just don't think something is going to happen to Cathy. Nothing that she doesn't want to happen."

"We don't know that it has," Leaphorn said. "Not for sure."

Krause's expression changed again. Immense relief. "It wasn't her blood?"

"That brings us to my question. Do you have any idea where we might find a sample of Miss Pollard's blood? Enough for the lab to make a comparison?"

"Oh," Krause said. "So you just don't know yet? But who else could it belong to? There was no one with her."

"You sure of that?"

"Oh," Krause said again. "Well, no, I guess I'm not. I didn't see her that morning. But she didn't say anything in the note about having company. And she always worked alone. We often do on this kind of work."

"Any possibility that Hammar could have been with her?"

"Remember? Hammar said he was doing his teaching work back at the university that day."

"I remember," Leaphorn said. "That hasn't been checked yet as far as I know. When the lab tells the police it's Miss Pollard's blood in the Jeep, then the alibis get checked."

"Including mine?"

"Of course. Including everybody's."

Leaphorn waited, giving Krause time to amend what he'd said about that morning. But Krause just stood there looking thoughtful.

"Had she cut herself recently? Donated any

blood? Any idea where some could be found for the lab?"

Krause closed his eyes, thinking. "She's careful," he said. "In this work you have to be. Hard as hell to work with, but skillful. I don't ever remember her cutting herself in the lab. And in a vector control lab getting cut is a big deal. And if she was a blood donor, she never mentioned it."

"When you came in that morning, where did you find her note?"

"Right on my desk."

"You were going to see if you could find it. Any luck?"

"I've been busy. I'll try," Krause said.

"I'll need a copy," Leaphorn said. "Okay?"

"I guess so," Krause said, and Leaphorn noticed that some of his cordiality had slipped away. "But you're not a policeman. I'll bet the cops will want it."

"They will," Leaphorn said. "I'd be satisfied with a Xerox. Can you remember exactly what it said? Every word of it?"

"I can remember the meaning. She wouldn't be in the office that day. She was taking the Jeep and heading southeast, over toward Black Mesa and Yells Back Butte. Working on the Nez plague fatality."

"Did she say she'd be trapping animals? Prairie dogs or what?"

"Probably. I think so. Either she said it or I took it for granted. I don't think she was specific, but she'd been working on plague. She still hadn't pinned down where Mr. Nez got his fatal infection."

"And that would have been from a prairie dog flea?"

"Well, probably. That *Yersinia pestis* is a bacteria spread by fleas. But some of the *Peromyscus* host fleas, too. We got two hundred off one rock squirrel once."

"Would she have had a PAPRS with her?"

"She carries one with her stuff in the Jeep. Was it still there when they found the vehicle?"

"I don't know," Leaphorn said. "I'll ask. And I have one more question. In that note, did she tell you why she planned to quit?"

Krause frowned. "Quit?"

"Her job here."

"She wasn't going to quit."

"Her aunt told me that. In a call Pollard made just before she disappeared, she said she was quitting."

"Be damned," Krause said. He stared at Leaphorn, biting his lower lip. "She say why?"

"I think it was because she couldn't get along with you."

"That's true enough," Krause said. "A hard-headed woman."

TWENTY-ONE

SUMMER HAD ARRIVED with dreadful force in Phoenix, and the air conditioning in the Federal Courthouse Building had countered the dry heat outside its double glass windows by producing a clammy chill in the conference room. Acting Assistant U.S. Attorney J. D. Mickey had assembled the assorted forces charged with maintaining law and order in America's high desert country to decide whether to go for the first death penalty under the new congressional act that authorized such penalties for certain crimes committed on federal reservations.

Acting Lieutenant Jim Chee of the Navajo Tribal Police was among those assembled, but being at the bottom level of the hierarchy, he was sitting uncomfortably in a metal folding chair against the wall with an assortment of state cops, deputy sheriffs, and low-ranking deputy U.S. marshals. It had been clear to Chee from the onset of the meeting that the decision had been long since made. Mr. Mickey was serving on some sort of temporary appointment and intended to make the most of it while it lasted. The timing of the death of Benjamin Kinsman opened a once-in-a-lifetime window of opportunity. National—or at least congressional district regional—publicity was there for the grabbing. He'd go for the historic first. What was happening here was known in upper-level civil service circles as "the CYA maneuver," intended to Cover Your Ass by diluting the blame when things went wrong.

"All right then," Mickey was saying. "Unless anyone has more questions, the policy will be to charge this homicide as a capital crime and impanel a jury for the death sentence. I guess I don't have to remind any of you people here that this will mean a lot more work for all of us."

The woman in the chair to Chee's right was a young Kiowa-Comanche-Polish-Irish cop wearing the uniform of the Law Enforcement Services of the Bureau of Indian Affairs. She snorted, "Us!" and muttered, "Means more work for us, all right. Not him. He means he guesses he don't have to remind us he's running for Congress as the law-and-order candidate."

Now Mickey was outlining the nature of this

extra work. He introduced Special Agent in Charge John Reynald. Agent Reynald would be coordinating the effort, calling the signals, running the investigation.

"There'll be no problem getting the conviction," Mickey said. "We caught the perpetrator literally red-handed with the victim. What makes it absolutely iron-clad is having Jano's blood mixed with the victim's on both of their clothing. The best the defense can come up with is a story that the eagle he was poaching slashed him."

This produced a chuckle.

"Trouble is, the eagle didn't cooperate. There wasn't a trace of Jano's blood on it. What we'll need to get the death penalty is evidence of malice. We'll want witnesses who heard Mr. Jano talking about his previous arrest by Officer Kinsman. We need to find people who can remember hearing him talk about revenge. Talking about how badly Kinsman handled him during that first arrest. Even bad-mouthing Navajos in general. That sort of thing. Check out the bars, places like that."

"Where'd this jerk come from?" the LES woman asked Chee. "He sure doesn't know much about Hopis."

"Indiana, I think," Chee said. "But I guess he's been in Arizona long enough to establish residency for a federal office election."

Mickey was closing down the meeting, shaking hands with the proper people. He stopped Chee at the door.

"Stick around a minute," Mickey said. "I want to have a word or two with you."

Chee stuck around. So did Reynald and Special Agent Edgar Evans, who closed the door behind the last departee.

"There're several points I want to make," Mickey said. "Point one is that the victim in this case may not have had a perfect personal record, you know what I mean, being a healthy young man and all. If there's any talk going around among his fellow officers that the defense might use to dirty his name, then I want that stopped. Going for the death penalty, you understand why."

"Sure," Chee said, and nodded.

"I'll get right to the second point then," Mickey said. "The gossip has it that you're engaged to this Janet Pete. The defense attorney. Either that, or used to be."

Mickey had phrased it as a question. He and Reynald and Evans waited for an answer.

Chee said: "Really?"

Mickey frowned. "In a case like this one, in a touchy business like this, culturally sensitive, the press looking over our shoulders, we have to watch out for anything that might look like a conflict of interest."

"That sounds sensible to me," Chee said.

"I don't think you're understanding me," Mickey said.

"Yes, sir," Chee said. "I understand you."

Mickey waited. So did Chee. Mickey's face turned slightly pink.

"Well, then, goddamnit, what's with this gossip? You got something going with Ms. Pete or what?"

Chee smiled. "I had a wise old maternal grandmother who used to teach me things. Or try to teach me when I was smart enough to listen to her," Chee said. "She told me that only a damn fool pays attention to gossip."

Mickey's complexion turned redder. "All right," he said. "Let's get one thing straight. This case is about the murder of a law officer in the performance of his duty. One of your own men. You're part of the prosecution team. Ms. Pete runs the defense team. You're no lawyer, but you've been in the enforcement business long enough to know how things work. We got the disclosure rule, so the criminal's team gets to know what we're putting into evidence."

He paused, staring at Chee. "But sometimes justice requires that you don't show your hole card. Sometimes you have to keep some of your plans and your strategy in the closet. You understand what I'm telling you?"

"I think you're telling me that if this gossip is true, I shouldn't talk in my sleep," Chee said. "Is that about right?"

Mickey grinned. "Exactly."

Chee nodded. He'd noticed that Reynald was following this conversation intently. Agent Evans looked bored.

"And I might add," Mickey added, "that if somebody else talks in their sleep, you might just give a listen."

"My grandmother had something else to say about gossip," Chee said. "She said it doesn't have a long shelf life. Sometimes you hear the soup's on the table and it's too hot to eat, and by the time the news gets to you it's in the freezer."

Mickey's beeper began chirping as Chee was ending that observation. Whatever the call was about, it broke up the cluster without the ritual shaking of hands that convention required.

Chee hadn't lucked into a shady place to leave his car. He used his handkerchief to open the door without burning his hand, started the engine, rolled down all the windows to let the oven-like heat escape, turned the air conditioner to maximum and then slid off the scorching upholstery to stand outside until the interior became tolerable. It gave him a little time to plan what he'd do. He'd call Joe Leaphorn from here to see if anything new had developed. He'd call his office to learn what awaited him there, and then he'd head for the north end of the Chuska Mountains, the landscape of his boyhood, and the sheep camp where Hosteen Frank Sam Nakai spent his summers.

From Phoenix, from almost anywhere, that meant a hell of a long drive. But Chee was a man of faith. He did his damnedest to maintain within himself the ultimate value of his people, the sense of peace, harmony and beauty Navajos call *hozho*. He badly needed Hosteen Nakai's counsel on how to deal with the death of a man and the death of an eagle.

Hosteen Nakai was Chee's maternal grand-uncle, which gave him special status in Navajo tradition. He had given Chee his real, or war, name, which was "Long Thinker," a name re-vealed only to those very close to you and used only for ceremonial purposes. Circumstances, and the early death of Chee's father, had magni-fied Nakai's importance to Chee—making him mentor, spiritual adviser, confessor and friend. By trade he was a rancher and a shaman whose command of the Blessing Way ceremonial and a half dozen other curing rituals was so respected that he taught them to student *hataalii* at Navajo

Community College. If anyone could tell Chee the wise way to handle the messy business of Kinsman, Jano and Mickey, it would be Nakai.

More specifically, Nakai would advise him on how he could deal with the problem posed by the first eagle. If it existed and he caught it, it would die. He had no illusions about its fate in the laboratory. There was a chant to be sung before hunting, asking the prey to know it was respected and to understand the need for it to die. But if Jano was lying, then the eagle he would try to lure to that blind would die for nothing. Chee would be violating the moral code of the Dine, who did not take lightly the killing of anything.

No telephone line came within miles of the Nakai summer hogan, but Chee drove along Navajo Route 12 with not a doubt that his granduncle would be there. Where else would he be? It was summer. His flock would be high in the mountain pastures. The coyotes would be waiting in the fringes of the timber, as they always were. The sheep would need him. Nakai was always where he was needed. So he would be in his pasture tent near his sheep.

But Hosteen Nakai wasn't in his tent up in the high meadows.

It was late twilight when Chee pulled his truck

off the entry track and onto the hard-packed earth of the Nakai place. His headlight beams swept across the cluster of trees beside the hogan. They also caught the form of a man, propped on pillows in a portable bed, the sort medical supply companies rent. Chee's heart sank. His grand-uncle was never sick. Having the bed outside was an ominous sign.

Blue Lady was standing in the hogan door-way, looking out at Chee as he climbed out of the truck, recognizing him, running toward him, saying: "How good. How good. He wanted you to come. I think he sent out his thoughts to you, and you heard him."

Blue Lady was Hosteen's second wife, named for the beauty of the turquoise she wore with her velvet blouse when her *kinaalda* ceremony initia-ted her into womanhood. She was the younger sister of Hosteen Nakai's first wife, who had died years before Chee was born. Since Navajo tradi-tion is matrilineal and the man joined his bride's family, practice favored widowers marrying one of their sisters-in-law, thereby maintaining the same residence and the same mother-in-law. Nakai, being most traditional and already study-ing to be a shaman, had honored that tradition. Blue Lady was the only Nakai grandmother Chee had known.

Now she was hugging Chee to her. "He wanted to see you before he dies," she said.

"Dies? What is it? What happened?" It didn't seem possible to Chee that Hosteen Nakai could be dying. Blue Lady had no answer to that question. She led him over to the trees and motioned him into a rocking chair beside the bed.

"I will get the lantern," she said.

Hosteen Nakai was studying him. "Ah," he said, "Long Thinker has come to talk to me. I had hoped for that."

Chee had no idea what to say. He said: "How are you, my father? Are you sick?"

Nakai produced a raspy laugh, which provoked a racking cough. He fumbled on the bed cover, retrieved a plastic device, inserted it into his nostrils and inhaled. The tube connected to it disappeared behind the bed. Connected, Chee presumed, to an oxygen tank. Nakai was trying to breathe deeply, his lungs making an odd sound. But he was smiling at Chee.

"What happened to you?" Chee asked.

"I made a mistake," Nakai said. "I went to a *bilagaana* doctor at Farmington. He told me I was sick. They put me in the hospital and then they broke my ribs, and cut out around in there and put me back together." His voice was trailing off as he finished that, forcing a pause. When he had breath again, he chuckled. "I think they left out some parts. Now I have to get my air through this tube."

Blue Lady was hanging a propane lantern on the limb overhanging the head of the bed.

"He has lung cancer," she said. "They took out one lung, but it had already spread to the other one."

"And all sorts of other places, too, that you don't want to even know about," Nakai said, grinning. "When I die, my *chindi* will be awful mad. He'll be full of malignant tumors. That's why I made them move my bed out here. I don't want that *chindi* to be infecting this hogan. I want it out here where the wind will blow it away."

"When you die, it will be because you just got too old to want to live anymore," Chee said. He put his hand on Nakai's arm. Where he had always felt hard muscle, he now felt only dry skin between his palm and the bone. "It will be a long time from now. And remember what Changing Woman taught the people: If you die of natural old age, you don't leave a *chindi* behind."

"You young people—" Nakai began, but a grimace cut off the words. He squeezed his eyes shut, and the muscles of his face clenched and tightened. Blue Lady was at his side, holding a glass of some liquid. She gripped his hand.

"Time for the pain medicine," she said.

He opened his eyes. "I must talk a little first," he said. "I think he came to ask me something."

"You talk a little later. The medicine will give you some time for that." And Blue Lady raised his head from the pillow and gave him the drink. She looked at Chee. "Some medicine they gave him to let him sleep: Morphine maybe," she said. "It used to work very good. Now it helps a little."

"I should let him rest," Chee said.

"You can't," she said. "Besides, he was waiting for you."

"For me?"

"Three people he wanted to see before he goes," she said. "The other two already came." She adjusted the oxygen tube back into Nakai's nostrils, dampened his forehead with a cloth, bent low and put her lips to his cheek, and walked back into the hogan.

Chee stood looking down at Nakai, remembering boyhood, remembering the winter stories in his hogan, the summer stories at the fire beside the sheep-camp tent, remembering the time Nakai had caught him drunk, remembering kindness and wisdom. Then Nakai, eyes still closed, said: "Sit down. Be easy."

Chee sat.

"Now, tell me why you came."

"I came to see you."

"No. No. You didn't know I was sick. You are busy. Some reason brought you here. The last time it was about marrying a girl, but if you married her you didn't invite me to do the ceremony. So I think you didn't do it." Nakai's words came slowly, so softly Chee leaned forward to hear.

"I didn't marry her," Chee said.

"Another woman problem then?"

"No," Chee said.

The morphine was having its effect. Nakai was relaxing a little. "So you came all the way up here to tell me you have no problems to talk to me about. You are the only contented man in all of Dinetah."

"No," Chee said. "Not quite."

"So tell me then," Nakai said. "What brings you?"

So Chee told Hosteen Frank Sam Nakai of the death of Benjamin Kinsman, the arrest of the Hopi eagle poacher, of Jano's unlikely story of the first and second eagles. He told him of the death sentence and even of Janet Pete. And finally Chee said: "Now I am finished."

Nakai had listened so silently that at times Chee—had he not known the man so well—might have thought he was asleep. Chee waited.

Twilight had faded into total darkness while he talked and now the high, dry night sky was adazzle with stars.

Chee looked at them, remembered how the impatient Coyote spirit had scattered them across the darkness. He hunted out the summer constellations Nakai had taught him to find, and as he found them, tried to match them with the stories they carried in their medicine bundles. And as he thought, he prayed to the Creator, to all the spirits who cared about such things, that the medicine had worked, that Nakai was sleeping, that Nakai would never awaken to his pain.

Nakai sighed. He said: "In a little while I will ask you questions," and was silent again.

Blue Lady came out with a blanket, spread it carefully over Nakai and adjusted the lantern. "He likes the starlight," she said. "Do you need this?"

Chee shook his head. She turned off the flame and walked back into the hogan.

"Could you catch the eagle without harming it?"

"Probably," Chee said. "I tried twice when I was young. I caught the second one."

"Checking the talons and the feathers for dried blood, would the laboratory kill it then?"

Chee considered, remembering the ferocity of

eagles, remembering the priorities of the laboratory. "Some of them would try to save it, but it would die."

Nakai nodded. "You think Jano tells the truth?"

"Once I was sure there was only one eagle. Now I don't know. Probably he is lying."

"But you don't know?"

"No."

"And never would know. Even after the federals kill the Hopi you would wonder."

"Of course I would."

Nakai was silent again. Chee found another of the constellations. The small one, low on the horizon. He could not remember its Navajo name, nor the story it carried.

"Then you must get the eagle," Nakai said. "Do you still keep your medicine *jish*? You have pollen?"

"Yes," Chee said.

"Then take your sweat bath. Make sure you remember the hunting songs. You must tell the eagle, just as we told the buck deer, of our respect for it. Tell it the reason we must send it with our blessings away to its next life. Tell it that it dies to save a valuable man of the Hopi people."

"I will," Chee said.

"And tell Blue Lady I need the medicine that makes me sleep."

But Blue Lady had already sensed that. She was coming.

This time there were pills as well as a drink from the cup.

"I will try to sleep now," Nakai said, and smiled at Chee. "Tell the eagle that he will also be saving you, my grandson."

TWENTY-TWO

WHERE WAS ACTING Lieutenant Jim Chee? He'd gone to Phoenix yesterday and hadn't checked in this morning. Maybe he was still there. Maybe he was on his way back. Check later. Leaphorn hung up and considered what to do. First he'd take a shower. He flicked on the television, still tuned to the Flagstaff station he'd been watching before sleep overcame him, and turned on the shower.

They had good showerheads in this Tuba City motel, a fine, hard jet of hot water better than the one in his bathroom. He soaped, scrubbed, listened to the voice of the television newscaster reporting what seemed to be a traffic death, then a quarrel at a school board meeting. Then he heard "—murder of Navajo policeman Benjamin

Kinsman." He turned off the shower and walked, dripping soapy water, to stand before the set.

It seemed that Acting Assistant U.S. Attorney J. D. Mickey had held a press conference yesterday evening. He was standing behind a battery of microphones at a podium with a tall, dark-haired man stationed uneasily slightly behind him. The taller man was clad in a white shirt, dark tie and a well-tailored dark business suit, which caused Leaphorn to immediately identify him as an FBI agent—apparently a new one to this part of the world, since Leaphorn didn't recognize him, and probably a special agent in charge, since he had come to take credit for whatever discoveries had been made in an affair that produced the sort of headlines upon which the Bureau fed.

"The evidence the FBI has collected makes it clear that this crime was not only a murder done in the commission of a felony, which would make it a capital crime under the old law, but that it fits the intent of Congress in the passage of the legislation allowing the death penalty for such crimes committed on federal reservations." Mickey paused, looked at his notes, adjusted his glasses. "We didn't decide to seek the death penalty casually," Mickey continued. "We considered the problem confronting the Navajo Tribal Police, and the police of the Hopis and Apaches and all the other reservation tribes, and the same problems shared by the police of the various states. These men and women patrol vast distances, alone in their patrol cars, without the quick backup assistance that officers in the small, more populous states can expect. Our police are utterly vulnerable in this situation, and their killers have time to be miles away before help can arrive. I have the names of the officers who have been killed in just—"

Leaphorn switched off the mortality list and ducked back into the shower. He had known several of those men. Indeed, six of them were Navajo policemen. And it was a story that needed to be told. So why did he resent hearing Mickey tell it? Because Mickey was a hypocrite. He decided to skip breakfast and wait for Chee at the police station.

Chee's car was already in the parking lot, and Acting Lieutenant Chee was sitting behind his desk, looking downcast and exhausted. He looked up from the file he was reading and forced a smile.

"I'll just ask a couple of questions and then I'll be out of here," Leaphorn said. "The first one is, do you have a report yet from the crime scene people? Did they list what they found in the Jeep?"

"This is it," Chee said, waving the file. "I just got it."

"Oh," Leaphorn said.

"Sit down," Chee said. "Let me see what's in it."

Leaphorn sat, holding his hat in his lap. It reminded him of his days as a rookie cop, waiting for Captain Largo to decide what to do with him.

"No fingerprints except the radio thief," Chee said. "I think I already told you that. Good wiping job. There were prints on the owner's manual in the glove box, presumed to be Catherine Pollard's." He glanced up at Leaphorn, turned a page and resumed reading.

"Here's the list of items found in the Jeep," he said, and handed it across the desk to Leaphorn. "I didn't see anything interesting on it."

It was fairly long. Leaphorn skipped the items in the glove box and door pockets and started with the backseat. There the team had found three filter-tip Kool cigarette butts, a Baby Ruth candy wrapper, a thermos containing cold coffee, a cardboard box containing fourteen folded metal rodent traps, eight larger prairie dog traps, two shovels, rope, and a satchel that contained five pairs of latex gloves and a variety of other items that, while the writer could only guess at their technical titles, were obviously the tools of the vector control trade.

Leaphorn looked up from the list. Chee was watching him.

"Did you notice the spare tire, the jack and the tire tools were all missing?" Chee asked. "I guess our radio thief didn't limit himself to that and the battery."

"This is all of it?" Leaphorn asked. "Everything that they found in the Jeep?"

"That's it," Chee said, frowning. "Why?"

"Krause said she always carried a respirator suit in the Jeep with her."

"A what?"

"They call 'em PAPRS," Leaphorn said. "For Positive Air Purifying Respirator Suit. They look a little like what the astronauts wear, or the people who make computer chips."

"Oh," Chee said. "Maybe she left it at her motel. We can check if you think it's important."

The telephone on Chee's desk buzzed. He picked it up, said, "Yes." Said, "Good, that's a lot faster than I expected." Said, "Sure, I'll hold."

He put his hand over the receiver. "They've got the report on the bloodwork."

Leaphorn said: "Fine," but Chee was listening again.

"That's the right number of days," Chee told the telephone, and listened again, frowned, said: "It wasn't? Then what the hell was it?" Listened again, then said: "Well, thanks a lot."

He put down the telephone.

"It wasn't human blood," Chee said. "It was

from some sort of rodent. He said he'd guess it was from a prairie dog."

Leaphorn leaned back in his chair. "Well now," he said.

"Yeah," Chee said. He tapped his fingers on the desktop a moment, then picked up the telephone, punched a button and said: "Hold any calls for a while, please."

"Did you see the dried blood on the seat?" Leaphorn asked.

"I did."

"How'd it look? I mean, had it been spilled there, or smeared on, or maybe an injured prairie dog had been put there, or dripped, or what?"

"I don't know," Chee said. "I know it didn't look like somebody had been stabbed, or shot, and bled there. It didn't really look natural—like what you expect to see at a homicide scene." He grimaced. "It looked more like it had been poured out on the edge of the leather seat. Then it had run down the side and a little onto the floor."

"She would have had access to blood," Leaphorn said.

"Yeah," Chee said. "I thought of that."

"Why do it?" Leaphorn laughed. "It suggests she didn't have a very high opinion of the Navajo Tribal Police."

Chee looked surprised, saw the point. "You mean we'd just take for granted it was her blood and wouldn't check." He shook his head. "Well, it could happen. And then we'd be looking for her body instead of for her."

"If she did it," Leaphorn said.

"Right. If. You know, Lieutenant, I sort of wish we were back in Window Rock right now, with that map of yours on the wall, and you'd be putting your pins in it." He grinned at Leaphorn. "And explaining to me what happened."

"You're thinking about where the Jeep was left? So far from anywhere?"

"I was," Chee said.

"Way too far to walk to Tuba City. Too far to walk back to Yells Back Butte. So somebody had to meet her, or whoever drove the Jeep there, and give them a lift," Leaphorn said.

"Like who?"

"Did I tell you about Victor Hammar?"

"Hammar? If you did, I don't remember."

"He's a graduate student at Arizona State. A biologist, like Pollard. They were friends. Mrs. Vanders had him pegged as a stalker, a threat to her niece. He'd been out here just a few days before she disappeared, working with her. And he was out here the day I showed up to start my little search."

Chee's expression brightened. "Well now," he said, "I think we should talk to Mr. Hammar."

"The trouble is he told me he was teaching his

lab course at ASU the day she vanished. Actually he wasn't. He called in sick. Haven't checked beyond that."

Chee nodded and grinned again. "I have a map." He pulled open his desk drawer, rummaged and pulled out a folded Indian Country map. "Just like yours." He spread it on the desktop. "Except it's not mounted so I can stick pins in it."

Leaphorn picked up a pencil, leaned over the map and made some quick additions to terrain features. He drew little lines to mark the cliffs of Yells Back Butte and the saddle linking it to Black Mesa. A dot indicated the location of the Tijinney hogan. With that Leaphorn stopped.

"What do you think?" Chee asked.

"I think we're wasting our time. We need a larger map scale."

Chee extracted a sheet of typing paper from his desk and penciled in the area around the butte, the roads and the terrain features. He drew a tiny *h* for the Tijinney hogan, an *l* for Woody's lab, a faint irregular line from the hogan to represent the track in from the dirt road, and a little *j* and *k* for where Jano and Kinsman had left their vehicles. He examined his work for a moment, then added another faint line from the saddle back to the road.

Leaphorn was watching. "What's that?"

"I saw a flock of goats on the wrong side of

the saddle and a track leading in. I think it's a shortcut the goatherd uses so he doesn't have to climb over," Chee said.

"I didn't know about that," Leaphorn said. He took the pencil and added an *x* near the Yells Back cliffs. "And here is where an old woman McGinnis called Old Lady Notah told people she had seen a snowman. The same woman? Probably."

"Snowman? When was that?"

"We don't know the day. Maybe the day Miss Pollard disappeared. The day Ben Kinsman got hit on the head." Leaphorn leaned back in his chair. "She thought she'd seen a skinwalker. First it was a man, then it walked behind a bunch of junipers and when she saw it again it was all white and shiny."

Chee rubbed a finger against his nose, looked up at Leaphorn. "Which is why you were asking me about that filter respirator suit, isn't it? You thought Pollard was wearing it."

"Maybe Miss Pollard. Maybe Dr. Woody. I'll bet he has one. Or maybe somebody else. Anyway, I'm going to go talk to that old lady if I can find her," Leaphorn said.

"Dr. Woody, he'd have access to animal blood, too," Chee said. "And so would Krause, for that matter."

"And so would Hammar, our man with the

bum alibi. Now I think it might be worth the time to look into that."

They considered this for a while.

"Did you know Frank Sam Nakai?" Chee asked.

"The *hataalii*?" Leaphorn asked. "I met him a few times. He taught curing ceremonials at the college at Tsali. And he did a *yeibichai* sing for one of Emma's uncles after he had a stroke. A fine old man, Nakai."

"He's my maternal granduncle," Chee said. "I went to see him last night. He's dying of cancer."

"Ah," Leaphorn said. "Another good man lost."

"Did you see the TV news this morning? The press conference J. D. Mickey called in Phoenix?"

"Some of it," Leaphorn said.

"He's going for the death penalty, of course. The sonofabitch."

"Running for Congress," Leaphorn said. "What he said about cops out here having no backup help, lousy radio communications, all that's true enough."

"It's a funny thing," Chee said. "I catch Jano practically red-handed standing over Kinsman. He was there, and nobody else was around. He had a fine revenge motive. And then there's Jano's blood mixed with Kinsman's on the front of Kinsman's uniform—just about where he would have cut himself on Kinsman's buckle if they'd been struggling. You have a dead-cinch conviction—and all Jano can do is come up with a daydream story about the eagle he poached slashing him—and there's the eagle right there with no blood on it, so he says not that eagle. That's the second eagle, he says. I caught one earlier and turned it loose." Chee shook his head. "And yet, I'm beginning to have some doubts. It's crazy."

Leaphorn let that all pass without comment.

"That other eagle story is so phony that I'm surprised Janet's not too embarrassed to give it to the jury."

Leaphorn made a wry face, shrugged.

"Jano claims he pulled out a couple of the first eagle's tail feathers," Chee said. "I saw one circling up there over Yells Back with a gap in its tail plume."

"So what are you going to do?" Leaphorn asked.

"Jano told me how to locate the blind where he caught the first eagle. I'm going to get myself a rabbit as eagle bait and go up there tomorrow and catch the bird. Or shoot it if I can't catch it. If there's no old blood in the grooves in its talons, or in its ankle feathers, then I don't have any more doubts."

Leaphorn considered this. "Well," he said. "Eagles are territorial hunters. It would probably be the same bird. But the blood could be from a rodent it caught."

"If there's dried blood anywhere, I'll take it in and let the lab decide. You want to come along?"

"No thanks," Leaphorn said. "I'm going to go find the lady with the goats and learn about that snowman she saw."

TWENTY-THREE

ACTING LIEUTENANT JIM Chee reached Yells Back Butte early and well prepared. He climbed the saddle while the light of dawn was just brightening the sky over Black Mesa, carrying his binoculars, an eagle cage, his lunch, a canteen of water, a quart thermos of coffee, a rabbit and his rifle. He found the tilted slab of rimrock just where Jano said it would be, straightened out the disordered brush that formed the blind's roof. He took out his medicine bag and removed from the doeskin pouch the polished stone replica of a badger, which Frank Sam Nakai had given him as his hunting fetish, and an aspirin bottle, which held pollen. He put the fetish in his right hand and sprinkled a pinch of pollen over it. Then he faced the east and waited. Just as the rim of the sun appeared, he sang his morning song and sprinkled an offering of pollen from the bottle. That done, he shifted into the hunting chant, telling the eagle of his respect for it, asking it to come and join in this sacrifice that would send it into its next life with his blessing and, perhaps, save the life of the Hopi whose arm it had slashed.

Then he climbed down into the blind.

By 10:00 a.m. he had watched two eagles patrolling the rim of the butte to the west of his position, neither the one he wanted. He'd found the feather he'd left behind on his original visit to the blind, retrieved it, wrapped it in his handkerchief and laid it aside. He'd consumed about fifty percent of his coffee and the apple from his lunch sack, and read two more chapters of *Execution Eve*, the Bill Buchanan book he'd brought along to pass the time. At 10:23, the eagle he wanted showed up.

It came from the east, drifting over Black Mesa in lazy circles that brought it nearer and nearer. Through gaps in the blind's brush roofing, Chee followed it through the binoculars, confirming the irregularity in its fan of tail feathers. He lifted the struggling rabbit out of the eagle cage, made sure the nylon cord on its leg was secure and waited until the bird's hunting circle was taking it away. Then he put the rabbit on the roof, squirmed into his best watching position and waited.

On its next circle it swept southward, lost altitude and patrolled over the rolling sagebrush desert away from the butte, disappearing from Chee's view. He put the rifle in a handier place and waited, tense. A moment later, the eagle reappeared, rising on an updraft just a few yards above the rim of the butte and not fifty yards from the blind, then soared above him to the left.

The rabbit had long since given up its struggles and sat motionless on the roof. Chee stirred the brush supporting it with the rifle barrel. Startled, it scrambled to the end of the cord, jerked at it, sat again. The eagle turned, tightened its circle directly overhead. Chee jerked the cord, provoking a fresh flurry of struggles.

And then the eagle produced a raucous whistle and swept down.

Chee pulled the rabbit back toward the center of the blind. As he did, the eagle struck it with a crash, blanking out the sky with extended wings. Chee tugged at the cord, pulling against the thrust of beating wings, reaching for the eagle's legs.

He was lucky. When it struck, the eagle had locked both sets of talons, one through the rabbit's back, the other on its head. Chee grabbed both legs and brought bird, rabbit and much of the brush roof falling down on him. He dragged his jacket over the eagle, folded it over head and wings and inspected the bird's legs. He saw fresh blood on its talons. At the base of the ruff feathers on its left leg, he found something black and brittle. Dried blood. Old rabbit blood, perhaps. Or Jano's. The lab would decide. Either way, Chee could rest now.

He pushed bird, rabbit and jacket into the eagle cage and secured the door. Then he leaned back against the stone, poured himself the last of the coffee, and inspected the damage to himself. It was minimal—just a single cut across the side of his left hand, where the eagle's beak had caught him.

The eagle extricated itself from his jacket, unlocked its talons from the rabbit, and battled frantically against the stiff metal wires that formed the cage.

"First Eagle," Chee said. "Be calm. Be peaceful. I will treat you with respect." The eagle stopped its struggles and fixed Chee with an unblinking stare. "You will go where all eagles go," Chee said, but he was sad when he said it.

Back at the Tuba City police station, Chee parked in the shade. He brought the eagle cage in and put it beside Claire Dineyahze's desk.

"Wow," Claire said. "He looks mean enough. What's he charged with?"

"Resisting arrest and biting a cop," Chee said, displaying the cut on his hand.

"Ugh. You ought to put some disinfectant on that."

"I will," Chee said. "But first I've got to report this capture to the Federal Bureau of Ineptitude in Phoenix. Could you get 'em for me?"

"Sure." She started dialing. "On line three."

He picked up the telephone on the adjoining desk.

The receptionist at the FBI office said that Agent Reynald was busy and would he leave a message.

"Tell him it concerns the Benjamin Kinsman case," Chee said. "Tell him it's important." He waited.

"Yes," the next voice said. "This is Reynald."

"Jim Chee," Chee said. "I want to tell you we have the other eagle in the Jano case."

"Who?"

"Jano," Chee said. "The Hopi who—"

"I know who Jano is," Reynald snapped. "I mean who is the person I'm talking to."

"Jim Chee. Navajo Tribal Police."

"Oh, yes," Reynald said. "Now what's this about an eagle?"

"We caught him today. Where do you want him delivered for the blood testing?"

"We already have the eagle," Reynald said. "Remember? The arresting officer impounded it when he took the perp into custody. It tested negative. No blood was on it."

"This is the other eagle," Chee said.

Silence. "Other eagle?"

"Remember?" Chee said, trying to include in the question the same measure of impatience that Reynald had used when he'd asked it. "The suspect's case will be based in part on his claim that the slash on his arm was caused by a first eagle, which he then released," Chee said, reciting it at about the rate a teacher might read a difficult passage to a remedial class. "Whereupon Jano claims he caught a second eagle, which he contends was the bird the arresting officer impounded. He contends that the blood—"

"I know what he contends," Reynald said, and laughed. "I didn't dream you guys—or anybody, for that matter—was taking that seriously."

While Reynald was enjoying his laugh, Chee signaled Claire to listen and to flick on the recording machine.

"Serious or not," Chee said, "we have the eagle now. When the FBI lab checks it for human blood in the talon grooves or the leg ruff feathers, it's either there or it isn't. That takes care of that."

Reynald chuckled. "I can't believe this," he

said. "You mean you fellas actually went out and caught yourself a bird to run through the lab? What's that supposed to prove? The lab finds nothing, so you keep catching eagles until you run out of them, and then you tell the jury Jano must have made it up."

"On the other hand, if Jano's blood—"

But Reynald was laughing. "And then the defense attorney will say you missed the one he released. Or, better still, the defense catches one for itself, and they put some of Jano's blood on it and present it as evidence."

"Okay," Chee said. "But I want to be clear about this. How does the Federal Bureau of Investigation want me to dispose of this eagle I have here?"

"Whatever you like," Reynald said. "Just don't dump it on me. I'm allergic to feathers."

"All right then, Agent Reynald," Chee said. "It's been a pleasure working with you."

"Just a second," Reynald said. "What I want you to do with that bird is get rid of it. All it can possibly do is complicate this case, and we don't want it complicated. You understand? Get rid of the damned thing."

"I understand," Chee said. "You're telling me to get rid of the eagle."

"And get to work on what you're supposed to be doing. Are you making any progress finding witnesses who can testify that Jano wanted some revenge on Kinsman? People who can swear he was angry about that original arrest?"

"Not yet," Chee said. "I've been busy trying to catch that first eagle."

That out of the way, Chee called the federal public defender's office and asked for Janet Pete. She was in.

"Janet, we have the first eagle."

"Really?" She sounded incredulous.

"At least I'm almost certain it's the right one. A couple of its tail feathers are missing, which matches what Jano told us."

"But how did you get it?"

"The same way Jano did. Used the same blind, in fact. Only the decoy rabbit was different."

"Has it gone to the lab yet? When will we know what they find?"

"It hasn't gone to the lab. Reynald didn't want it."

"He what? He said that? When?"

"I called him just a little while ago. He said what it boiled down to was nobody would believe Jano's story and if we dignified it by checking another eagle for his blood, you'd just say we'd caught the wrong eagle and want us to go out and keep catching them. And so forth."

"The sonofabitch," Janet said. There was silence while she thought about it. "But I guess I can see his logic. A negative find wouldn't help his case. Finding Jano's blood on that bird might hurt it. So it would be either no help or a loss for him."

"Unless he wanted justice."

"Well, I don't think he has any doubt Jano killed Kinsman. You don't, do you?"

"I didn't."

"You do now? Really?"

"I want to know if he's telling the truth."

"You may have to let a jury decide."

"Janet, twist Reynald's arm. Tell him you insist on it. Tell him if he won't have the tests done you'll petition the court to order it."

Long silence. "Who caught the eagle? How many people know it's caught?"

"I caught it," Chee said. "Claire Dineyahze has it sitting beside her desk right now. That's it."

"Was there dried blood on the feathers? Anywhere else?"

"Not that I could be sure of," Chee said. "Something dried on its feathers. Tell the bastard if he won't order the lab work you'll get it done yourself."

"Jim, it's not that simple."

"Why not?"

"A lot of reasons. In the first place, I won't

even know about the eagle until Reynald tells me. If he doesn't think it has any importance, he won't."

"But there's the evidence disclosure rule. Mickey has to tell the defense attorney what evidence he has."

"Not if it's not important enough for him to use. Mickey will say he didn't even intend to mention the eagle in connection with the blood on Kinsman. The defense can use it if it likes. He'll say he considers it too foolish to require any response."

"All that's probably right. So you tell him that you know the eagle was caught, tell him—"

"And he says, How do you know this? Who told you?"

"And you say a confidential informant."

"Come on, Jim," Janet said impatiently. "Don't sound naive. The federal criminal justice world is small and the acoustics are good. How long do you think it took me to know that Mickey had been warning you about leaking stuff to me? My confidential informant said she got it thirdhand, but she said Mickey called it 'pillow talk.' Did he?"

"That's what he called it. But do it anyway."

Chee listened while Janet outlined the sort of trouble this would cause for Acting Lieutenant Jim Chee. True, he wasn't a federal employee, but the links between the U.S. justice system and the Tribal Justice operations were strong, close and often personal. And it meant a headache for her, too. She badly wanted to win this case, at the very least to save Jano from the death penalty. It was her first in this new job and she wanted it to be clean, neat and tidy, not a messy affair with her looking like an inept loose cannon who didn't understand the system. And so forth. And while he listened, Chee knew what he had to do. And how to do it. And that the effects might change the direction of his life.

"Tell you what," he said. "You tell Mickey that you have access to a tape recording, with two credible witnesses to certify it's genuine. Tell him that on this tape, the FBI agent whom Mr. Mickey put in charge of the Jano case can be clearly heard ordering a policeman to get rid of evidence that might be beneficial to the defense."

"My God!" Janet said. "That's not true, is it?"

"It's true."

"Did you tape a telephone call with Reynald? When you told him you had the eagle? Surely he didn't give you permission to tape something like that. If he didn't, that's a federal offense."

"I didn't ask him," Chee said. "I just taped it, with a witness listening in."

"That's against the law. You could go to jail. You'll surely lose your job."

"You're being naive now, Janet. You know how the FBI feels about bad publicity."

"I won't have anything to do with this," Janet said.

"That's fair enough," Chee said. "And I want to be fair with you, too. Here's what I'll have to do now. I'll get on the telephone and find out how I can get the necessary laboratory work done. Maybe at the lab at Northern Arizona University or Arizona State. I have to be here at the office until noon tomorrow. I'll check with you then—or you can call me here—so I'll know what's going on. Then I'll take the bird on to the lab and I'll have them send you a copy of their report."

"No, Jim. No. They'll charge you with evidence tampering. They'll think of something. You're being crazy."

"Or maybe just stubborn," Chee said. "Anyway, give me a call tomorrow."

Then he sat back and thought about it. Had he been bluffing? No, he'd do it if he had to. Leaphorn's lady friend would know someone on the NAU biology faculty who could run the tests—and do it right so it would hold water in court. And if they found it wasn't Jano's blood, then maybe Jano was just a damn liar.

But Chee wasn't kidding himself about his motivation. One of the reasons he'd told Janet about the tape was to give her a weapon if she needed it. But part of that was purely selfish— the kind of reason Frank Sam Nakai had always warned him against. He wanted to find out how Janet would use this weapon he'd handed her.

For that, he'd have to wait until tomorrow. Maybe a few days more, but he thought tomorrow would tell him.

TWENTY-FOUR

CHEE SLEPT FITFULLY, the darkness in his little trailer full of bad dreams. He got to his office early, thinking he would get a stack of paperwork out of the way. But the telephone was at his elbow and concentration was hard.

It first rang at eighteen minutes after eight. Joe Leaphorn wanted to know if he could get a copy of the list of items found in Miss Pollard's Jeep.

"Sure," Chee said. "We'll Xerox it. You want it mailed?"

"I'm in Tuba," Leaphorn said. "I'll pick it up."

"You on to something I should know about?"

"I doubt it," Leaphorn said. "I want to show the list to Krause and see if he notices anything funny. Something missing that should be there. That sort of thing."

"Did you locate Mrs. Notah?"

"No. I found some of her goats. Somebody's goats, anyway. But she wasn't around. After I waste some of Krause's time this morning, I think I'll go there and look again. See if she can add anything to what she told McGinnis about the skinwalker who looked like a snowman. Did the FBI pick up that eagle?"

"They didn't want it," Chee said, and told Leaphorn what Reynald had said without mentioning taping the call.

"I'm not too surprised," Leaphorn said. "But you can't blame the people. I've known a lot of good agents. It's the system you get with political police. I'll let you know if Mrs. Notah saw anything useful."

The next two calls were routine business. When call number four arrived, Claire didn't just buzz him. She waved and wrote FBI in the air with her finger.

Chee took a long breath, picked up the telephone, said, "Jim Chee."

"This is Reynald. Do you still have that eagle?"

"It's here," Chee said. "What do—"

"Agent Evans is en route to pick it up," Reynald said. "He'll be there about noon. Be there, because he'll need you to sign a form."

"What are you—" Chee began, but Reynald had hung up.

Chee leaned back in his chair. One question was now answered, he thought. Janet had told Reynald she knew about the eagle, prodding him into action, or she had told J. D. Mickey, who had told Reynald how to react. That solved the first part of the problem. The FBI would have the lab test the eagle. He would know sooner or later whether Jano had lied. That left the second question. How had Janet used the club he'd handed her?

In the periods between his bad dreams the night before, he had worked out three scenarios for Janet. In the first, she would simply stand aside, as she had suggested she would, and see what happened. If nothing happened, when he appeared on the witness stand as Jano's arresting officer, she would lead him to the eagle during cross-examination.

"Lieutenant Chee," she would say, "is it true that you were told by Mr. Jano that he had caught a second eagle after the first one slashed his arm, and that you made an attempt to recapture that first eagle?" To which he would have to say: "Yes."

"Did you capture it?"

"Yes."

"Did you then take the eagle to the laboratory at Northern Arizona University and arrange for an examination to be made to determine if it had Mr. Jano's blood on its talons or feathers?"

"Yes."

"And what did that report show?"

The answer to that, of course, would depend on the laboratory report.

He could now rule out that scenario. She hadn't stood aside. She had intervened. But how?

In scenario two, the one for which he ardently longed, Janet went to one of the key federals, told him she had reason to believe the first eagle had been caught and demanded to see the results of the blood testing. Mickey or Reynald, or both, would evade, deny, argue that her request was ridiculous, imply that she was ruining her career in the Department of Justice if she was too stupid to understand that, demand to know the source of this erroneous leak, and so forth. Janet would bravely stand her ground, threaten court action or a leak to the press. And he would love her for her courage and know that he was wrong in not trusting her.

In scenario three, the cause of the previous night's bad dreams, Janet went to Mickey, told Mickey that he had a problem—that Lieutenant Jim Chee had gone out and captured an eagle that he insisted was the same eagle her client would testify had slashed his arm and he had then released. She would recommend that he take custody of said eagle and have tests done to determine if Jano's blood was on it. Whereupon Mickey would tell her to just relax and let the FBI handle collection of evidence in its routine manner. Then Janet would say the FBI had decided against checking the eagle. And Mickey would ask her if Reynald had told her that. And she'd say no. And he'd say how did you find out then. And she would say Lieutenant Chee had told her. And he'd say Chee was misleading her, trying to cause trouble. And about there Janet would realize that she had already caused career-blighting trouble in Mickey's mind and the only way that could be fixed was by using Chee's secret weapon. She would then pledge Mickey to secrecy. She would let him know that in telling Chee he wouldn't get the eagle tested, Reynald had carelessly allowed his telephone conversation to be taped and that on that tape Agent Reynald could be heard imprudently ordering Chee to get rid of the eagle and thus the evidence.

What would this prove? He knew, but he didn't want to admit it or think about it. And he wouldn't have to until Agent Evans arrived to pick up the bird. And not even then, if Evans's conduct didn't somehow tip him off.

Edgar Evans arrived at eleven minutes before noon. Through his open office door Chee watched him come in, watched Claire point him to the eagle cage in the corner behind her, watched her point him to Chee's office.

"Come in," Chee said. "Have a seat."

"I'll need you to sign this," Evans said, and handed Chee a triplicate form. "It certifies that you transferred evidence to me. And I give you this form, which certifies that I received it."

"This makes it awful hard for anything to get lost," Chee said. "Do you always do this?"

Evans stared at Chee. "No," he said. "Not often."

Chee signed the paper.

"You need to be careful with that bird," he said. "It's vicious and that beak is like a knife. I have a blanket out in the car you can put over it to keep it quiet."

Evans didn't comment.

He was putting the cage in the backseat of his sedan when Chee handed him the blanket. He spread it over the cage.

"I thought Reynald had decided against this," Chee said. "What made him change his mind?"

Evans slammed the car door, turned to Chee.

"You mind if I pat you down?"

"Why?" Chee asked, but he held out his hands.

Evans quickly, expertly felt along his belt line, checked the front of his shirt, patted his pockets, stepped back.

"You know why, you bastard. To make sure you're not wearing a wire."

"A wire?"

"You're not as stupid as you look," Evans said. "And not half as smart as you think you are."

With that, Evans got into his car and left Jim Chee standing in the parking lot looking after him, knowing which tactic Janet had used and feeling immensely sad.

TWENTY-FIVE

For Leaphorn it was a frustrating day. He'd stopped at Chee's office and picked up the list. He studied it again and saw nothing on it that told him anything. Maybe Krause would see something interesting. Krause wasn't at his office and the note pinned to his door said: "Gone to Inscription House, then Navajo Mission. Back soon." Not very soon, Leaphorn decided, since the round trip would be well over a hundred miles. So he drove to Yells Back Butte, parked, climbed over the saddle and began his second hunt for Old Lady Notah.

After much crashing around the goats again, twenty-one in all unless he had counted some twice (easy to do with goats) or missed some others, he didn't find Mrs. Notah. Recrossing the saddle required much huffing and puffing, a couple of rest stops, and produced a resolution to watch his diet and get more exercise. Back at his truck, he drank about half the water in the canteen he'd carelessly left behind, and then just rested awhile. This cul-de-sac walled in by the cliffs of Yells Back and the mass of Black Mesa was a blank spot for all radio reception except, for reasons far beyond Leaphorn's savvy in electronics, KNDN, Gallup's Navajo-language Voice of the Navajo Nation.

He listened to a little country-western music and the Navajo-language open-mike segment, and while he listened he sorted out his thoughts. What would he tell Mrs. Vanders when he called her this evening? Not much, he decided. Why was he feeling illogically happy? Because the tension was gone with Louisa. No more feeling that he was betraying Emma or himself. Or that Louisa was expecting more from him than he could possibly deliver. She'd made it clear. They were friends. How had she put it about marriage? She'd tried it once and didn't care for it. But enough of that. Back to Cathy Pollard's Jeep. That presented a multitude of puzzles.

The Jeep had come here early, as the note from Pollard suggested. Jano said he had seen it arrive, and he had no reason Leaphorn could think of to lie about that. It must have left during the brief downpour of hail and rain, not long after Chee had arrested Jano. Earlier, Chee would have heard it. Later, it wouldn't have left the tire prints in the arroyo sand where it had been abandoned. So that left the question of who was driving it, and what he or she had done after parking it. No one had come down the arroyo to pick up the driver. But an accomplice might have parked near the point where the access road crossed the arroyo and waited for the Jeep's driver to walk back to join him or her along the rocky slope.

That required some sort of partnership, not a sudden panicky impulse. Leaphorn's imagination couldn't produce a motive for such a conspiracy. But he came up with another possibility. No cinch, but a possibility. He started the engine and drove off in search of Richard Krause.

A stopoff at Tuba showed Krause's office still empty with the same note on the door. Leaphorn refilled his gasoline tank and started driving. Krause wasn't at Inscription House. The woman who responded to Leaphorn's knock at the Navajo Mission office door said the Health Department man had left about thirty minutes earlier. Going where? He hadn't said.

So Leaphorn made the long, long drive back to Tuba City, writing off the day as a loser, watching the sunset backlight the towering thunderheads on the western horizon and turn them into a kind of beauty only nature can produce. By the time he reached his motel, he was more than ready to call it quits. Calling Mrs. Vanders could wait. Tomorrow he'd rise earlier and catch Krause before he left his office.

Wrong again. The note on the door the next morning suggested that Krause would be working in the arroyo west of the Shonto Landing Strip. An hour and sixty miles later Leaphorn spotted Krause's truck from the road, and Krause on his knees apparently peering at something on the ground. He heard Leaphorn coming, got to his feet, dusted off his pant legs.

"Collecting fleas," he said, and shook hands.

"It looked like you were blowing into that hole," Leaphorn said.

"Good eye," Krause said. "Fleas detect your breath. If something is killing their host mammal and they're looking for a new host, they're very sensitive to that. You blow into the hole and they come to the mouth of the tunnel." He grinned at Leaphorn. "Some say they prefer garlic on your breath, but I like chili." He stared at the tunnel month. Pointed. "See 'em?"

Leaphorn squatted and stared. "Nope," he said.

"Little black specks. Put your hand down there. They'll jump on it."

"No thanks," Leaphorn said.

"Well, what can I do for you?" Krause said. "And what's new?"

He removed a flexible metal rod from the pickup bed and unfurled the expanse of white flannel cloth attached to the end of it.

"I'd like you to take a look at this list of stuff found in the Jeep," Leaphorn said. "See if it's missing anything that should be there, or if there's anything on it that tells you anything."

Krause had folded the flannel around the rod. Now he pushed it slowly into the rodent hole, deeper and deeper. "Okay," he said. "I'll just give 'em a minute to collect on the flannel. Then when I pull it out, the flannel pulls off the rod and folds over the other way and traps a bunch of fleas."

Krause slipped the flannel off the rod, dropped it into a Ziploc bag, closed it, then checked himself for fleas, found one on his wrist, and disposed of it.

Leaphorn handed him the list. Krause put on a pair of bifocals and studied it. "Kools," he said. "Cathy didn't smoke so those must be from somebody else."

"I think it notes they were old," Leaphorn said. "Could have been there for months."

"Two shovels?" Krause said. "Everybody carries one for the digging we do. Wonder why she had the other one?"

"Let me see it," Leaphorn said, and took the list. Under "on floor behind front seat" it listed "long-handled shovel." Under "rear luggage space," it also listed "long-handled shovel."

"Maybe a mistake," Krause said, and shrugged. "Listing the same shovel twice."

"Maybe," Leaphorn said, but he doubted it.

"And here," Krause said. "What the hell was she doing with this?" He pointed to the rear luggage space entry, which read: "One small container of gray powdery substance labeled 'calcium cyanide.'"

"Sounds like a poison," Leaphorn said.

"It damn sure is," Krause said. "We used to use it to clean out infected burrows. You blow that dust down it and it wipes out everything. Pack rats, rattlesnakes, burrowing owls, earthworms, spiders, fleas, anything alive. But it's dangerous to handle. Now we use 'the pill.' It's phostoxin, and we just put it in the ground at the mouth of a burrow and it gets the job done."

"So where would she get this cyanide stuff?"

"We still have a supply of it. It's on a shelf back in our supply closet."

"She'd have access to it?"

"Sure," Krause said. "And look at this." He pointed to the next entry: "'Air tank with hose and nozzle.' That's what we used to use to blow the cyanide dust back into the burrow. It was in the storeroom, too."

"What do you think it means—her having that in the Jeep?"

"First, it means she was breaking the rules. She doesn't take that stuff out without checking with me and explaining what she wants it for, and why she's not using the phostoxin instead. And second, she wouldn't be using it unless she wanted to really sterilize burrows. Zap 'em. Something big like prairie dogs. Not just to kill fleas."

He returned the list to Leaphorn.

"Anything else on there you'd wonder about?"

"No, but there's something that should be on that list that isn't. Her PAPRS."

"You always have that with you?"

"No, but you'd damn sure have it if you were going to use that calcium cyanide dust." Krause made a wry face. "They say the warning is you smell almonds, but the trouble is, by the time you smell it, it's already too late."

"Not something you'd use casually then."

Krause laughed. "Hardly. And before I forget it, I found that note Cathy left me. Made a copy for you." He fished out his wallet, extracted a much-folded sheet of paper, and handed it to Leaphorn. "I don't see anything helpful on it, though."

The note was written in Pollard's familiar semilegible scrawl:

Boss—Heard stuff about Nez infection at Flag. Think we've been lied to. Going to Yells Back, collect fleas and find out—Will fill you in on it when I get back. Pollard.

Leaphorn looked up from the note at Krause, who was watching his reaction, looking penitent.

"Knowing what I know now, I can see I should have got worried quicker when she didn't get back. But, hell, she was always doing things and then explaining later. If at all. For example, I didn't know where she was the day before. She didn't tell me she was driving down to Flag. Or why." He shrugged, shook his head. "So I just thought she'd gone tearing off somewhere else."

"I wonder why she didn't tell you she was quitting," Leaphorn said.

Krause stared at him. "I don't think she was. Did she tell her aunt why?"

"I gather it was something about you."

Krause had spent too many summers in the sun to look pale. But he did look tense.

"What about me?"

"I don't know," Leaphorn said. "She didn't get specific."

"Well, we never did get along very well," Krause said, and began putting his equipment in the truck. The legend on his sweat-soaked T-shirt said, SUPPORT SCIENCE: HUG A HERPETOLOGIST.

TWENTY-SIX

Two telephone notes were stuck on his spindle when Chee got to his office. One was from Leaphorn, asking Chee to call him at his motel. The second was from Janet Pete. It said: "The eagle's being tested today. Please call me."

Chee wasn't quite ready for that. He dialed Leaphorn's number first. Yesterday the Legendary Lieutenant had wanted to show Krause the list of stuff found in the Jeep. Maybe that had developed into something.

"You had breakfast?" Leaphorn asked.

"I'm not much for eating breakfast," Chee said. "What's on your mind?"

"How about joining me for coffee then at the motel diner? I want to go back out to Yells Back Butte. Can you get away? I think I should have an officer along."

An officer along! "Oh," Chee said. He felt ela-
tion, quickly tinged with a little disappointment.
The Legendary Lieutenant had done it again. Had
unraveled the puzzle of who had abandoned the
Jeep. Had maintained the legend. Had again out-
thought Jim Chee. "Sure. I'll be there in ten minutes."

Leaphorn was sitting at a window table, putting butter on a stack of pancakes. He put the
note on the table in front of Chee and smoothed
it out.

"I showed the list to Krause," he said. "There
were a couple or three surprises."

"Oh," Chee said, feeling slightly defensive. He
hadn't noticed anything amiss.

"Mostly technical stuff way over our heads,"
Leaphorn said. "This blower here, for example,
and the container of calcium cyanide. I figured
that was just one of their flea killers. Turns out
they don't use it these days except in some sort
of unusual circumstances." He looked up at Chee.
"Like, let's say they needed to wipe out a whole
colony of prairie dogs."

Chee leaned back in his chair, understanding
again why he admired Leaphorn instead of re-
senting him. The man was giving him a chance
to figure it out for himself. And of course he had.

"Like, let's say, the colony Dr. Woody is working with."

Leaphorn was grinning. "That occurred to me, too," he said. "I don't think Woody would have wanted that to happen."

Chee nodded. And waited. He could tell from Leaphorn's expression that more was coming.

"And then there's this," Leaphorn said. "I asked Krause why there would be two of these long-handled shovels in that Jeep. He said everybody carried one because of the digging they do, besides getting stuck in the sand. But just one."

Chee leaned back again, considering that. "Be useful to have one if you wanted to dig a grave."

Leaphorn nodded. "That also occurred to me. Maybe toss it in, not knowing there was already one in the Jeep."

"So somewhere between Yells Back Butte and where the Jeep was left we might be checking on easy places to dig and looking for freshly dug dirt."

"I'd suggest that," Leaphorn said.

"I'm also asking people to check for bicycle tracks along the Goldtooth road. But there's not much chance they'll find any. Too dry."

This caused Leaphorn's eyebrows to rise. "Bicycle?"

"I noticed Woody had a bicycle rack bolted to the back of that mobile lab truck," Chee said. "There wasn't a bike on it."

Leaphorn slammed his hand on the tabletop, rattling his plate. "I must be getting old," he said. "Why didn't I think of that?"

"It wouldn't be a hard bike ride," Chee said, "from where the Jeep was left back to Yells Back. He could have stepped out of the Jeep onto rocks, lifted the bike out, and carried it back to the road."

"Sure," Leaphorn said. "Sure he could. But it would have been clumsy to carry the shovel, too. I've had my brain turned off."

Chee doubted that. It reminded Chee of watching the Easter egg hunt on the White House lawn on television. Seeing the big brother overlook an egg so the little kid could find it.

The waitress arrived and offered refills. But now both of them were in a hurry.

They took Chee's patrol car, roared down Arizona 264, turned right onto the road to Goldtooth, jolted over the washboard bumps.

"Seems like old times," Leaphorn said. "Us working together."

"You miss it? I mean, being a cop?"

"I miss this part of it. And the people I worked with. I don't miss the paperwork. I'll bet you wouldn't, either."

"I hate that part of it," Chee said. "I'm not good at it, either."

"You're acting now," Leaphorn said. "Usually

after you've done that a while, they offer you the permanent position. Would you take it?"

Chee drove for a while without answering. Clouds were building up already, fleets of great white ships against the dark blue sky. By late evening yesterday they had towered high enough to produce a few drops of rain here and there. By this afternoon the monsoon rains might actually begin. Long overdue.

"No," Chee said. "I guess not."

"When I heard you'd applied for the promotion, I sort of wondered why," Leaphorn said.

Chee glanced at him, saw only a profile. Leaphorn was staring at the clouds. "I imagine you could make a pretty good guess. Part prestige, mostly the money's better."

"What do you need it for? You still live in that rusty old trailer, don't you?"

Chee decided to turn the cross-examination around.

"You think they'll offer me the job?"

Long silence. "Probably not."

"Why's that?"

"I suspect the powers that be will get the impression that you would not be a proper team player. You wouldn't cooperate well with other law enforcement agencies," Leaphorn said.

"Any agency in particular?"

"Well, maybe the FBI."

"Oh," Chee said. "What have you heard?"

"It has been said that the FBI would hesitate to handle sensitive business with you over the telephone."

Chee laughed. "Man, oh man," he said. "How fast the word does travel. Did you hear that this morning?"

"Last night already," Leaphorn said.

"Who?"

"Kennedy called me from Albuquerque. Remember him? We worked with him a time or two, and then the Bureau transferred him. He was asking me about a thing we were looking into just before I retired. He's retiring himself at the end of the year and he wanted to know how I liked being a civilian. Asked about you, too. And he said you had made yourself some enemies. So I asked him how you managed that."

"And he said I'd taped a telephone call without permission," Chee said. "Thereby violating a federal statute."

"Yeah," Leaphorn said. "Did he have it right?"

Chee nodded.

"It's nice you don't want that promotion then," Leaphorn said. "Had you decided that before or after you turned on the tape recorder?"

Chee thought for a moment. "Before, I guess. But I didn't really realize it."

They turned up the track toward Yells Back

Butte, circled around a barrier of tumbled boulders and found themselves engulfed in goats. And not just the goats. There, beside the track was an aged woman on a large roan horse watching them.

"Lucked out," Leaphorn said. He climbed out of the patrol car, said *"Ya'eeh te'h"* to Old Lady Notah and introduced himself, reciting his membership in his born to and born for clans. Then he introduced Jim Chee, by maternal and paternal clans and as a member of the Navajo Tribal Police at Tuba City. The horse stared at Chee suspiciously, the goats milled around, and Mrs. Notah returned the courtesy.

"It is a long way to Tuba City," Mrs. Notah said. "And I have seen you here before. I think it must be because the other policeman was killed here. Or because the Hopi came to steal our eagles."

"It is even more than that, mother," Leaphorn said. "A woman who worked with the health department came here the day the policeman was killed. No one has seen her since. Her family asked me to look for her."

Mrs. Notah waited a bit to see if Leaphorn had more to say. Then she said: "I don't know where she is."

Leaphorn nodded. "They say you saw a skinwalker somewhere near here. Was that the day the policeman was killed?"

She nodded. "Yes. It was that day it rained. Now I think it might have been somebody who helps the man who works in that big motor home."

Chee sucked in his breath.

Leaphorn said: "Why do you think that?"

"After that day I saw that man come out of his place carrying a white suit. He walked way up the slope with it, and through the junipers, and then he put it on and put a white hood over his head." She laughed. "I think it is something to keep the sickness off of them. I saw something like that on television."

"I think that's right," Leaphorn said. And then he asked Mrs. Notah to try to tell them everything she had seen or heard around Yells Back Butte that morning. She did, and it took quite a while.

She had risen before dawn, lit her propane burner, warmed her coffee and ate some fry bread. Then she saddled her horse and rode there. While she was rounding up the goats, she heard a truck coming up the track toward the butte. About sunup, she had seen a man climb up the saddle and disappear over the rim onto the top of the butte.

"I thought it must be one of the Hopi eagle-catchers come to get one. They used to come out here a lot before the government changed the boundary, and I had seen this same man the afternoon before. Just looking around," she said. "That's the way they used to work. Then they would come back before daylight the next morning and go up and catch one."

Chee asked: "Did you tell anyone about this?"

"I was down by the road when a police car came by. I told him I thought the Hopis were going to steal an eagle again."

Chee nodded. Mrs. Notah had been Kinsman's confidential source.

Next in Mrs. Notah's narration was the arrival of the black Jeep.

"It was going too fast for those rocks," Mrs. Notah said. "I thought it would be the young woman with the short hair, but I couldn't see who it was."

"Why the woman with the short hair?" Leaphorn asked.

"I have seen her driving that car before. She drives too fast." Mrs. Notah emphasized her disapproval with a negative shake of her head. "Then I had to go get that goat there." She pointed at a black and white male that had wandered far down the track. "Maybe a half-hour later, when I moved the goats back up near the butte, I saw

somebody moving behind the trees, and then I
saw the thing in the white suit."

She paused, rewarded them with a wry smile.
"I went away for a while then, and on the way
back to the goats, I heard a car coming, very,
very slowly, up the trail. It was a police car, and
I thought, That policeman knows how to drive
over rocks. When I came back to the goats, I saw
the man who works in that motor home was
over at the old Tijinney hogan. He was right in
there, and I thought *bilagaana* don't know about
death hogans, or maybe that's the skin-walker.
A witch, well, he don't care about *chindis*."

"What was he doing?" Leaphorn asked.

"I couldn't see much over the wall from where
I was," she said. "But when he came out, I could
see he was carrying a shovel."

Chee parked his patrol car on the hump overlooking the Tijinney place. They walked down together, Chee carrying the shovel from the trunk
of his car, and stood looking over the tumbled
stone. The hard-packed earthen floor was littered
with pieces of the fallen roof, blown-in tumbleweeds, and the debris vandals had left. It was flat
and smooth except for a half dozen holes and
the filled-in excavation where the fire pit had
been.

"That's where it would be," Chee said, pointing.

Leaphorn nodded. "I've been doing nothing for about a week but sitting in a car seat. Give me the shovel. I need a little exercise."

"Well, now," Chee said, but he surrendered the shovel. For a Navajo as traditional as Chee, digging for a corpse in a death hogan wasn't a task done lightly. It would require at least a sweat bath and, more properly, a curing ceremony, to restore the violator of such taboos to *hozho*.

"Easy digging," Leaphorn said, tossing aside his sixth spadeful. A few moments later he stopped, put aside the shovel, squatted beside the hole. He dug with his hands.

He turned and looked at Chee. "I guess we have found Catherine Pollard," he said. He pulled out a forearm clad in the white plastic of her PAPR suit and brushed away the earth. "She's still wearing her double set of protective gloves."

TWENTY-SEVEN

DR. WOODY OPENED his door at the second knock. He said: "Good morning, gentlemen," leaned against the doorway and motioned them in. He was wearing walking shorts and a sleeveless undershirt. It seemed to Leaphorn that the odd pink skin color he'd noticed when he'd first met the man was a tone redder. "I think this is what they call serendipity, or a fortunate accident. Anyway, I'm glad you're here."

"And why is that?" Leaphorn asked.

"Have a seat first," Woody said. He swayed, supported himself with a hand against the wall, then pointed Leaphorn to the chair and Chee to a narrow bed, now folded out of the wall. He seated himself on the stool beside the lab working area. "Now," he said, "I'm glad to see you because I need a ride. I need to get to Tuba City and make some telephone calls. Normally, I would drive this thing. But it's hard to drive. I'm feeling pretty bad. Dizzy. Last time I took my temp it was almost one hundred and four. I was afraid I wouldn't make it out."

"We'll be glad to take you," Chee said. "But first we need to get answers to some questions."

"Sure," Woody said. "But later. After we get going. And one of you will have to stay here and take care of things." He leaned forward over the table and ran his hand over his face. Leaphorn now noticed a dark discoloration under his arm, spreading down the rib cage under the under-shirt.

"Hell of a bruise there on your side," Leaphorn said. "We should get you to a hospital."

"Unfortunately, it's not a bruise. It's the capil-laries breaking down under the skin. Releases the blood into the tissue. We'll go to the Medi-cal Center at Flagstaff. But first I have to do some telephoning. And someone should stay here. Look after things. The animals in the cages. The files."

"We found the body of Catherine Pollard bur-ied out there," Chee said, "Do you know any-thing about that?"

"I buried her," Woody said. "But, damnit, we don't have time to talk about that now. I can tell you about it while we're driving to Tuba City.

But I've got to get there before I'm too sick to talk, and these cell phones won't work out here."

"Did you kill her?"

"Sure," Woody said. "You want to know why?"

"I think I could guess," Chee said.

"Silly woman didn't give me a choice. I told her she couldn't exterminate that dog colony and I told her why. They might hold the key to saving millions of lives." Woody laughed. "She said I'd lied to her once and that was all she allowed."

"Lied," Chee said. "You told her the rodents weren't infected. Was that it?"

Woody nodded. "She put on her protective suit and was getting ready to pump cyanide dust into the burrow when I stopped her. And then the cop saw me burying her."

"You killed him, too?" Chee said.

Woody nodded. "Same problem. Exactly the same. I can't let anything interfere with this," he said, gesturing around the lab. Then he produced a weak chuckle, shook his head. "But something is. It's the disease itself. Isn't that ironic? This new, improved, drug-resistant version of *Yersinia pestis* is making me another lab specimen."

He was reaching into a drawer as he said that. When his hand came out it held a long-barreled pistol. Probably .22 caliber, Chee guessed. The right size for shooting rodents, but not something anyone wanted to be shot with.

"I just don't have time for this," Woody said. "You stay here," he said to Leaphorn. "Look after things. I'll ride with Lieutenant Chee. We'll send somebody back to take over when I get to the telephone."

Chee looked at the pistol, then at Woody. His own revolver was in the holster on his hip. But he wasn't going to need it.

"I'll tell you what we're going to do," Chee said. "We're going to take Mr. Leaphorn with us. As soon as we get out of this radio blind spot, we'll call an ambulance to meet us. I'll send out a patrolman to take care of this place. We'll turn on the siren and get to Tuba City fast."

Chee stood and took a step toward the door and opened it. "Come on," he said to Woody. "You're looking sicker and sicker."

"I want him to stay," Woody said, and waved the pistol toward Leaphorn. Chee reached and grabbed the gun out of Woody's hand and handed it to Leaphorn. "Come on," he said. "Hurry."

Woody was in no condition to hurry. Chee had to half-carry him to the patrol car.

They raised the dispatcher just as they bounced away from the radio shadow of Yells Back Butte. Chee told him to send an ambulance down the road to Goldtooth and an officer to guard Woody's mobile lab at the butte. Leaphorn sat in the back with Woody, and Woody talked.

He'd found two fleas in his groin area when he awakened the day before and immediately redosed himself with an antibiotic, hoping the fleas, if infected at all, were carrying the unmutated bacteria. By this morning a fever had developed. He knew then that he had the form that resisted medication and had killed Nez so quickly. He had hurriedly compiled his most recent notes in readable form, put away breakable items, stored the blood samples he'd been working on in the refrigerator for preservation and started the engine. But by then he felt so dizzy that he knew he couldn't drive the big vehicle out. So he'd begun a note explaining where he stood in the project, to be passed along to an associate at the Center for Control of Infectious Diseases.

"It's there in the folder on the desk with his name on it—a microbiologist named Roy Bobbin Hovey. But I forgot to mention that he'll want an autopsy. The name and number are in my wallet in case I'm out of it before we get to a telephone. Tell him to do the autopsy. He'll know what organs to check."

"Your organs?" Leaphorn asked.

Woody's chin had dropped down to his breastbone. "Of course," he mumbled. "Who else?"

Chee was driving far too fast for the wash-board road and watching in the rearview mirror.

"How were you able to hit Officer Kinsman on the head?" he asked. "Why didn't he cuff you?"

"He was careless," Woody said. "I said, Aren't you going to put those handcuffs on me, and when he twisted around to reach for them, that's when I hit him."

"Then when we left with Kinsman, you drove the Jeep out and abandoned it and poured the blood on the seat so it would look like a murder-kidnapping? Right? And took your bicycle along so you could ride it back from there? Is that right?"

But by then, Dr. Woody had drifted off into unconsciousness. Or perhaps he didn't think the answer mattered.

They met the ambulance about ten miles from Moenkopi, warned the attendants that Woody was probably in the final stages of bubonic plague and sent it racing off toward the Northern Arizona Medical Center. At his station, Chee fished out the note from Woody's wallet, left Leaphorn talking with Claire, and disappeared into his office to make the telephone call.

He emerged looking angry, flopped into a chair across from Leaphorn, wiped his forehead, and said: "Whew, what a day."

"Did you get the man?" Leaphorn asked.

"Yeah. Dr. Hovey said he'll fly out to Flagstaff today."

"Quite a shock, I guess," Leaphorn said. "Learning your associate is a double murderer."

"That didn't seem to bother him. He asked about Woody's condition, and his notes, and who was looking after his papers, and where he could pick them up, and were they being cared for, and how about the animals he was working with, and was the prairie dog colony safe."

"Like that, huh?"

"Pissed me off, to tell the truth," Chee said. "I said I hoped we could keep the sonofabitch alive until we can try him for killing two people. And that irritated him. He sort of snorted and said: 'Two people. We're trying to save all of humanity.'"

Leaphorn sighed. "Matter of fact, I think Woody *was* trying to save humanity."

TWENTY-EIGHT

FOR CHEE, THE next hours were occupied by the work of wrapping it up. He called the Northern Arizona Medical Center, got the emergency room supervisor, and told the woman Woody was en route in an ambulance and what to expect. Then he called the FBI office in Phoenix. Agent Reynald was occupied. He got Agent Edgar Evans instead.

"This is Jim Chee," he said. "I want to report that the man who killed Officer Ben Kinsman is in custody. His name is Woody. He is a medical doctor, and a—"

"Hold it! Hold it!" Evans said. "What're ya talking about?"

"The arrest this morning of the man who killed Kinsman," Chee said. "You better take notes because your boss will be asking questions. After being read his rights, Dr. Woody made a full confession of the assault on Kinsman to me, in the presence of Joe Leaphorn. He also confessed to the murder of Catherine Pollard, a vector control specialist employed by the Indian Health Service. Woody is critically ill and is now en route to the hospital at Flag in an amb—"

"What the hell is this?" Evans said. "Some kind of joke?"

"In an ambulance," Chee continued. "I recommend you pass this information along to Reynald, so he can get it to Mickey, so Mickey can drop the charges against Jano," Chee said. "If you want to do a television spectacular with this, the Navajo Police office at Tuba City can tell you where you can find the Pollard body and the details you need about how you, the FBI, solved this crime."

"Hold it, Chee," Evans said. "What kind of—"

"No time for silly questions," Chee said, and hung up.

Next he worked his way down the list of law enforcement agencies put to work by J. D. Mickey on the Kinsman case and gave them the pertinent information. Then he called the Public Defender Service in Phoenix. He got the office secretary. Ms. Pete was not in. Ms. Pete had left about an hour ago en route to Tuba City. Yes, there was a telephone in her car. Yes, she would notify Ms. Pete that she should contact him at Tuba City to receive information critical to the Jano case.

"I think she was going to Tuba to talk to you, Lieutenant Chee," the secretary said. "But this 'critical information.' She'll ask me about that."

"Tell Ms. Pete she was right about the Kinsman case. I arrested the wrong man. Now we have the right one."

Then he called Leaphorn's room at the motel. No answer. He called the desk.

"He's over at the diner," the clerk said. "He said if you called to come on over and join him."

Leaphorn had been busy, too. First he had called the law firm of Peabody, Snell and Glick and persuaded a receptionist that he should be allowed to talk to Mr. Peabody himself. He'd told Peabody the circumstances and suggested that, in view of Mrs. Vanders's fragile health, someone close to her should break the news to her. He'd explained that Miss Pollard's body would not be released to the family until the crime scene crew exhumed it properly and the required autopsy had been completed. He'd given him the names of those who could provide further information.

That done, he had called Louisa and recited into her answering machine the details of what had happened. He'd told her he was checking out, would drive back to Window Rock, and would call her from there tomorrow. Then he'd taken a shower, rescued what was left of the soap and shampoo from the bathroom to add to his emergency supply, packed, left a message for Chee at the desk, and strolled over to the diner to eat.

He was enjoying the diner's version of a Navajo taco and watching a Nike commercial on the wall-mounted television when Lieutenant Chee walked in, spotted Leaphorn and came over. He moved Leaphorn's bag from a chair and sat.

"You leaving town?"

"Home to Window Rock," Leaphorn said. "Back to washing my own dishes, doing the laundry, being a housewife." He had to speak up because the Nike ad had been followed by a used-car commercial, which involved noise and shouting.

"I wanted to thank you for the help," Chee said.

Leaphorn nodded. "I thank you in return. It was mutual. Like old times."

"Anyway, if I can ever—"

But now he was talking over a promo for what the Phoenix station called a news break. A pretty young man was telling them there had been a startling development in the Ben Kinsman murder case and he would take them to Alison Padilla, who was "live at the federal building."

Alison was not as pretty as the anchorman, but she seemed competent. She told them that Acting Assistant U.S. Attorney J. D. Mickey had called a press conference a bit earlier. She would let him speak for himself. Mr. Mickey, looking stern, got right to the point.

"The Federal Bureau of Investigation has taken into custody a suspect in the homicide of Officer Benjamin Kinsman and in the death of an Indian Health Service employee who has been missing for several days. The FBI has also developed information which verifies statements made by Robert Jano, who had previously been arrested by the Navajo Tribal police and charged with the Kinsman murder. Charges against Mr. Jano will now be dismissed. More information will be released as details become available."

While Mickey was reading this, Officer Bernadette Manuelito walked in. Chee waved her over, pointed to a seat. Mickey was now waving off questions and ending the conference, and the camera switched back to Ms. Padilla, who began providing background information.

"Lieutenant," Officer Manuelito said. "Mrs. Dineyahze asked me to tell you the U.S. Attorney's office is trying to reach you." She pointed to the screen. "Him."

"Okay," Chee said. "Thanks."

"And the U.S. Public Defender Service. They said it was urgent."

"Okay," Chee said again. "And, Bernie, you remember Mr. Leaphorn, don't you? From when we were both working at Shiprock? Have a seat. Join us."

Bernie smiled at Leaphorn and said she had to get back to the station. "But did you hear what that man said? I think that's awful. He made it sound like we screwed up."

Chee shrugged.

"It's not fair," she said.

"They tend to do that," Leaphorn said. "That's why a lot of the real cops resent the federals."

"Well, anyway, I just think—" Bernie paused, looking for the words to express her indignation.

Chee wanted to change the subject. He said: "Bernie, when did you say they were having the *kinaalda* for your cousin? Now that we have the FBI handling the Kinsman case, I'm not going to be so busy. Would it still be okay if I came?"

The beeper in her belt holster made its unpleasant noise. "It would be okay," Bernie said, and hurried out the door.

Leaphorn picked up his check, looked at it, fished out his wallet and dropped a dollar tip on the table. "That drive from here to Window seems to get longer and longer," he said. "Got to get moving."

But at the door he paused to shake hands with a woman coming in and chat for a moment. He pointed back into the room and disappeared. Janet Pete had arrived from Phoenix.

She stood in the doorway a moment, scanning the tables. She wore boots and a long skirt with a patterned blouse, and her silky hair was cut short like the chic women on the television shows wore theirs these days. She looked tired, Chee thought, and tense, but still so beautiful that he closed his eyes for a moment and looked away.

When he looked again, she was walking toward him, her expression saying she was glad she had found him. But it revealed nothing else.

Chee stood, pulled back a chair for her and said: "I guess you got the message."

"The message, but not the meaning." She sat, adjusted her skirt. "What does it mean?"

Chee told her how they had found Pollard's body, about Woody's confession that he had killed Kinsman when Kinsman found him burying the woman, about Woody's desperate sickness. She listened without a word.

"Mickey was just on television announcing the murder charge against your client is being dropped," Chee said. "Nothing left now but the 'poaching an endangered species' charge. It's a second offense, done while on probation for the first one. But under the circumstances I'd imagine the judge will just sentence Jano to the time he's already spent locked up waiting for the big trial."

Janet was looking at her hands folded on the table in front of her. "Nothing left but that," she said. "That and the wreckage."

He waited for an explanation. None came. She simply looked at him quizzically.

"Let me get you a cup," Chee said. He pushed back his chair, but she shook her head. "I got your call about the eagle being tested," Chee said. "I intended to call you back, but things got too busy. How did it come out? Mickey made it sound like they found blood."

"It doesn't matter now, does it?"

"Well, sure," Chee said. "It would be nice to know Mr. Jano wasn't lying to us."

"I haven't seen the report yet," Janet said.

He sipped his coffee, watching her. The ball was in her court.

She took a deep breath.

"Jim. How long had you known about this Woody? That he'd killed Kinsman?"

"Not very long," Chee said, wondering where this was leading.

"Before you told me about catching the eagle?"

"No. Not until this morning."

She looked down at her hands again. Calculating all this, he thought. Adding it up. Searching for a conclusion. She found it.

"I want to know why you told me you'd taped Reynald's telephone call."

"Why not?"

"Why not!" The anger showed in her face as well as her voice. "Because as you certainly knew I am a sworn officer of the court in this case. You tell me you have committed a crime." She threw up her hands. "What did you think I would do?"

Chee shrugged.

"No. Don't just kiss it off. I'm serious. You must have had a reason for telling me. What did you think I would do?"

Chee considered that. By traditional Navajo ethical standards he wouldn't be required to tell the absolute truth unless she asked the question a fourth time. This was time two.

"I thought you'd either push the FBI to get the eagle tested or you'd handle it yourself."

"That's not what I meant. What would I do about the taped call? And for that matter about the agent in charge asking you to destroy evidence."

"I thought the information would be useful.

Give you leverage if you needed it," Chee said, thinking: That's the third time.

She stared at him, sighed. "You're not good at pretending to be naive, Jim. I know you too well. You had a reason—"

Chee held up his hand, ending this just short of the fourth question. Why make her ask it? He spoke carefully.

"I thought you would go to Mickey and tell him that you had learned Jano's first eagle had been caught, that the FBI declined to test it on grounds that it would be a waste of time and money and had ordered the eagle disposed of. I presumed that if you did this, Mickey would tell you he agreed with the FBI. He would suggest that you, a rookie member of the federal justice family, should be part of the team and drop the issue. Then you would either agree or you would defy Mickey and tell him you would have the eagle tested yourself."

He paused, then drew a deep breath, looked away.

Janet waited.

Chee sighed. "Or you might start by telling Mickey that you had become aware of a potential risk to the case. The Navajo Police had caught the eagle, the FBI agent representing Mickey had ordered it destroyed and the telephone call during which he had done this had been taped. Therefore you would urgently recommend that he order the first eagle tested immediately and make the results public."

Janet's face was flushed. She looked away from him, shook her head, looked back.

"And what would I say when Mickey asked who had made this unauthorized felonious tape? And what would I tell the grand jury when Mickey called it to investigate?"

"He wouldn't call a grand jury," Chee said. "That would drag Reynald in, Reynald would pass the buck back to Mickey, and then Mickey's political hopes are down the tube. Besides, he'd have no trouble at all figuring out who taped the telephone call."

"And you certainly knew that. So what did you do? You deliberately wrecked your career in law enforcement. You put me in an intolerable position. What happens if there is a grand jury? What do I testify?"

"You'd have to tell the simple truth. That I had told you I had illegally taped Reynald's call. But Mickey will never call the jury."

"And what if he doesn't? There's still the fact that you admitted a felony to me and I, also an officer of the court, failed in my duty to report it."

"And the FBI knows you failed to report it.

But the FBI knew it, too, and didn't report it either."

"Not yet," she said.

"They won't."

"And if they do, what then?"

"You say that Jim Chee told you he had, without authorization, taped a telephone call from Agent Reynald." Chee paused. "And that you had believed him."

She stared at him. "Had believed him?"

"Then you say that after you had reported this to the assistant U.S. attorney, Jim Chee informed you that while Reynald had made the remarks exactly as reported, Chee had no such tape."

Janet was rising from her chair. She stood looking down at him. How long? Five or six seconds, but memory doesn't operate on conscious time. And Chee was remembering the happiest day of his life—the moment when their romance had become a love affair. He had imagined their love could blend oil and water. She would become a Navajo in more than name and work on the reservation. She would forget the glitter, power, and prestige of the affluent Washington society that produced her. He would set aside his goal of becoming a shaman. He would become ambitious, compromise with materialism enough to keep her content with what he knew she must see as poverty and failure. He'd been young enough to believe that. Janet had believed it, too. Believed the impossible. She could no more reject the only value system she'd ever known than he could abandon the Navajo Way. He hadn't been fair to her.

"Janet," he said, and stopped, not knowing what else to say.

She said: "Damn you, Jim," and walked away.

Chee finished his coffee, listened to her car starting up and rolling across the parking-lot gravel. He felt numb. She had loved him once, in her way. He knew he'd loved her. Probably he still did. He'd know more about that tomorrow when the pain began.

BOOKS BY TONY HILLERMAN

SERIES

The Blessing Way
Dance Hall of the Dead
Listening Woman
People of Darkness
The Dark Wind
The Ghostway
Skinwalkers
A Thief of Time
Talking God
Coyote Waits
Sacred Clowns
The Fallen Man
The First Eagle
Hunting Badger
The Wailing Wind
The Sinister Pig
Skeleton Man
The Shape Shifter

STANDALONES

Finding Moon
The Fly on the Wall

NONFICTION

Seldom Disappointed: A Memoir

HarperCollins*Publishers* | HARPER
DISCOVER GREAT AUTHORS, EXCLUSIVE OFFERS, AND MORE AT HC.COM.

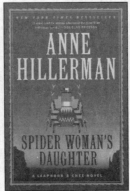
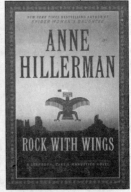
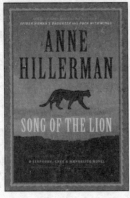
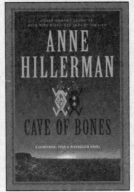
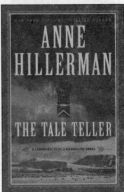

Res¹ Punch say 1st
Say voice nk
*Alexa
1st continue Reading them watch for Blue light
— up